A STONE IN HER SHOE

Jo Burgess

UPFRONT PUBLISHING
LEICESTERSHIRE

ISBN 1 84426 001 1

First Published 2002 by
UPFRONT PUBLISHING LTD
Leicestershire

A STONE IN HER SHOE

Dedicated to my dearest friend Peta Colin

A Stone in Her Shoe
An autobiography written in the stream of consciousness by Jo
Burgess

Chapter One

Her mother was as fragile as a piece of Dresden, her father boasted. She was fair and athletic through her Norwegian and German mother and proud beyond measure of her English descent from the Conqueror. She stood five feet one inch tall, and Corinna was like her, except that she was tall, and while her mother was as feminine as a butterfly, from the age of eight Corinna knew she was a boy inside.

There were banister bars in the new house; they reminded her of when she was four and she could see the boys through the balcony railings of the buildings, their knees grey and knocked about, kicking up dirty water in the gutters.

'No shoes, poor little monkeys,' said her mother.

She remembered many things about those early times, but most were told her by her mother. When their father came home from the war, the flats had had to come down and they had come to live here, in the country. She had nearly forgotten the boys, but the banisters reminded her.

There were twenty-nine banister bars. Sitting on the top stair, she could see secretly into the hall below. Red and blue squares fell on the floor from the street-door glass. Standing dark and close, blocking out the light, stood a shadow. The bell rang.

Granny opened the door and sun filled the hall.

'No reply,' she said.

She shut the door, fumbled with the envelope and the sheet of paper, and took out a handkerchief and gently blew her nose, sniffing.

'It's a boy, Evelyn! A boy!' she called.

Corinna slid down the stairs and ran into the kitchen. Her mother was sitting with the yellow bowl in her lap beating the cake mixture before scooping it into the tin.

'Mummy, why is Granny crying?'

Her mother went on beating the cake mixture.

'Granny's not really crying – it's nothing to worry about. Sometimes people cry for joy and Auntie Mat's had a little boy, and Granny never had a little boy, that's all.'

She stopped beating the cake mixture and pressed her forehead against hers.

'I want to be a boy, Mummy.'

'I think you're a tomboy already.'

She knew she must not cry. She was eight, but the words screamed in her head, 'I want to be a boy! Not just a tomboy!'

She knew it was a wrong thing to do because God had made her a girl, but she was certain she was a boy inside.

She felt she would burst out of her skin if she didn't run out and throw herself into the air on the swing where no one could see she was crying, watching the whole sky tremble with anger.

When the trembling stopped, she jumped off the swing and tore up to the terrace where Benjamin was playing with his soldiers in the old zinc bath.

'Zoom!' he shouted. 'Boom!' and the Royal Navy sank.

She was sorry about his neck being bandaged up, but he was a boy – he had everything – the soldiers, the railway and the carpentry set she had wanted for Christmas.

'We're having a puppy!' she said, towering over him in his open-air bed.

He was fidgeting under the pillow. The pistol! He had it!

'That's mine! Give it to me!'

'Girls don't have pistols, silly,' he lisped.

His esses were all mixed up and he flinched as if she might hit him.

She stood glaring down at him until his face crumpled and she grabbed the pistol and ran over the grass ridge, over the ditch full of dead Germans, down the garden to the oak tree.

Benjamin didn't climb. This was her tree. Hers and David's. She didn't mind David being a boy. He read stories, and he told them to her while sitting up in the branches. Then he'd test the branches to get higher still. He was there now, his yellow hair sticking up. He had come over the fence from his garden. She hid the pistol in the secret place in the long grass.

'Look!' he called. 'Conkers!'

She had to start again and run and jump on to the first branch without touching. This was their law. David had stopped climbing and leaned down to hold out his hand to her.

'That's my champion – would you like it?'

She climbed nearer to see. It was his King.

'Will you be my sweetheart?' he asked.

The dark brown conker slid into her hand and out of her hand into her pocket. She shook her head. She said nothing. He had given her his King – it was a pledge. They were comrades. She didn't want to be anything else.

The school was across the fields. All the children of the new houses went together, through the passage at the top of the avenue, and over the fields leading to the great trees along the main road to school. After school, they came home again together through the passage.

David was already at the end of the passage one day when classes were finished, a crowd of boys round him, his cap on one side.

'Hallo!' he said.

He always said, 'Hallo,' but this time he looked different. All the boys got behind him and pushed him up to her, and quickly he leaned forward and kissed her. Then he turned and ran, his hand on his cap, all the boys after him making a long hissing sound.

She rubbed her mouth hard. Amanda giggled, running down the hill at her side into the house. Corie flew through the kitchen and up the stairs, feet banging, up to the bathroom to gulp cold water and wash her mouth, sobs in her throat.

'David kissed Corie, I saw him!' Amanda sang out loud enough for the entire world to hear.

'What a lot of nonsense!' her mother said shortly. 'Come and eat up your tea. Plenty of time for that sort of thing.'

All night David's face was in her eyes. She was too hot and she threw off the bedclothes. If it had been raining she would have gone out to feel it on her face.

How could David do that when he knew without her telling him that she was a boy inside? It made her angry with God for getting her mixed up, and for getting David sent away to school.

And then it was all quiet again. In the winter, their father taught them to sing. The flames shot up the chimney and he held the poker like a sword. That was what he liked, singing in the firelight on Sunday evening. He had a fine tenor their mother said. He taught them to roundelay.

'After me then – the same words, only low.'

Sword raised.

Down by the stream,
Slowly now! Down by the stream,
Where the watermelons grow,
Louder! Where the watermelons grow.

The room was full of voices in the firelight, the faces bright and sleepy, all their eyes on the sword. At the last verse, the sword came down.

'Altogether now,' their father's voice rang loud and clear.

My rent I owe
Slowly! My rent I owe.

In Buenos Aires they had sung that, all the fellows when he was eighteen and working on the great railway, searching for gold and gambling away all his luggage and references.

Endless tales he told them. One farmer had sent him to get in the cows. He put him on a horse, but by the time he had got the cows in, there wasn't a pint of milk in the lot of them. Then he came home to fight the war and found Evelyn waiting for him. For four years he was in the trenches. Not many chaps could say that. Eight days he was in a shell hole sending messages. His CO said he'd get a medal for that, but he was killed that day. The ninth day, the sniper nearly got him. A bullet had touched his hair, there, a silver streak in his black hair.

'I had to kill him with a bayonet – that's war.'

He shrugged as if it still hurt him to have killed a young man like that.

'Couldn't sleep in a bed for months when it was all over.'

'They were very clean, the Germans,' he said. 'They'd take our trench and when we got it back it was concreted, lavatories built. They had no lice on their side.'

Then he threw his head back and sang.

When we get to Berlin the Kaiser he will say,
Ach ach mein Gott
Vot a blommin' fine lot
Are the tenth Rifle Brigade.

It was the comradeship that had mattered. Never would he forget the comradeship. He stopped talking and the singing died away. The room grew warm and sleepy. Somewhere in the world there was a comrade to sing with, march with, sleep with in a dugout. A comrade walking down a lonely road, a girl with shining eyes, slipping into step beside her.

'Why don't women go to war?'

'They'd run away as soon as the firing started!'

'What about Grace Darling? And Nurse Cavell?' her mother asked.

When their father came home from the war, Grandpa taught him the streets of London for the police test to drive a taxi. That was how they had a taxi all to themselves to take them to the sea.

'The best marriage in the family,' Grandpa said, 'even if Evelyn makes him keep the taxi two miles down the road and walk home in the dark because of the neighbours.'

He was the best father in other ways – he brought home a puppy Pomeranian, black as coal. Her mother named him Prince after a pup she had had when she was a child. They all took Prince to their hearts, but Corinna knew he was her dog. In all the old sepia photographs Prince was up in her arms.

When he was fourteen, her father said, he and a pal had borrowed bicycles and cycled hundreds of miles to Lowestoft and back in two days, sleeping under hedges. The next day they couldn't walk. Both of them were in bed for a week. Every time they went to the sea, he told them this tale and added bits to it. He stood in the sand, rubbing his hands together, looking at them all baked in hot sand, noses peeling, fighting over the float oars and told them tales about when he was a boy.

One day at Clacton, a tidal wave came rising over the sand. He was standing in the sand laughing when he saw it. In a flash he had whisked their mother up in his arms.

'The food!' she cried. 'The food!'

The leg of mutton, the lettuce, the white bread, the little cakes. They were starving with not a thing to eat.

'We'll have to go to Ma's before we eat instead of after and take pot luck on what she has in the larder,' he said.

They ate the larder inside out, laughing all the time, and ate all the afternoon. After tea, they were to take Aunt Annabel and Uncle Jack back to London. By the time they had carried all the paraphernalia, the packages, buckets, spades, coats and beach shoes into the taxi, there was nowhere to sit.

'Good thing we left Prince with Granny for the day,' Corinna said, even though she missed him.

She bagged the tip-up seat, and sat behind her father.

'I shall drive a taxi when I'm grown up.'

Benjamin sprang to life.

'Girl's can't drive taxis! And can't sit in front!'

He was allowed to sit in front with Uncle on the toolbox side because he was a boy. He would be able to drive a taxi and go to war, as if he could fight with his baby white moon face. With a bang she slammed the taxi door, making God's mosquitoes dancing under the trees shiver.

It was dark going home. Shadows fell in the corners of the gigantic hood making mysterious patterns on their faces – Auntie, Amanda, her mother. How pale her mother looked, black round her closed eyes, tired. They were too much for her, Granny said. *What did they do?* she wondered.

Through the sliding window came her father's dreamy voice, singing. Darker and darker the helmet of darkness settled on them. The wooden wheels rattled on the old track; the hooves of the horses clipped and clattered on the cobblestones. A rustle at the window! Highwayman! Pistols cocked! Yellow flashes of lights fell over the sleeping faces; the earth shook. She was awake! The taxi was falling sideways; it was going over. Her hand shot out and opened the door to the sky and jumped. A man as tall as a tree, shouted at her, 'You nearly copped it!'

His lorry lights squeezed up her eyes. Men were

standing on the taxi side.

'Mummy!'

The whole taxi was black and silent, all the men shouting. Then silence, listening.

'Children?' a strained little voice came calling out of the dark.

The men stood on the taxi arguing about how to lift everyone out of the dark body. Her father gripped her arm as if he would fall if he let go. He was shaking his head as if he had been hit, saying over and over he couldn't see; it was the headlights. She strained away from him, determined to climb on the taxi and open the door.

'She can't walk.'

Her voice faded away and came back.

'She can't walk,' she shouted.

No one heard. The men were still arguing. She felt she would go mad, her head all tied up inside.

'Come with me, children.'

A tall strange lady came out of the dark holding her hands out to them. Holding hands, they walked across the grass to where the house stood, all the windows lit. Inside in the sitting room it was quiet. Benjamin crept up to her and put his hand in hers. She held it hard and Amanda's the other side. The ladies couldn't understand what they were saying about their mother until the door burst open and their father was there with her in his arms.

'Here she is.'

He carried her in and put her on the sofa, his face red, his trilby tilted back, coughing smoke from his cigarette. They had been rescued! There were gigantic cups of cocoa for everyone, and everyone was laughing.

Uncle Jack was the hero – he had pushed Benjamin clear of the taxi roof as it went over and saved his life. But Uncle was in hospital with a broken ankle from where the toolbox had landed on his leg in the ditch.

'Home in two or three days,' their mother said. 'Daddy'll fetch him.'

Benjamin sat up.

'In the taxi?'

'In the taxi – and he can come home to tea and you can make a fuss of him then.'

'The same taxi!'

That seemed a miracle to everyone.

'It was God's mercy the wind blew out the lamps,' her father said, 'or there might not have been a taxi at all.'

He had taken off his trilby and put it on the floor and the red had gone out of his face, even though he looked sheepish with the ladies of the house making such a fuss of him.

It was singing all the way home.

Her father called through the little window, 'Derby next week. Just think about that! It's going to be my lucky day – I can feel it. And we'll have a new car to go in – promise.'

And suddenly the car was there in the local garage and the garage at home needed to be creosoted to put it in.

Her father spent the afternoon painting all the sides except the fence side.

'Here, Corie.' He handed her a brush.

'See if you can get in there.'

Draped in an old overall of her mother's, she squeezed into the gap keeping the brush tilted up to prevent the juice from running back under her arm. Benjamin and Amanda stood watching, trying brushes and dipping sticks into the creosote.

She had reached the centre of the side when she saw Benjamin push himself into the other end. No one knew how the fighting started.

Brushes flicked like whips leaving a tail of dirty brown liquid hanging in the air that fell on Benjamin and made him scream and kick out and knock the can over, causing her to drop her brush in a pile of dusty dirt.

'Go away! This is my side!'

'Where's Daddy?'

'Gone to get some more.'

Amanda started the giggles, and when Amanda giggled everything fell to pieces.

'Come out of there at once!'

Her mother's voice stopped her punching Benjamin just as she was winning.

'Can't, I'm stuck!' Benjamin wailed.

She pushed Benjamin and he fell through his end of the gap into the yard. She had won. She felt six inches taller and began to laugh. The brushes were whizzing again, leaving long dirty sheets of sticky mess everywhere. Their hair was sticking up, their mother's face was red with anger and they couldn't stop laughing.

'I don't care – he's a silly little boy!'

Her mother's stick hit her shin bone.

'That's enough! Up to the bathroom.'

The first thing Grandpa said when he came to see them on Sunday was, 'That creosote's inflammable, Will. Highly dangerous mix – tar, oil and petrol fumes.'

'I'll line it with asbestos,' her father said, still throwing buckets of hot soapy water down the yard to take away the metallic blue film on it. Her father never did line it with asbestos and it lasted all the days of their childhood. The immediate damage was done with a cane.

'Corie – you will go to Mr Blake's and ask for a cane. No, don't argue. You won't do as I say and I shall have to get a cane.'

Corinna went with Amanda.

'Let's say it's for the drains,' said Amanda.

'What you want is a plunger,' said Mr Blake.

He knew her mother well and that was a lot of money.

She felt so miserable walking home with the plunger,

her feet died, and walking back with it her voice died too.

'Mummy says she wants a cane, please,' she whispered, handing him the sixpence, chancing whether he guessed or not.

Her mother stood the cane in the corner by the gas stove, a symbol of authority, until Corinna, the ringleader, saw the shame of it and her mother's plight, and put it in the shed in case the drains ever were blocked.

When the day for the Derby came, their faces had lost the dirty golden streaks. They all waited in the new car while her father telephoned the headmistress to say she had had a bilious attack. She watched him speaking.

What would Miss Evans say at assembly?

'How well you look Corinna! Bilious, were you? I do hope you enjoyed your day at Epsom. That will be one hundred lines in the hall.'

She thought out the lines. 'I promise, on my honour, to tell fibs only when I have to, like my father, and to lift my head as he does, eyes far away, while making them up.'

Keeping her fingers crossed, she hoped fervently that Miss Evans would believe the tale about the bilious attack because, of course, she knew she would write no such thing, however much she would like to.

Her mother had chosen a jockey in pink stripes, a rank outsider at one hundred to one. Her father stopped the Pearly King to speak to him for luck. She chose a horse because he looked quick.

'Well,' said her father, 'you may have beginner's luck – he happens to be a good one.'

In front of the bookie she stood close to her father, wrapped up in the warmth from his body and the smell of tobacco all round him. He was a fool, but there wasn't much he didn't know about horses. That was why he'd never make a bookie, Grandpa said.

The horses were like giant phantoms. When the bell had

gone their nostrils expanded and they looked excited enough to run away, out across the world.

'They're off!'

The whole earth shook with the thunder of their hooves and she could see nothing because crowds of men had gathered round them and she was right down in the middle. The shouting grew louder. Her father gripped her arm and pulled her out.

'Thought I'd lost you. Keep with me. You've won a pound or two.'

The bell had gone again before they could reach the bookie and they stood still to watch the next race. She couldn't see it, but she kept her eyes on her father's face, keeping close to him under the shouting while be banged one hand into the other, shouting, 'Attaboy! Attaboy!' over her head.

'Hold on to me tight. Mummy's won too. Come along.'

If she let go, she would get killed under all those feet, crushed to death. She gripped his sleeve and let her feet skim over his. At the office window, she opened her hand for the pile of two-shilling pieces.

'Two pounds!' said her father. 'Not bad. The paddock, then back to Mummy, but see the horses first.'

'Do they have women jockeys?'

'Never. You're too big anyway. Benjamin more likely.'

'Well, I'm going to be one and I shall ride like a cowboy, with no saddle.'

The jockey was patting his horse, rubbing its neck and long white nose, but the horse's mouth was bleeding. He shuddered as if all his muscles were broken. The enormous eyes, luminous and wet, looked straight into hers over the jockey's hand. She longed to speak to him, touch him, stop his eyes bulging, and soothe away his swollen veins.

'I wouldn't make the horse's mouth bleed if I were a jockey – not even to win the race.'

'Ah, well, he pulled him too hard I 'spect. Come on.'

He gripped her hand and ran over the rough grass, past the gypsies' caravans, straight up to the new car with a shout, puffing smoke, tossing his trilby in the air, opening the car door and emptying his pockets into her mother's lap deep in the front seat.

'There! How's that? Twenty quid! And I've made a packet myself this afternoon.'

'And I won two pounds!' she said even louder, dropping the florins gaily into her mother's lap.

'Mind, the gypsies'll see,' said her mother sharply, covering the silver with her coat.

She was happy. Her face was rosy with happiness, but then she didn't know about the horse.

Corinna flopped down in the back seat and rubbed her fingers over Prince's black silky head. He would know just how she felt about the horse.

'The horse's mouth was bleeding – the jockey pulled him too hard.'

'Never mind that,' her father said, rebuking her. 'We're going to France on this race, Ostende too. How about that? Ypres, the Menin Gate, Passchendaele. I'll show you where I was in the war.'

In the war! The Great War! That would be the most marvellous thing ever to happen! At last she would see where they had fought and died, the places of heroism, the lanes where comrades walked, the plains of no-man's-land, the monuments to the fallen. She would see it all! No one stopped talking all the way home.

There were passports to get and tickets and times of trains and boats, and one of those little French dictionaries to buy so that they could ask for *des errf* and *jambong* and all the things Granny would tell them how to say. She stopped. She had forgotten the horse. He had won the race and he had been whipped and his bit had been too tight. He had shuddered and sweated and his mouth had been full of blood. It was wrong to do that to a horse so that you could go to Passchendaele. It made her feel ill.

She rubbed Prince's little pricked ears and told him about the horse in whispers, how she longed to ride him, telling him horses like someone who really loves them riding on their backs. Every time she woke in the night, she felt herself riding the horse like a cowboy, but when she woke in the morning her head was full of the war and Belgium and no-man's-land.

First, there was Tilbury. The soldiers had left from here, the wind cutting into their faces through the gap in the stone walls. Out to sea they went, the engines deep below roaring. She left the rail and ran across no-man's-land to the corner by the steps to her mother, grabbing the chair handles and holding tight, her stomach shaking.

'Gosh! The wind was like a wall. I couldn't walk.'

'Find Benjamin, there's a good girl. In that door.'

All she could see was the great slice of green jelly cut into the sea by the boat. Long black shadows came and went in her eyes. She was falling, falling.

'I feel sick!' she shouted into the wind.

'Sit still! Put your head down.'

She heard, but could do nothing. She had one idea, to run through the great doors down to the lower deck, frantically looking for the lavatory. Inside people sat on the floor or lay on low benches holding paper bags. Someone gave her one and she hung on to it just in time. She gripped all the rails she could see, up the steps, along the deck, back to her mother, and sat on the deck by the chair.

'Better? Sit still. Nelson was always sea sick, so you're in good company.'

'Passports and tickets ready, please,' a sailor's voice echoed over their heads.

She was saved.

'Nearly in – in good time to get settled for the night,' said her mother.

'Look – houses!'

Benjamin was beside himself, frantic with the desire to be everywhere at once. He and Amanda couldn't stop running. The wheelchair rattled over the gangplank and ran on to the quayside as if caught up in the excitement.

'I remember that pub,' her father said. 'We could get something to eat in there later.'

Along the seafront, past the boats moored by the harbour wall and past the houses, was the Ostende wall.

'Come on, run! Jump!'

Holding hands in a line, they skimmed down the wall to land with a great bump in the wet sand, the sea coming round their feet. The world stopped spinning and their shoes were full of seawater.

'Where's Mummy?' Benjamin wept, the great crybaby.

She grabbed his hand and ran him to their mother.

'He wants ice cream, don't you?'

'Ask Daddy, he has the francs.'

Their father stood them along the kerb. She held the wheelchair on one side and the other two the other.

'All the traffic goes the wrong way – see,' he said.

He had become the responsible parent.

'Drive on the right – look.'

Lines of foreign-looking bicycles and cars and trams came down the road.

'Come on, now! Charge!'

And they were over.

Outside the yellow café at a yellow table, they sat in the sun, all eating ice creams while waiting for food.

'*Cinq oeuf* means five eggs each,' her father said, rubbing his hands on his knees as if he were at home.

That was what the waiter brought, five eggs each, but their father ate the most.

19

Corinna was to go on a tram with her father to find somewhere for the night. Her mother would stay on the beach with Amanda and Benjamin. How far away they looked playing in the sand, as if they had been left on an island. Sudden fear slashed into her.

'I can't leave Mummy, someone may come up!'

'Don't be silly! We'll be only ten minutes.'

Under the tram platform, the road slid away like the sea at the back of the boat. Aft. She raised her telescope and the coast of England fell below the horizon.

'England expects…'

A lady came out of the tram and stood next to her against the rail, very elegant, very foreign, like her mother in photographs of when she was young. Her mother said perfume was not nice, it disguised uncleanliness, but the lady was beautifully dressed, silky and soft perfectly clean with a perfume like flowers. Next to hers on the rail, the lady's hand looked like her mother's with small bones, little veins, fingers looking quick even when they were still, but her mother wouldn't have had that huge red stone halfway up one finger.

She wriggled her arm to draw back the frayed cuff of her blazer. It used to be cousin Vernon's and she had insisted on wearing it. The lady smiled at her and she took a deep breath and stood still. On one side of her was her father with his warm tobacco smell and on the other the perfume of the lady, the most beautiful lady.

The tram had stopped. Her father grabbed her by the arm and hoisted her off the tram, and they were on the road among fruit barrows all along the kerb, crowds of people talking loudly and laughing, and shops with red and green and white awnings.

Her father was talking to a tall bald man with a teacloth over his arm speaking strange words.

'Why call him patron?'

'He's the boss. Come on.'

Up the stairs she followed him to a huge bedroom with five beds and an enamel jug for the water on the wash-stand, right over the café. Shaving water would be at the door *ici – here*. Even the doorknob was square and covered in flowers like an ornament.

'Can we go back to Mummy?'

'In a jiffy. Don't worry so much.'

All day they had been in the sand, in the sea, or walking through the streets. Everything they saw was strange to their eyes, everything they heard strange to their ears. It was French, but not in France. Her father's French was soldier's French, but better than nothing, unless it was eggs you wanted.

'*San fairy anne*. What does that really mean?'

'Not a sausage, ducky.'

There was a twinkle in his eyes.

Her head was full of words – Menin Gate. Flanders. Ypres, words like a great noise. Now they fell into a pool of calm, an oasis. They were together in a foreign land, with their mother in the wheelchair her hand white as marble in the lamplight on the chair arm, the wheels spinning, their feet clattering on the pavement through the streets, foreign voices calling. They would all sleep in the same room over the café. They were all together, that was what mattered. This was their home for the night, safe and sound.

'Tomorrow we'll get a charabanc to Ypres. Never thought I'd go there again.'

Miles and miles of white crosses spread to the horizon. It made her eyes ache just to see them, and nearby her father wandered among the tombstones, her mother's eyes never leaving his face from the coach window. When it was time to go, he still wandered there, his face wet with tears, frowning at memories – his pal with half his face gone, the eight days in a dugout with a sniper in the tree over his head.

This was the land of comrades, the land where they had fought the Germans, now covered by white stone slabs.

'A comrade is a fellow you would give your life for.'

Their names were cut in the stone walls of the arch, the Menin Gate, that was the memorial, where they read: THEIR NAMES LIVETH FOR EVERMORE.

Two steps down led into the little shop, and immediately on the counter in front of her lay a box full of penknives. She picked one up. It was chunky with everything in it – two long blades, a small one, a corkscrew, a tin-opener.

'Could I have Ostende on the side?'

The assistant behind the counter shook her head.

'This is Ypres; this is not Ostende,' she said in beautiful English.

'But Ypres is not a proper place.'

'*San fairy anne*,' said her father, and the penknife slid deep into her blazer pocket, Ostende on the side.

At the frontier, they had to get out of the coach so that soldiers could rummage through the seats. She was allowed to stand with her mother, and when the soldier came she moved so that he could not see the bulky parcel in her mother's lap.

'Nothing there. Au revoir! *Merci!*'

He had gone, trailing his rifle.

'Bastards,' said their father. 'Trying to charge English people for a few paltry mementoes and all we did in the war.'

When they reached home, there were three solid brass Menin Gate ashtrays for the grates.

'One for each of you three in the years to come, a memory of the Great War, and your father a hero in it', their mother said, because she loved him.

Chapter Two

There was the question of the leeches.

'Leeches!'

'They experimented and one hung on too long,' her mother said. 'All that I ask is that God will let me have it all – keep it from you children.'

The hospital was on a hill in London. Trams ran outside.

'Why do they always look like prisons?' her father asked. 'And no children allowed.'

Over the weeks, Corinna grew good at hanging on the outside window sill to peep inside to their mother, the other two grizzling under her feet because she was the leader.

At last her father came out smiling.

'Coming home – we'll manage.'

That day they all washed the kitchen floor and swept the passages, shook the mats in the garden and made Prince bark himself silly.

'Sixpence each for helping – and no arguments!'

The flat was the only one with a garden. The others had nothing – no roses up to the door. But it was much bigger than the house in the country, which was a good thing, and when they had been to Wigmore Street to buy an indoor chair, their mother could go all over it and take charge. After that the aunts came to a quiet party for her mother.

'An old gentleman comes a long way on a bus to see me play netball,' Corinna said to Aunt Alice.

She felt her mouth go dry. She couldn't say he was Miss Mathew's father and Miss Mathew was the fourth form mistress.

'And then there are the essays all about fighting boys,' Corinna said with hesitation.

'Miss said, "Very good, but you're too old for that." What did she mean?'

She was not to take the eleven-plus after all, and not to read too much, the doctor had said. It was a nervous cough, don't push her. She's just highly strung and rather delicate needs plenty of games and fresh air. When girls are twelve, Cora had said, they have to wear a pad because they bleed. Boys wear a rubber bag because they have white stuff.

Cora was top of the class. She was Jewish, her father said.

'Jews are like that,' he said. 'Clever and clean even if they do you as soon as look at you. I'll have to talk to Mummy.'

Later, he took her on the tram to get a new wireless set.

'I want to speak to you,' he whispered in smoky puffs into her forehead. 'It's about growing up.'

Quiet fell throughout the tram. The passengers sat or stood like statues, listening.

'It's about boys and girls. Young men will always try with a girl – you have to be very careful.'

She pressed close to him trying to will him to stop because she knew everything already, but he took another breath.

'Never – never let a fellow – if a girl does before they're married, he'll never be able to trust her afterwards.'

Her face was on fire and she kept her head near his shoulder, holding herself tightly together. There was nowhere to hide, no way to stop him, until someone shouted and people pushed past. The tram had stopped. He let go of the ceiling strap and clutched the wireless close.

'Come on. We're there.'

He jumped off and she jumped after him. It was over.

Nothing could happen unless you let it, and you never let a boy kiss you on the mouth. Amanda let all the boys kiss her on the mouth, but she didn't have babies. How could Amanda be a flirt and not have babies? Round and round in her head the question raced all the way home, ringing in her ears through the street door into the kitchen as she followed her father. Prince scampered round her as she stood looking expectantly at her mother. Her father edged the wireless on to the table.

'I couldn't get anywhere. You'll have to try!'

Her mother wasn't worried.

'She'll be all right. She's a good girl.'

As if that made any difference. Amanda was bad and the same would happen to her, except that she didn't want any babies and Amanda wanted four.

Something much worse happened that night. Prince was lost. He had wandered out of the side gate into the road and was stolen. Day after day she ran home from school, pushed open the door, and listened, but heard nothing. She woke in the night listening, everyone listening for his tiny feet.

'Good luck gone for good,' said their father.

That very night Granny died. (*Quietly*) Sobbing her mother laid her veil on the glove box. The house was so quiet, it too seemed to have died. Everything was miserable – Granny dead, Prince gone. Now they were moving.

'Go and practise the piano now.'

She stood at the window peering into the black space between the stars – that must be heaven. If she looked hard enough. But Granny was in the room, looking at her over her pince-nez, darning.

'Granny!'

'*S'il vous plaît* – sound the *I*.' Granny was in her head! She ran down the long passage to the kitchen and banged open the door. Amanda and Benjamin sat at the table scribbling.

'Tea's ready,' said her mother. 'That's enough for tonight.'

In the big old sitting room, her mother moved her chair closer to the fire.

'The new school's lovely. It's brand new, with a sports field all round it.'

There was white in her face that was unhappiness. Corinna felt sick. She wanted to cry. She moved along the sofa instead.

Her mother was very quiet, then she said, 'I must speak to you, Corie,' and she knew it was about babies and things like rough men and boys in the dark – never let them touch you. 'It's not only about babies, it's about periods.'

Her mother fidgeted a bit.

'You can't have babies unless you have periods.'

In a way that was a relief.

'Well, I don't want any babies so that's all right. I shan't have periods.'

She lay back on the sofa and stretched out her legs towards the fire. She decided to concentrate on the animals standing or lying on the little white shelves over the fireplace. Rosebuds there were, with cupids climbing up them. Every animal was doubled in the mirror behind, and all had come from Granny's house. A pig with WON'T BE DRUV on its side, that was best. She knew all the time in her stomach that there was more to come, and worse.

Her mother edged the chair nearer to the fire.

'You're twelve now, not a little girl any more.'

Her voice sounded strained.

'You'll get a sign of blood, like blood but not really blood – in your water perhaps – or in the bath.'

She sat upright against the firelight.

'Just tell me when it happens. I don't want you to be afraid, that's all. It's in the Bible,' she said to help her along. 'Adam had to work by the sweat of his brow. Eve had to have children or the world would stop going round.'

She paused.

'It's only for a few days every month.'

'Every month!'

Corinna jumped up and stalked to the window looking up the steps to the pavement.

'Every month! I'll go to work. I'm not having that.'

All round her was the trap. God had made it. She couldn't breathe and she felt tight in her skin.

'Don't be cross now – there's a good girl. We don't choose. God makes us men or women.' Her mother's thin voice softly added, 'You can still do all – most – of those things you like. Not swimming, of course, netball perhaps.'

Her lips were pale, her eyes on the fire.

'Perhaps!'

It was all to do with religion and she wanted to scream. She was not a girl. She was a boy inside. She wanted to burst out of herself. She would do all the things she wanted to as boys did. She was as good as any boy playing football – she was captain of the netball team.

Her mother sighed and bent down to move hair from her forehead.

'Mummies do what they think is right. You'll know when you grow up.'

There was no stopping the anger that boiled over in her until she was shouting.

'Aunt Alice says you'd never have been so ill if you hadn't had us!'

'Nonsense!'

Her mother perked up in their defence.

'I'd've been much worse more likely – besides, that has nothing to do with it. These things come from the sins of the fathers. That's in the Bible too unto the third and fourth generation.'

'Then the Bible isn't fair!'

Corinna was standing looking out of the window, hot with rage against God, when she saw a beautiful woman coming to the door. A lady, in a wide-rimmed cream hat with a long rolled umbrella, daintily stepped down the stone steps from the pavement. She froze.

'A lady is coming to the door.'

Her mother sat bolt upright, her facing going red.

'Ah! That's Miss Wilton – I'd forgotten. She's coming about Benjamin. She's getting him into a college. Now, be a good girl and let her in.' She tried to tidy the front of her blouse and smooth out her lap as if nothing was wrong.

A storm broke out in the room. Corinna was bursting with rage. She would not open the door. Let the woman die.

'I can write essays, Benjamin can't. It's not fair!'

She was shouting again.

'Come along now! Open the street door and pick up your satchel, there's a good girl.'

There was something in her voice, like tears.

'No!'

There was silence. Her mother looked so white and small, trying to be strong. All that noise, that screaming, was in her own head. How could she run out of the room and leave her. It would take her mother ages and ages to open the door. Corinna snatched up her satchel and strode down the hall, shouting in her head at God who had made her a girl, flung open the street door and scowled at the lady under the wide-brimmed hat who was getting Benjamin into college.

Early in the spring they moved. Snow lay everywhere – on rooftops, fence tops, the branches of trees. Snow stood in little columns between the upright bars on the front gate. Double pneumonia their mother had. She lay in the front bedroom where the lino was not yet laid and Aunt Rebecca who had only came for a week was still with them. The snow stuck to the outside walls of the house.

She could see from the window all the houses and gardens had vanished in a field of snow that ran down to the river and out to the horizon. God was in the silence and in the endless cloud of snow under the sky.

'Please, God!'

'That you, Corie?' a faint little voice said. 'My watch,' her mother went on, holding it out, her hand falling on to the quilt.

Wet hair lay flat on her forehead and there was a strange faded white in her face.

'It has diamond sides – you and Amanda have those – Benjamin's to have the long strips of diamond pieces to make a nice tiepin.'

'Leave Mummy now. She must sleep.'

That night was as long as eternity, but in the morning Aunt Rebecca came into the bedroom and slung the curtains apart.

'Mummy's better! Come in quietly, all of you.'

Corinna laid her head on her mother's hand in the bed and cried and cried. Then she went into the bathroom to thank God in case she should want Him again. When she stood up, she looked out of the window and saw boats sailing on the river below. The snow had gone.

'Now we must get the girls to school.'

They bumped the wheelchair down the hill, the air so cold it hurt their noses.

'Mrs Eliot?'

The headmaster had a nice voice, but his mouth was twisted so that his teeth moved when he spoke as if he were eating. He took the chair handles and pushed it into the centre of the room.

'So – you've brought your little girls to my school.'

Little girls, indeed! Corinna stood taller for him to see how tall she was.

Her mother liked him. She looked all pink and perky.

'The boy's at college – the girls've had no settled education.'

At her elbow, books started in long lines and filled every wall round the room. Some had gold letters on leather covers like those at Grandpa's, some were blue-covered, some brown or red, some were old, some brightly new. Books and books.

All the time her mother spoke, his eyes were on her face.

'The school's the newest in the country,' he said, 'all on one level.'

The uniform was to be light and dark blue. He gave Corinna a silver badge of interwoven Latin so small no one could read it. Then, walking slowly round his desk, he put his hand over one of her mother's on the rug.

'Shell shock, my dear, excuse me.' He rubbed his hand over Amanda's curls and to Corinna he said, 'And you come in one day and tidy my books. Would you like that?'

Home again, Corinna put the kettle on to make her mother tea and made Amanda cut the bread. Then Benjamin came in and they all began to shout.

'Children! All of you,' her mother called from the sitting room. 'Do as Corie tells you. Benjamin, come here.'

In some moods, Corinna could see he was just a silly little boy in his Etons, his satchel bulging with Latin and French books he couldn't read. She couldn't think of words powerful enough for the sarcasm she felt. At other times, she just hated him, like now.

'Well, I'm not washing-up,' she said. 'It's his turn.'

She stomped up the stairs, leaving him with her mother and Amanda, and stood at the bedroom window and shouted at God the eternal question – 'Why is it that only girls have to wash up?'

The sky was grey and silent. She felt the disapproval of God telling her it would be her fault if her mother was sent to hospital. It always came to this, first the anger and then, just as she had won, she felt sorry. Slowly she dragged herself down the stairs to make her mother tea.

There would be no time that summer to put down the new concrete path, their mother was too ill. It had been a mistake to come here. Her father bit the side of his finger. They had to move nearer to the hospital and she had to go for treatment immediately because the arthritis was affecting her eyes.

'School?' Corinna's mouth was so dry the word would hardly come. He gave her a little smile. He wanted to tease, but he didn't.

'You can go by bus,' he said, 'but Amanda'll have to move, the Council says.'

He took their mother in the new car to the hospital. The whole house went cold and empty. The wind blew with them up from the river after school and howled round the house wall. She opened the street door and all their feet stamped in together to scare away the devil. She gave the orders.

'Here's your milk. Drink it. You wash up. I've got other things to do.'

In a flash, every little cake bulging with currants, the pile of bread and butter and jam, all were gone. Coats lay everywhere, satchels were on the floor. She flew over them up the cold stairs to lie on her bed and read. She had to know where Pip took the cake to the prisoner before it was time go to. When she looked up again, the light was fading from the sky.

On the way down the hill, the empty wheelchair banged, its hard wheels hitting kerbs. The metal frame rattled in sympathy with the noise of their feet and bumped to a stop under the bus stop lamppost with the rain blowing into their faces and the long dark road shining wet. She gripped the chair handles.

'Stand near me, keep near the chair.'

Any minute Benjamin would cry.

'Bus's coming.'

The warning broke out of her like a trumpet call. The bus stopped. A little upright figure stood on the step. Bandages! That was the first impression – white bandages round their mother's head. She felt the other two go stiff with her. Their mother's eyes were covered with white bandaging. The conductor leapt off to help her down to the kerb. His action released them.

'Mummy!'

Upright and stiff, she balanced herself on the pavement, moving her stick towards them and raising her head so that she could see them under the bandage, and smiled, fumbling for the chair. Amanda stamped her foot, crying, Benjamin began to whimper. Their mother laughed and pulled the rug on to her lap.

'Silly old doctors – made me look like I don't know what – a real mess!'

They all laughed. Corinna pushed the chair while Amanda skipped all the way in the dark singing with Benjamin.

'Silly old hospital! Silly old doctors!'

She went up to her room to ask God why these things should happen to her mother. He didn't answer. That was because He made them unhappy so that they would know the difference when they were happy. Their mother said that, but she was too angry to keep on making excuses for Him.

She stood up on the top of the new bus all the way home from school, the rain in her hair like a sailor on the lookout mast. Long, long ago this was the country. Horse-drawn buses had come down this road when her mother was a child and it was a narrow lane with trees on each side. Milk had slopped out of the buckets that the milkmaids had carried on to the grass to make piecrusts.

Breathing fire, the horses stopped. She jumped off the bus step and stood still. All was quiet in the long dark road and the big old house down there in the dark. Then she took a deep breath and ran.

'You're soaked! Off with your things!'

'Can't breathe – can't!'

'You should get inside.'

'Claustrophobia!'

Benjamin had French and Latin in his satchel, but she had the pistol in hers, the *History of England*, and an apple. In the kitchen, she slung the satchel away from Benjamin under the table and pushed his books out of the way. She had to cut thirteen slices of bread, four slices each and one extra – she was starving. Amanda took her four and slid off the chair.

'I want dripping – I'll get it.'

They could do as they liked at school teatime, help themselves and be good. Sometimes they had thirteen slices each, but tonight there was fruitcake after because their mother and father were going to see Uncle Herbert about a new taxi and supper would be late.

'Whoopee! Dracula's on! Let's go! I've read it and it made my ears go funny.'

When they got home that night it was pitch dark. The house looked like a great black hole with bricks round it. The gate groaned. The key stuck in the lock. Corinna threw open the street door and flattened herself against the wall. Vampires and bats filled the hall, all suckers of blood. She was the leader, she had to go in first. She flung herself arms stretched out into the black hole – to the light switch.

'I wasn't afraid,' Benjamin said. He pushed past, majestically striding in.

She watched him stride to the kitchen door and braced herself.

'You were. You cheated. I was first.'

He turned under the case where the servant's bells were still fixed over the door, glowering at her.

'You asking for a fight?'

His black eyebrows were in a straight line. 'Girls can't fight!'

'Don't be silly. The boys chase you to school!'

The electric light turned his face into a mask with holes for eyes and mouth. His face went black, his body a pillar of stone filling the doorway. She pushed herself forward.

'Scared?' She was poised for action, full of hate for his pale, cold face and the disdain in his eyes.

Over his head a piece of brown, varnished wallpaper flapped down the frosted glass. His hands were on her throat. He was shaking her, his legs entangled with hers and she fell with him on top of her. Hot waves of pain stabbed her chest and his breath blew into her face.

'Give in!'

'No.'

He was puffing air like a horse. No, she would not give in. She would die rather. He let go and sprang to his feet. He had gone, his trouser legs swishing over her face, the boards on the stairs creaking. She scrambled up and into the kitchen.

'You shouldn't fight.'

Amanda cut a chunk of fruitcake and pushed it over the table. Corinna reached the sink. In a bowl of warm water, she opened out her hands. In her head over and over she was still seeing herself lying helpless on the floor. He was three years younger and much heavier than she was, and much stronger.

'I should've been a boy, then I'd be stronger.'

'Well, you're not. Girls don't fight.'

'I don't feel like a girl.'

'It's nice being a girl. Amy Johnson's a girl. She's flown

all that way in an aeroplane.'

Her heart still pounded, her head full of fear of what might have been. Her back hurt, as did her throat and her eyes. She wanted to cry. She would never fight him again with body strength that was worthless.

'I shall learn everything instead of fighting. I shall learn and learn, French, history, stories, I shall know more than he does, like Grandpa. Knowledge is power, Grandpa said, and for that you have to read and read.'

She buried her hands in the warm soapy water, then in a towel.

'I swear to learn everything. Amanda, you've got to remember that – it's an oath.'

But it was too late. It was time to leave school. There was no money, times were bad and millions out of work. She could see how her father hated saying it.

'You'll like it at work, meet lots of people, young people. Grandpa went to work when he was nine, learnt French fluently before he was eighteen and played the violin too.'

He didn't believe that would help, but he had to say it, drumming his fingers on the kitchen table and staring into space.

It was difficult to see if the headmaster had tears in his eyes because of the shellshock, but he watched her walk away from his door all the way down the cloister. Every step she could feel him there.

'Into a shop! What a waste – in a better world you'd go on to become a teacher.'

She reached the big doors and still she couldn't turn to wave. The doors closed and she ran up the steps to the main road, and stopped. Eileen had remembered; she was waiting by the railings. Corinna slowed down to walk towards her. Eileen being there made all the difference.

'Hallo!'

Eileen turned and stared at her.

'Hallo,' she said.

No, she had forgotten. She must be waiting for Gertrude. All she really wanted was for Eileen to like her. Eileen, with her smooth dark hair and shining blue eyes.

'You're like a boy,' she had said her strong straight hands holding the model ship, replacing it with a look of admiration back on the bookcase. Why was it wrong to say that? Why did Eileen feel guilty and her face turn pink?

Like a knight of old, she walked with Eileen to the bus stop where all the others could see.

'This is my last day at school,' she said.

Eileen looked at her and smiled, but her eyes flickered.

'I shall miss you,' she said, but with an empty sound, already thinking of other things, and her soft plump cheeks looked rosier because she felt awkward and didn't know what else to say.

But that didn't matter. The moment was coming – the top deck of the bus was visible as it came round the corner. Slowly it stopped in front of them making her heart lurch. This was the moment she had to say it.

'Eileen—'

The rest had gone. Her mouth was paralysed. The mocking look had come back into Eileen's eyes because she knew the words without their being said, but it vanished in the soft touch of lips on her face. Corinna swung on the bus handrail and ran up the steps. She had kissed Eileen.

Below, Eileen stood with her face lifted to the drizzling rain, blowing a kiss. Then she tossed her head and turned away.

It would be best, said her mother, to take an apprenticeship in London. No need to look for the store. There it was, a giant building, windows full of elegantly dressed figures, in a side street with a secret passage and a door marked STAFF ENTRANCE. This was the office. Her mother climbed the long steep flight of stairs, one step and a stop to get ready for the next. Corinna kept her eyes on the little door at the top. They were nearly there when it flew open and a tall thin lady stood staring down at them.

'Mrs Eliot? I am Jean Letts. Miss Letts.'

A small pot of red liquid stood on one end of the desk like a storm beacon. At the other stood a typewriter, a sheet of white paper ready. Out of the distance came the questions and answers – fourteen years old, yes, English good, and maths too, which was a fib.

'She's going to miss her netball,' her mother added, trying to sound cheerful.

'Aha,' said Miss Letts. 'We have our own netball team – Saturday afternoons.'

That was spiffing! It would be like school after all, except that she would have to wear silk stockings and a black dress with a white collar. And she would get seven shillings and six pence a week and free lunch.

At the end of the interview, they were soon eating toast and drinking tea in a teashop as if they were starving. The waitress pretended not to see them until she felt like it.

'They used to call me lightning,' her mother said. 'You could hardly call this one that.'

All the excitement of the day fell into quietness. When she was warm and cosy her mother began to talk about the suffragettes, about her own father emigrating to South America when he was eighteen, and about the old times and Grandpa's three illegitimate sons, and the punishment that came when two died and one was a criminal.

'Then why have him to tea on Sundays?' Corinna asked.

'Because Granny would have wanted it.'

Outside on the pavement, her mother stood back against the big windows, drinking in the fumes and the constant eye-teasing movement, the ear-splitting hooters and scorching tyres of braking cars, her face shining with joy.

Her old perky self came out in her home ground, London, encouraged now that her eldest was about to become an apprentice.

'We might see Will – you never know – it's a small world.' She watched the taxis sail by like trawlers on the Thames.

The ribbon department was her first assignment. Her first customer was a big white lady with a cigarette, loud and jolly, who had three children. In her profession she could afford them, the other girls said laughing.

'Three yards of red silk ribbon half an inch wide,' she said.

The large white hand hung in the air. On every finger was a heavy magnificent ring.

That one.

She dabbed at a reel in the tray.

The red ribbon oozed out of the slit in the little black machine like a tongue of blood – three children – that meant lots of blood saved up for nine months – the nipple a pink bud in a purple nest slipping out of baby's mouth – in one end and out of the other – all that mess – fetch doctor, baby's bleeding!

Better to be clever and rich and then you didn't have to have babies.

Terribly hot it was. Something moved in front of her. The woman was peering at her over the counter – the little clock read thirty yards. Thirty yards! A pile of red ribbon lay at her feet. She shook all over, then took out a pencil and wrote very clearly on the paper end: 30 YARDS. She cut off three yards and made it into a little roll and tucked it in a bag.

The woman said, 'Thank you.'

She went, her head shaking with laughter, her left hand swinging the little green bag. Silence fell everywhere; no one had noticed. She rolled the rest of the ribbon back on its spool and slipped the spool into the glass-fronted drawer. On the way home, she bought her mother a chocolate éclair – it was a holy thing to do in case someone had noticed.

She began to hate the shop, escaping by staring out of the great door. She felt she would die if she didn't get out in the fresh air and she was so tired she couldn't play netball. In no time at all, she had a cold with a fever and special leave at home.

'Does your hand hurt?'

The sword was deep between her mother's eyes, her knuckles big and shiny where she pressed the frock hem against the table edge.

'Only when I'm sewing. Don't fret now. You've got to keep quiet or doctor'll be cross.'

'I could sew that for you. I wouldn't cobble it up, promise!' Corinna answered her.

'No – I can manage. You go on reading and talking to me...'

'Well,' said the doctor the second time he came, 'an X-ray, I think.'

Aunt Rebecca took her to the hospital and they had tea in the Empire Club afterwards. She was to have ultra-violet rays for six weeks and see the specialist after that, the sister said.

Aunt Rebecca taught Corinna how to break a roll not to cut it, and how to eat meringue glacé so that it didn't shoot across the room. It was like a lesson and she liked lessons. Two little ladies with black bands round their necks watched, whispering like two little birds by the fire. She told her mother about the Club and Aunt Rebecca's fox fur and the little legs making her feel sick.

'What did the doctor say?'

'He said I had a temperature.'

'Next time ask him if he thinks you should go to Switzerland to stay with Aunt Mat for a while.'

Switzerland! As soon as it was said, she knew she was going. The idea grew day by day – she would learn German, she would make it happen; she would go into a new world full of sun and mountains. She would see John, who was four when they went the last time and was now eleven, a little Swiss boy, speaking German.

In the tiny cell lying on the hard bench she watched the doctor wash his hands and come towards her wiping them. He bent over her, listening through the stethoscope and when he stood up she dared to ask him. He looked very tired, like a removal man in his soft black shoes and his dirty white coat, with bulging pockets. When she asked him, he swung his stethoscope in tiny circles as he stood and looked at her, and breathlessly she waited. He said nothing. He turned to go and began to walk out, then he turned back and said quickly and quietly so that she could hardly hear.

'Yes – yes – of course – go if you can.'

'He's writing our doctor a note,' she burst out in the kitchen. 'I'm a suspect case he told the sister.'

She stopped. Her mother had gone white.

'What does that mean? Suspect – of what?'

'Chest trouble, I 'spect. You just need watching.'

It was only then that it struck her – it would be more than a holiday; she would have to leave her mother. It struck her in the stomach with a thud.

'How long – how long will it take?'

'You get better. Stop coughing and you can come home. I'll put the fare money in the Post Office ready to send to you.'

Panic propelled her to her mother's side.

'I don't want to go really,' weights in her feet. 'I don't cough all the time, sometimes hardly at all.'

'Doctor wants you to. He says it'll save trouble later.

You'll be home in no time at all.'

'I'll write often, of course. If you're sure you'll be all right.'

'Stop arguing and go, there's a good girl. You'll be glad all your life.'

Chapter Three

They were singing at the station – 'Tipperary', 'Goodbye Dolly I must leave you' – all the songs her father used to sing in the firelight. Girls with gaily coloured scarves, young men carrying skis like bayonets, laughed and broke out of the train singing.

'Toff's home from the mountains,' said her father. 'Get a porter as soon as the train stops. Tip him right away.'

His black hair was full of shining smuts. Amanda and Benjamin at his side frowned up at her.

'Here!'

He pushed a coin into her hand over the window top. Two shillings!

'That's for tipping, extra. Telegraph Mummy.'

The train jolted; the engine hissed, started off and stopped. Then it was away.

She had a queer feeling in her stomach, tight. She was alone and grown up. It was like going into no-man's-land – when your numbers up you die.

'You can do it,' said her mother, her voice fading, 'an' don't forget to eat, then you'll be all right.'

First she ate the egg sandwiches and opened *Tom Sawyer*. Already the train was slowing down.

'Dover!'

She wasn't supposed to ask the Cooks man at Calais, but he flicked his fingers and a porter came to carry the cases. He led her with the porter across the railway lines buried in grass to the platform.

The Cooks man spoke to the porter in French, saluted her and left. The cases were tossed through the train window and the porter ran round into the carriage to put them on the rack.

'*Merci*! Mamselle.'

She bounced into the corner seat, took out a towel and rolled it up for a pillow. Gosh she was tired! A thousand pictures in her head - her mother's face, the Cooks man. She drifted to sleep and woke, the train gliding silently into the Gare du Nord.

'*S'il vous plaît?*'

Her voice was so quiet she couldn't hear it herself. 'St Lazare, please,' she said louder.

One driver out of the whole line of taxi drivers looked at her, a dark haired young man, who hoisted the cases into the back, opened the door for her and shut it, all in a jiffy.

'Paris!'

She leaned forward on the edge of the seat and saw everything at once – street lights, taxis flying out from side turnings, a woman in red slippers carrying a long loaf, café tables on the pavements.

If she had had a comrade with her, they would have gone into a café and drunk black coffee with cream, while dipping and eating those long white biscuits. Then they would have walked by the river to see the bookstalls in the painting that Grandpa had, but was Granny's from Paris long ago.

'Gare St Lazare, Mamselle.'

She held out her hand full of English money. He couldn't cheat her because of the war. When he had gone, she pulled the cases on to the platform through the entrance to a line of waiting porters.

'Le train pour Brig?' she managed, but all their dark ferocious-looking faces said nothing.

The strength was draining from her legs when one man came forward and looked at the ticket again.

'Ah, *Anglaise*! *Le train pour Brig*!'

She tipped this one the extra florin. He stepped backwards and bowed.

The journey really started with the long all-night train. She poured herself a cup of tea from the flask and opened the packet of cheese sandwiches. Her mother would be having tea, or supper, everything would be all right. The wheels droned under her, on and on.

'*Billet*! *S'il vous plaît*!'

Without stopping, a short fat man lurched past her to the window and pushed it up and rolled down the blind.

He smiled and examined her ticket.

'*Bon nuit*!'

The door clicked shut. Nothing could be heard, but the steady rumble of the train.

She lay down again, her ears full of French. If only it were inherited like blood she could have had it from Granny. The train jolted and steamed on. Deliberately, she closed her eyes and slept.

Descendez! *La frontiere*!

Get out! She could see under the blind a long low crack of light running across the horizon. Stiff with sleep, she walked down the platform following passengers into a high-roofed shed where they stood stamping their feet, columns of cigarette smoke hovering over their heads.

'Passport – *s'il vous plaît*.'

At her end of a line of trestle tables, an official sat staring at her. He took her passport and examined it, hesitating while her heart stopped. With the faintest of smiles, he handed it back to her.

'*À la Suisse*!' he said, his long white hand referring her to the official next to him.

She had been handed over from France to Switzerland!

With a whoop of joy, she flew back to her seat, opened up the rug previously despised as too used, and fell into it, asleep.

'*Frühstück!*'

A young man in a white jacket had stuck his head in the door and gone again. She let up the blind, squinting in the sharp sunlight shining on brilliant snowy slopes that rose to mountain peaks.

With hand in her overcoat pocket gripping her passport and ticket, she lurched after him until he stopped at a small counter made of wooden boxes in a corner of the luggage van.

'One shilling for coffee,' he said brightly.

Passengers all round her were speaking English. She kept her eyes down so that no one would speak to her, gratefully drinking the whole bowl of coffee and replacing the bowl on the box. Then she battled her way back to her compartment to find a huge official blocking the door.

'*Billet – Fahrkarte – bitte.*'

Her first German!

'Brig?' she asked, her voice rising with excitement.

She waited while he studied the ticket, then he smiled and let out a long chaos of French and German all mixed up, rolling his eyes under heavy brows and waving his arms.

Lötschenberg she recognised in the chaos, and was instantly alarmed to see him pull her cases off the rack and leave them on the floor while he retreated as the train rumbled into a tunnel.

She stood at the window, riveted by the alternating dark and brilliant strips of sunlight cutting in over the train as they crossed crevices, looked down on clouds below, and plunged back into darkness. Here lived eagles, bringing prey from the valleys for their young like a stolen lamb or a rabbit.

The door opened. The official had come back. He said nothing. He brusquely picked up the cases and walked off.

The train had stopped on top of a mountain. The official left her and the cases on the platform and vanished into the buffet. She stood still, wary.

With pale faces and in dark heavy clothes, mountain peasants burst out of nowhere. They pulled her luggage labels and shouted into her face.

'*Billet? Billet?*'

They were all talking at once. The whistle blew, and the train jolted.

'Ver you go to?'

English!

'Brig! Brig!'

'*Dies Frutigen – geh!*'

The woman pushed her aboard. She jumped down again and grabbed her big case and the train moved. She scrambled up the steps again heaving it after her. A porter had grabbed the other case and was running now at a great speed to throw it in to her. She stood in the open doorway waving. All their swarthy peasant faces smiled broadly at her. The door slammed.

She pulled the cases into the first compartment and on closing the door looked up into the grinning face of the official. He took her ticket. He tilted back his head to look at her under the peak of his cap.

'Ah, Brig,' he said and bowed himself out.

She burst out laughing.

'Zippee!'

That she would write about to her mother.

The tune of the wheels had changed, they were running down into the open valley. The train dipped and hummed. The rails ran into the little town and along the road between houses and shops full of people. Skiers filled the station, sitting on walls and on luggage trucks. Some had arms in slings or heads bandaged. They were English people, mad and laughing. She opened the door and jumped out.

She had forgotten what Aunt Mat looked like, recognising her suddenly.

'Auntie!' she called.

A boy nearly as tall as Benjamin but thinner appeared at her side under a fur hat.

'John?'

'Post office first,' said Aunt Mat. 'Telegram to your mother.'

She watched Aunt Mat fill out the form and hand it to the man behind the counter.

'Give special love from me – please.'

'I did,' Aunt Mat without a blink.

A slice of lemon floated on the tea and the eyes of all the Swiss working men in the buffet watched her.

'I'd rather have water next time, please.'

'Oh no! You can't drink the water here, you'd get typhoid.'

'How can anyone live here then?'

'Lemonade. I'll give you a dash of my wine.'

John slopped his lemonade drinking too quickly because he was too shy to stay. His shy eyes were downcast under the pushed up ridge of his balaclava. He grabbed his cap and shot off, his long woollen stockings ruckling under leather shorts.

'I want to be a boy!'

The words hit her. She looked down at her own hands, just like a boy's! And in her jacket pocket was the Ostende penknife. Never would John have one like that.

The yellow slatted seats of the local train vanished under a line of villagers. All their dark eyes secretly looked at her, though their heads were hidden under headscarves. Their boots clobbered under their long heavy coats, and they talked and talked.

'Schwitzer-deutsch,' said Aunt Mat. 'Impossible. No one writes it so no one can learn it.'

The train stopped. John banged the cases down and left them, coming back a moment later pulling a little yellow truck with a long handle. Snow dripped from the station roof on to her head. It stood as high as she was along the sides of the road, like a wall.

'Boots first,' said Aunt Mat, 'then a balaclava.'

She walked like a ballerina, her long fur coat sweeping the snow as she balanced herself on the snow ruts, watching her feet without bending her head. It was easy to believe what Grandpa had said. She was wild and imaginative. She had run away from home to go on the stage when she was twelve.

'Vineyards under the snow, see? A metre under, look!'

Aunt Mat pointed with her alpine stick to the land running level with the top of the stone wall by the road.

'Listen – that's the air singing. It comes from the glacier – up there.'

Women with long baskets full of chopped wood walked ahead of them down the village high street, stopping to talk with truck drivers passing by.

'No pavements,' Aunt Mat called out. 'Look out for the trucks.'

She had stopped.

'Pauli!' she called up the steps of the post office.

On the top step, a young man in a blue shirt was tying up a bulging sack held between his knees. '*Meine Nichte*, Corinna,' Aunt Mat called up as he left the sack and came down.

He stood blinking in the sun, sunburnt and fair, shaking hands with a dry firm grasp and shyly looking at her.

'My sister's eldest girl, come to get some good Swiss air – she needs plenty of it.'

It was startling to hear Aunt Mat's casual English in a Swiss village street.

'The Swiss air will cure you of all,' Pauli said laughing.

'No, madame? And you, mamselle,' he smiled at her, 'you will come to speak English to me, *n'est-ce-pas?*'

'You can't have that young man,' said Aunt Mat. 'He's betrothed to a rich girl – it's all arranged for the land.'

It sounded like a grim tale of olden times, full of tears.

'Here we are!'

Aunt Mat had stopped at the foot of a flight of steps leading to the first floor of a tall white house.

'Where's that John?'

He had been and he had gone. The cases were in the middle of a little room that was newly painted and white-washed. A boulder as high as the window top stood outside, and a clothes line ran from the house into the woods behind.

'In here!' Aunt Mat called.

She was standing at a great black stove, its chimney rising into the ceiling, taking a ladle from a hook on the wall and opening the copper lid at the back to scoop hot water into a bowl.

'We'll have a bathroom soon. Look, there's the house – it'll be ready in the spring.'

Holding the ladle, she flung back the shutters to reveal a skeleton house alone in a meadow. The windows were black holes, and it had no roof, no doors.

Below the open window under a black balaclava and a man-sized sweater, John was tugging his sledge on to the road.

'You coming?' he called in a weird foreign voice.

Catching Aunt Mat's laugh she flew out, followed by warnings to John to be careful, she's not used to your rough ways.

'The feet go on the bar,' he said. 'If you are alone it is head first – lying flat – *nicht?*'

She gripped him round the waist and tucked her feet in as the sledge lurched forward. Stinging snow hit her face, the wind tore through her hair and the sledge had wings. Endlessly, endlessly faster they went.

Crash!

'Jump!'

The sledge had slumped sideways and ploughed into a heap of snow.

Water in a black stream burst over them and with a great gulp sucked the sledge under.

She jumped and landed on firm snow, laughing, watching John go under with the sledge until he stood in black water up to his waist holding on to the rope. Without a thought, she threw herself flat and held out her hand, and he, all his manliness gone, gave her the rope.

'The devil's pulling it,' she called.

From red his face went white. Feverishly he tugged the rope. Another great s–u–c–k and it sprang free, leaving him sitting in the snow, his overcoat heavy with black slime and his face dark in anger. She threw the rope end to him and sloshed her way back to the house laughing. On the top step, she met him again, all his temper gone. He jerked his head towards the alp where a line of little figures showed clearly against the sky.

'Skiers going home,' he said, every word sounding foreign.

He was a foreigner; that was why he knew about skiers and that they were going home, not because he was clever. He was hooking his sledge up on the wall when the veranda door flew open.

'The buggers!' said Aunt Mat. 'An' she's only been here five minutes.'

But there was laughter in her eyes as she got the zinc bath ready by the stove, and took Corinna's clothes while she squeezed into the hot water.

The black scum rose and plopped over the edge of the bath, the towels turned black, and the tiled floor glazed over. Towels and water everywhere, until with Aunt Mat's overcoat over her nightdress, she sat at the table watching Aunt Mat shoot bucket after bucket of dirty water down the sink to run free on the meadow below.

'*Mein Gott!*' said Aunt Mat ten times over. 'John!'

She kept her eyes on Aunt Mat bathing John whilst she stole a glance at Wilhelm Tell where John had left it open. Splashing water he squealed and giggled, just like a girl, but he was just a boy like Benjamin, only his boy thing was smaller.

'Polenta and scrambled eggs,' said Aunt Mat, her eyes on Corinna's face.

The strange foreign taste made her grimace making Aunt Mat laugh.

'You'll get used to it – it's only nutty.'

It was five o'clock on Aunt Mat's clock, teatime at home. The telegram would have arrived. The polenta swam in tears. How tired she was!

The sun had gone, the shutters were shut and the windows fastened. The house was surrounded by darkness. Every time the door closed, the little wooden cross tapped in John's room. She would rather have gone up to the loft where John was to sleep. She lay in the dark and Aunt Mat came. Quick rough hands pulled up the blankets, switched off the light, and were gone. That was because she was too shy to kiss goodnight.

There were strange cracks in the roof, and a long low whistle high up. Like an eagle she had flown down the long meadow, and knew just what to do to save John. They had been like Scott and Oates frozen, with beards full of ice.

She shut her eyes tight – please God, take care of Mummy while I'm away.

'Come on sporty! Up and out in the sun!'

From a far away land of light and joy, she woke with a bang. Sharp sunlight in her eyes shot her to her feet – Aunt

Mat had flung open the shutters.

Through the open window she saw the entire valley lay surrounded by mountains. Snow-fresh air streamed in. No curtains. No lino. No carpets. She ran down the passage skidding on the bare floor, glimpsing wooden walls and beams on white ceilings, in a world of sunlight.

'Shopping this morning,' said Aunt Mat, pouring hot water into a bowl. '*Mach' schnell!*'

She flew back to the bedroom, the bowl held high, washed and dressed and rushed back to the veranda to eat scrambled eggs and piles of toast. Aunt Mat was ready and gone. She caught up with her at the village pump.

Under the eyes of the women at the pump, she slowed down slyly watching their hands in the icy running water swishing clothes about, lifting them piece-by-piece and slapping them on the trough side.

'Don't have to be shy – they don't speak English,' Aunt Mat said in a voice as clear as a bell.

Aunt Mat spoke her own Anglo-French-German while walking beside the Konsum sacks of lentils, oats, barley, sugar and flour. Like a duchess, she bought half a kilo of dies and das until all the goods were ready and gathered up and carried out to the little four-wheeled cart.

'Come along, sporty, we'll go to Sion tomorrow.' She strode out into the sun, Heinzelmännchen at the truck wheels, and stopped at the Poste.

'Along the passage you'll find the guichet,' said Aunt Mat.

'*Bonjour* mamselle!'

Pauli was standing at a table covered with loose letters. Smiling shyly, he came over to her while rolling down his shirtsleeves. She was sorry he had called her mamselle, but that was only being polite. She stood strong and straight to show him she was not a silly girl.

'Briefmarke for home, bitte,' she said carefully.

'How long you stay with your auntie?'

'The summer, perhaps.'

'You will come often? Speak English with me? *N'est-ce-pas?*'

He smiled.

'*Adieu*! Au revoir, *merci*!'

She pelted after Aunt Mat up the hill and pounded up to the veranda breathless with excitement. He would be a real friend and teach her French.

Day after day, snow covered the mountains and the valley, and clouds froze in the sky. When they lifted, spring would be here, hey presto, like magic!

John had spaced all his books over the big kitchen table so that she had no room. He was just like Benjamin, but John was making spider-leg letters in his exercise book – German script, and was quite red with anger at her being there. She cleared a space and laid out Dr Otto's German grammar, Aunt Mat's special book. The only way to learn how to read the extracts at the end was to learn the grammar, all of it.

'*Der! Die! Das!*' she said aloud.

'*Mein Gott!*' Aunt Mat almost shrieked. 'What a language! You can't learn like that! You have to go out and speak it!'

'How can I do that? They only speak gibber-ditsch.'

It was a good word. It made her laugh, giggling until John slammed books and stamped up to his room.

'Girls are silly – silly!'

Aunt Mat brushed the table clean – all the books were to be put away, and the animals needed settling down for the night. She stopped giggling out loud, but it would not stop inside.

It was quiet in the stable, and dark, full of soft noises as the animals stirred and snuffled. Aunt Mat hung the lamp on the wall so that beams of light fell into the stall of the white goat.

Leaning on the low partition wall, she was soon mesmerised by the teat, the milk spouting out, the gold chain on Aunt Mat's wrist swinging with the rhythm of the pull, and had to wrench her eyes away to look over the partition wall where the pigs pushed and snuffled and grunted in the dim light. Aunt Mat didn't like milking goats or feeding pigs, but she wrapped the piglets in flannel in the winter to save them from the cold.

'Little bugger,' she said to the white goat. She gave the teats a final pull, then she tossed back her head and called out merrily, 'That's all for the day!' Standing up, she patted the goat as if she were a dog, saying, 'And don't forget – a clean dress for the morning and polish up your French.'

They had to catch the Poste bus to get halfway to Sion, then march on down the long white stone road through the vineyards, brushing snowcaps off the walls.

By the Stone Age rocks standing like weather-beaten giant snowmen at the road bend, her feet began to drag.

'When do we eat, Auntie? I'm starving.'

She stopped where the road dropped down to the valley, dumping her rucksack on a vineyard wall, ferreting in it and taking out an apple.

'Coming, my girl,' cried Aunt Mat, sitting beside her, taking out the long white bread rolls and the dried meat sliced so fine it was transparent, as well as a chunk of fruitcake from her mother. 'And Swiss chocolate to finish off, with a sip of red wine.' She stood the wine bottle carefully in the grass.

Sitting beside Aunt Mat, her legs stretched out and her feet dangling down the rough grass slope to the road, there was no time to talk, only to eat, eat, eat.

'Well,' said Aunt Mat, screwing up the paper bags and shaking out the napkins. 'It's a damn sight easier to take it in our stomachs than on our backs.'

She poured the wine into a wine glass and sipped,

laughing, shaking out her headscarf and tying it back on again.

'Have a dash in your lemonade, I'll let you,' she said, lifting her glass and pouring a spoonful into the lemonade bottle. 'Sante!'

Then it was on and down to Sion, past the butcher, turning their eyes away from the lumps of beef hooked up out on the pavement, and into the chemist where Aunt Mat bought winter oil for the piglets. They stood at the counter of a shop with models of ladies in dresses no one ever saw in the village, to buy a little purse for her mother, but one not too small for the housekeeping money.

Soon the rucksacks were full and overflowing and Aunt Mat led the way straight into La Jardiniere where the ice cream cake was something she had never dreamed of and they sat at a table like English visitors.

'It's wonderful what the egg money will do,' said Aunt Mat. 'And here comes Pauli.'

He came swinging the postbag for the bank, looking like Rupert Brooke or Prince Rupert of the Rhine, bowing and taking off his Swiss trilby.

'*Bonjour*, Madame Glenz, Mamselle.'

He shook hands like an old friend.

'Oswald, he comes tomorrow, *n'est-ce-pas*?'

'Of course,' said Aunt Mat in her best English as he bowed.

'Au revoir! Adieu!'

'How did he know Uncle was coming?'

'We live in a village,' said Aunt Mat.

Uncle Oswald had come home to work, to collect the men who worked for him to dig the vineyards, and to open up the waterways that ran between the vines. On the platform, he looked like a French officer with his long black moustache. Now he was the Swiss landowner of a great number of Klafters.

'Dinner everyday at eleven o'clock,' he said. 'That was Napoleon's law and that is what the men want.'

He also said Napoleon had planted the poplar trees that stood along the highway the whole length of the valley. He spoke as everyone did of Napoleon, as if he had known him, because he had slept in Grosspapa's house and tied his horse to the balcony post.

'I shall put up a plaque,' he said, 'now that I am president of the village council. That is my first job.'

'Pleasing Napoleon a few years late,' said Aunt Mat, 'and adding by chance to the value of the house.'

She paused, chuckling.

'And John's inheritance,' she added.

Uncle Oswald held the long white loaf against his chest and cut chunks off it. Then he held the Gruyere in the palm of his hand and sliced thin pieces off that, laying them in a line on the napkin spread on the top of the vineyard wall, showing her how to eat as neatly as a gentleman off the blade of a penknife. All his men were scattered along the wall, the women with the food and wine and the children playing.

John came with Hubert and Erich, from his class but bigger then he. They dropped down the vineyard walls to the river and didn't mind her going with them, even though she was a girl, down to the noise of the water making little lakes full of frogs behind the village rubbish dump.

'Frogland,' she called it, and John took it as a joke and told the boys what it meant, boasting because she had made him a sword they had admired.

'Tell them I'll teach them English if they like,' she said.

But they muttered amongst themselves and refused to speak to her any more. She knew they were going to kill the frogs by cutting their legs off and she didn't like that. She left them and wandered off to sit on an old log in the water and watched the frogs until the sun went over the mountain top. They croaked together in a goodnight chorus, then vanished into the mud.

'You can tell those boys if they kill the frogs I'll tell the priest,' she shouted to John.

But he pretended not to hear.

She walked back through the long meadow and through the vineyard. Uncle and all the men had gone and the boys were far behind, but when she later found John kicking off his boots on the veranda, he went red.

'They are jealous,' he said. 'Just ignorant, stupid village boys, but they are my friends.'

He frowned and couldn't speak to her all the evening because he was ashamed of them.

She wrote all about it to her mother, but it made her miserable. She didn't want to tell Aunt Mat it was because she was a girl.

'You can go up to the woods to help Uncle with the logging in the morning. That'd do you good,' said Aunt Mat the next day over supper.

She always seemed to know when something was wrong.

'Oh, yes, please!'

Like magic the glums had gone.

'Uncle can show me how to use the big saw.'

It wasn't the big saw that mattered. That took two men, but she helped to saw the long logs on the alp and bring them down in the hay cart, ready to be split.

In a day, she could split a log with the axe in one blow, as Uncle taught her, stacking the pieces rich in resin into each other, like bricks but made in triangles, against the house wall in the Hof below.

'You are the champion log-maker, *nicht?*' said Uncle Oswald, which quite made up for Hubert and Erich.

'Grosspapa,' said Aunt Mat, 'is dying. He's an old bugger, but we have to pay our respects.'

He lay dying in the room where Napoleon had slept with his horse tied to the balcony post, his hat and cloak on the floor by the stove where the faggots dried, and his muddied boots kicked off across the knotty, bare wood floor. One of the greatest men this world has ever seen, was Grosspapa's opinion.

He was drinking schnapps out of a bottle under his blankets, watching her with his sharp brown eyes in his old lean face. He saw that she was different, as bold as any of the boys, and able to jump twenty feet off the vineyard wall and not make a fuss when she sprained her ankle. She had to hobble across the room to let him speak to her.

'Evelyn's Mädchen,' he said, whispering with age.

He opened his eyes for one second to look at her, then closed them again, his long bony hands clutching the sheet under his chin.

'*Setz dich.*'

All his sons were in the room, their pipes sending up thick clouds of smoke that made her cough.

'*Em Engel in eine Wolke!*' he said, trying to chuckle, his old voice harsh and difficult to understand.

Aunt Mat laughed.

'An angel in a cloud! My word!'

It pleased her greatly, except that it was only for a girl. All the others laughed softly, the men stopping talking to look at her. The old man moved, his hand groping over the side of the bed to find the schnapps.

'Never too ill to drink, I see,' Aunt Mat scoffed.

The daughters sat silent, fingering their rosaries.

'Promenade?' he had asked her mother, quite like a gentleman in his straw boater while staying with them in London.

Now, like a saint he lay, dark and holy. Terrified they had been of him all their lives, but when he was in the open coffin in front of the house, Aunt Mat said, they would all be rich.

As soon as the funeral was over, Uncle Oswald went to see about selling some land on the alp. They all set off, the solicitor's clerk, the land agent, the bank clerk and Uncle.

'Gone for three weeks, *mein Gott*! Three weeks to sell a piece of land as big as a handkerchief,' Aunt Mat said, and started to sing again.

She was singing and cleaning the kitchen window when she yelled, 'Louis!' and there he stood in the open doorway. He took Aunt Mat's hand and kissed it, bowing. He sipped his tea like an Englishman sitting on the veranda in the shade, with his black moustache, white cuffs and long legs in dark city trousers.

'*Enchanté*, Mamselle! *Enchanté*!'

He bowed to her before turning back to Aunt Mat.

'And Oswald?'

He smiled all the time Aunt Mat spoke.

'Then you will come with me to Zermatt?'

The faintest pink rose in Aunt Mat's face.

'Corie, too, and John, of course.'

Uncle Oswald wouldn't like it, but obviously they would go, driving all day long from dawn to night to the Matterhorn, to Zermatt.

From the moment that she put her foot in the little iron step and sprang into the dicky seat of the magnificent roadster, and John scrambled up the other side, she knew this was the most exciting thing ever to happen. They were smothered with blankets and John was leaping about like a crazy animal.

Aunt Mat, in a frenzy that he would fall over the top, spoke through clenched teeth, 'Sit still, for God's sake!'

Louis's low voice soothed her. Corinna gripped the pen-knife in her pocket for luck, hearing Louis's voice come after her.

'They'll enjoy it out there. This wind will blow the rain

away.'

He was wrong about the rain, but it didn't matter. It was like flying in a cloud. Clouds always come down when you set off to see the peaks, Aunt Mat said. Water fell everywhere making deep puddles in the mackintosh cover. John's hair lay flat like a black straw hat. They all clumped into the hospice through the small entrance hall, and on into a small dining room with bare wooden tables and benches.

'Off with your things – we'll all get pneumonia,' Aunt Mat said, laughing gaily, piling coats and shoes round the great silver stove. 'Look!' she cried, bending down to peep through a small low window at a moving cloud. A space opened, revealing the unmistakable head of the Matterhorn.

One glimpse and it had gone, but Aunt Mat was happy, drumming on the polished wood surface of the table. She even forgot to fuss over John because Louis was telling her tales about journeys he had made and people he knew.

In a long brown gown, a monk walked slowly in bringing a tray of rolls, soup, cheese, red meat and a bottle of wine. He spoke so quietly none of them could hear him, then he bowed and went. No charge. Aunt Mat chuckled.

'Eat as much as you like, but they expect something in the box.'

The food was good. Logs in the stove blazed. In no time they would all be asleep. Everyone laughed because it was raining cats and dogs and the worst thing in the world that could happen would be if Uncle Oswald walked in, but it had to come to an end because Louis telephoned the guard and came back to say they could go no farther. The road was closed, although the rain had passed over.

Aunt Mat stood up and pulled her fur hat straight and marshalled them all out and back to the car in a world of grey cloud. She tucked her John deep in the dicky seat, saying, full of fun, 'And you, sporty,' before tucking her in too.

All the way down, she imagined herself an eagle, squeezing up her eyes against the cold mountain mist, flying over the valley with powerful wings and eyes as sharp as only eagles' eyes can be.

Gradually the mist changed. The valley lay below and the tip of the village church showed by the river. Everything grew sleepy and warm. Down and down into the haze of white dust they drove, past the first houses to stop at the bottom of the steps to the flat.

Still dreaming, she looked up and saw Pauli, letters in his hand, frowning down at Louis from the veranda. Without a word, but with a brief nod to Aunt Mat, he came down the steps and turned up the road. Louis standing rigid at the car door.

'*Mein Gott!*' said Aunt Mat. 'When Oswald gets back, it'll be haymaking – just look at the meadow.' Even Aunt Mat didn't know what else to say.

Louis took Aunt Mat's hand and looked straight into her eyes and said goodbye. It was a sad thing to do. She left them and raced up the steps and found a letter from her mother.

Chapter Four

Aunt Mat was quite right. The first thing Uncle Oswald said when he came back from the alp was, 'I must tend to the haymaking.'

Bleached with sun, the long grass rustled on the meadows. Up at first light, he and the men had only half the cutting done by midday.

'All hands on deck!' called Aunt Mat. 'John! Corie!'

Like a fisherman drawing in a net, Aunt Mat drew the long wooden rake through the broken hay, her black hair tied up in a red scarf and strong brown arms golden against her long white dress.

'Rakes in the Hof,' she called.

It was a shame to spoil the waves of hay that were like the sea rolling in. Corinna picked a long rake from the Hof and drew it through the tough resisting yellow stems following Uncle Oswald through the field.

In the centre it was hotter. Flies stuck to her legs and arms, while sweat trickled down her face.

'Die hair ist like gold!' called Uncle Oswald, stopping cutting to mop his brow with a huge white handkerchief. Then he shouted, 'Camille!'

His eyes falling behind her, a great smile broke out on his face. A tall young man was coming through the loose hay, hands in pockets, his black hair rising and falling with his stride.

As neatly as if it were his rifle, Uncle Oswald dropped his scythe. His big brown hand clamped round his pipe. He seized Camille, making him grin and turn red.

Speaking French, he said, '*Comment ça va? Bien?*'

Turning to her he went on, 'Corie, dies my leedle brodder. Six feet tall, *nicht!*'

Uncle Oswald laughed and blew his nose.

They all had big brown eyes, only John had blue like Aunt Mat's. Camille shook her hand, smiling, showing the whitest teeth in the world.

'Sure. Sure. I am pleased to meet you.'

American English straight from New York; ten days on the boat.

'Good journey?'

Uncle Oswald couldn't stop talking and laughing.

'Ja! Sure! Alles gut, lots of dollars, working hotels all over.'

'Mad and bad he was,' said Aunt Mat, 'but you have to like him.'

He stole fish from the river at midnight and sold it to hotels far away in the mountains before dawn. Before he went away, he had run wild in the village, chased the girls with a scythe and had been inside the police cell many a night.

'Now he's a reformed character, they say.'

Sometimes Aunt Mat laughed like a wicked old witch, but she must have trusted him or she would not have asked him to take Corinna to register with the police, which she should have done ages ago, even though he rolled his eyes to make her laugh. Aunt Mat pressed her best blue striped dress for her to go in, although she would rather have worn a skirt and blouse.

She called down the steps after her, 'You haven't cleaned your shoes! For Lord's sake, don't make a mess of yourself in the first five minutes.'

This made Camille wink at her as they set off.

A line of small village boys followed them to the station, close enough to listen to Camille's American drawl telling her about his two years in the States, how he had arrived with no English and in one week could speak enough, enough to live. They watched Camille buy the tickets because he had lots of money and he looked rich in his best suit, his hair smoothed down, and he laughed all the time.

'*Liebschatz*?' asked the officer in the small room behind the police station.

Camille shook his head, red and uncomfortable.

'What was that? *Liebschatz*?' she whispered.

'Sweetheart,' he said, waiting until they were outside the office.

In the café on the pavement eating ice cream, he talked again about New York, but Corinna was watching some girls laughing at another table.

He would bring her again in three months, he said adding, '*Wenn du hier bist.*'

He gently smiled at her.

'*Noch Eis un' Torte, ja*? Sure.'

'Yes, please – I think I will be.'

She was sure she would still be there, but more than anything she wanted to speak to the girl glancing at her and pretending not to, sitting in the dappled shade with sun falling over her summer dress of whites and blues and her black hair tied back.

'We must go,' said Camille, standing up ready. 'Or we shall miss the train.'

It was a dream, soft and warm. She walked out of the café after Camille, glancing back and catching the girl's eyes. A longing rose in her, and she made up a dream of how she would walk after her, catch up with her, laughing and talking, climbing the rocks below the waterfall where it was dangerous, and if the girl slipped she would rescue her and of a thousand other adventures they would have of danger and escape, and always she would save the girl and feel her close.

Camille had a long stride. It was impossible for her to

keep in step as she did with Aunt Mat, but she liked the way he walked with her through the village with his thumbs in the corners of his trouser pockets, his head strong and straight on his shoulders and called to villagers.

'*Geht's gut? Comment ça va?*'

Aunt Mat detested the hot summer, chucking out anything resembling a rug, a blanket, anything warm, and banishing it to the Hof.

'Any old hut will do – I've got to get out of here—'

Aunt Mat's voice went tight.

'Oswald, are you listening? As soon as you've gone back, we'll have to go. Matthier has one to let above Leuk.'

Like a business gentleman he left to go back for the summer season.

'You be here when I come back, *nicht*? Keep your auntie company, *n'est-ce-pas?*'

She nodded.

'Yes, please. I'd like that.'

'Your auntie, she has never laughed so much,' he said.

They all three waved him out of the station, and the funny thing was that Aunt Mat laughed much more when he had gone. She ordered the mule and cart at once and started to pack, singing and singing. Everything was packed swiftly – blankets, pillows, sheets, tea towels, boxes of saucepans, brushes and the three cases. Aunt Mat tucked the blanket down over the rest so that nothing could fall off, her bony fingers showing off all her rings because it was safer to wear them than to leave them in the house.

The mule stood staring down at the Simplon. Leo jerked the rein. He was in charge of the mule, though only nine years old, but the mule moved one leg then another and stopped. She could have made him go quicker than that. How she longed to hold the leather in her hands.

'Mules are like that,' said Aunt Mat. 'Stubborn, but strong and steady. *Mein Gott!* We're off!'

They plodded through the village past the church.

'Putting themselves right for another day of sin,' said Aunt Mat scornfully.

John kept his head down as they passed the church. Only last evening he had come running in shutting all the shutters and shouting that the priest had said all those motes in the sun's rays were souls of the dead. He was sulking now at his best leather shorts since Leo had long trousers like a man.

'Not everyone can go into the mountains like us, even if we do have to walk for the whole day to get there,' said Aunt Mat.

And no one else in the world had a mule and an Aunt Mat like Queen Boadicea walking beside her chariot. Up and up they went three hours, four. They had picnics on the rocks when, rising to fresher air, the clouds were below.

'Look up!' called Aunt Mat. 'Not down, and you'll see the Matterhorn today.'

But time passed and they had to leave the Matterhorn and turn into the valley, up towards the peaks, treading on pine needles with strong resin in the air.

'We're there!'

'We're in the mountains! Nothing but goats!'

'I'm starving.'

'All the way up you've been eating bread and cheese and red meat – and drinking whisked eggs neat and you're starving – *mein Gott!*' But Aunt Mat was rummaging under the blanket to find the boxes of saucepans and food.

'Ravioli?'

A mountain hut, nothing fancy, of tough wood and with legs made of piles of flat stones, on the edge of a tiny village was their goal. Inside it was a Hansel and Gretel hut with three beds, three rooms and a kitchen. A balcony all the way round, and a bucket outside.

'Well, it's clean!'

Aunt Mat's voice made echoes like a church bell.

'No wireless! Oil lamps! No chickens to feed!'

In one step, the lady of the village had made the transition to queen of the alp and stood on the balcony, narrowing her eyes to survey the terrain.

'And if a letter comes?'

Aunt Mat turned the ravioli in the saucepan with a long wooden spoon, thinking.

'Pauli will send it – if you're lucky.'

It took four days for a letter to come and Leo brought it up from the village. Corinna turned the envelope over. In the corner was a small scribble – BESTE GRÜSSE, PAULI! She dropped down the tufty grass bank to the stream and sat on a flat stone to read it.

'We're going to the Gemmi tomorrow,' John's voice came echoing up to her. 'Right up in the mountains!' He was down in the stream, naked in the icy water. No, she could not do that, stand in icy water, but tomorrow she would show him how to climb a mountain.

Aunt Mat's hard-as-wood old boots, oiled over the black toes and tied with laces wound round metal eyes, three pairs of thick socks, and Aunt Mat's old rucksack, and she was ready. The rucksacks bulged with long white loaves and packets of sliced red meat, bottles of eggs whipped into a froth to drink, homemade cake and the bottle of red wine.

John sulked his way out of the village kicking stones because Aunt Mat made him carry his own lemonade, the picnic plates and knives and a glass for Aunt Mat's wine wrapped up in the tea towels.

'God help you if you break it!'

Corinna stopped to look at him.

'It's too heavy,' he snarled, dumping himself on a vineyard wall.

His hair was standing up like hedgehog spikes, his socks were hanging round his boots, and his shorts, bought long because he grew so fast, came down to his grubby knees.

'Rumpelstiltskin!' she yelled. She started to giggle and only Aunt Mat's bursting into song stopped her.

Ignoring them, Aunt Mat struck out along the track. John laughed and sprang boulder to boulder between the road bends, finding edelweiss in the rocks. The air lifted them up and up, the track ahead zigzagging up the mountain getting lost and coming out again into the sun, up and up until Aunt Mat became a tiny statue standing alone in the valley. Corinna and John sat on the rocks and watched her come closer until she stopped, clear and laughing, pointing with her stick down the sky.

'Look – the Matterhorn – there!'

A glimpse and it was lost in the shimmer of a thousand peaks falling away forever.

Alone in the land of rocks, the Gemmi Hotel stood grey and silent, a notice board at the front door saying it was closed for repairs. A line of pigeons perched on it making little stacks of visiting cards to leave behind.

'Well, they can't charge us for sitting here,' said Aunt Mat, spreading out the food on the wide stone steps. 'Come on, drink and be merry and let the world go hang.'

Soon the sun would be gone from the road to the hut, and as soon as it touched the peak Aunt Mat's stick had pointed to the skyline, they had to go, dropping down the narrow track, racing against the falling sun, back to the hut in the woods.

It was cosy in the hut after a day climbing rocks and wandering through the meadows to find the source of the hot spring water bubbling up in a field at the foot of the Gemmi.

'One day, they say, a hotel will be built here with baths for people to bathe in, like Buxton,' said Aunt Mat, filling the lemonade bottle to take back to the hut to wash in. 'When you're rich, you must bring your mother here.'

Sometimes such dreams come true.

The oil lamps made pools of bright light in all the rooms. On the scrubbed kitchen table Aunt Mat tipped out her handbag, counted her money and sorted out her papers. Two snapshots fell on to the table, sepia photographs taken in America when she was twenty.

It was a sad story. She could see by the look in Aunt Mat's eyes and the way she held the faded pictures, as if she would never let them go.

'That's Liz, that one we called Billy. We all worked in the club together.'

There they sat, the three of them, on the steps of a big wooden veranda, on holiday with Aunt Meg who had married and gone to live there and had five boys and a girl to do the donkey work.

'It was Billy who was rather special,' said Aunt Mat. 'When we came home from America, Billy and Liz left the club and went to live in Scotland.'

She tucked the snapshots back into her bag.

'Billy's family had a big house there. Her brother played the bagpipes in the hall before dinner.'

It was wrong to get too fond of a girl if you were a girl. Aunt Mat didn't say that, but it sounded as if she did. She didn't tell Aunt Mat her wanting to be a boy, or that she was a boy inside.

Sometimes Aunt Mat would stop mending John's shirts and read, most often from two piles of magazines full of pictures they had brought up with them, one pile about medical things because John was going to be a doctor one day, the other about the history of Europe and all the royal families because she had known many of them at the club.

It was quiet in the little hut, with darkness close round it under the pines. Aunt Mat talked just to her because John was in bed. Later, she and Aunt Mat would go in to the big double bed and snuggle up to sleep under the soft duvet.

Mountains were always cold in the night.

Corinna would have liked to cuddle Aunt Mat. She lay thinking about it, but she could not bring herself to put out her arm and say, 'Cuddle me.' She tucked herself into Aunt Mat's back and listened for her falling into sleep, thinking how she had been very beautiful when she was young, her face like a painting, pure and noble, with lovely wide eyes and black hair swept back with strands falling forward, jet black as it was now. But now her face had lines across her forehead. Then Corinna asked God to take care of her mother before she fell asleep.

One night, she slipped off the bed while asleep and woke on the hard wooden floor. She jumped back in, snuggling close to Aunt Mat and putting her arm over her hip to hold herself in, but Aunt Mat woke and snatched herself away. It was a shock like a smack.

In the morning Aunt Mat had no time even to sing. She was too busy banging and shaking out the blankets on the veranda as if they had spooks in them, and she had to make up the little bed by the stove.

'Corinna, you sleep here. Can't have you falling out of bed, sporty.'

There was just time for another day of wandering in the chasm full of mystery and cobwebs, the silent trees reaching up from below and towering in the sky, the birds having gone into the meadows. Among the trees were the ladders. Aunt Mat knew they were there, but hidden – eight ladders going up to the alp used by the villagers to save a day's journey.

'There! Half a ladder. I can see them, Auntie! In the leaves, look.'

John was already there, a wriggling little boy beating her to the ladder, climb up it, and stand on the first ledge. He rose like a monkey, his grey socks over his boots inches from her nose, up one ladder and along the ledge to reach the second.

He sat on the second ledge, elbows on knees, a luminous ecstasy on his face and she shot across behind him and grabbed the ladder, up, three, four, a queer tightening in her back.

'Don't look down!'

Aunt Mat's voice came behind her like a thunderclap, her breath heavy as she fumbled with her stick, peering at the rock through her spectacles. Fling! Aunt Mat's walking stick flew into the air.

'Throw away your sticks! I nearly went with it. Do as I say!'

She hesitated – this was Uncle's best stick, with edelweiss carved in the wood all the way up.

'Let it go!' shouted Aunt Mat. 'It's a hindrance.'

It was no use arguing halfway up a mountain. Silently it went, like a winged creature. She pressed her head on the ladder rung to watch it go.

'Look up!' yelled Aunt Mat.

She looked up to see John standing on the next ledge, his face white, his mouth shut tight, pressing his body against the ladder. He was frozen, frozen with fright, swaying with vertigo.

'There's lots more ladders,' he said in a little whimper.

Corinna reached the ledge and pushed him aside. The rungs rose above her, the sky began to open, and at the last rung she let go. In the dawn Woolf and his men had reached the plain and taken Quebec. She held her breath and scrambled to the top.

Aunt Mat took off her headscarf, brushing herself down with her hands.

'Lord knows what Oswald'll say when he finds all his best sticks gone.'

The alp was a great rough field of grass and rocks and the snow lay thick on all the mountain tips along the horizon.

Not an animal was to be seen, neither a house nor a tree. No bird song.

'Land of the spirits, the villagers says.'

Aunt Mat shook out her headscarf and retied it.

'But life needs the earth and that's down there, in the valley.'

Corinna liked that: the land of the spirits. Or Olympus, as Grandpa called it. It reminded her of her mother, the stillness, and brought a lump to her throat.

'Come on, dreamer, eat up. We're got to cross the alp – I'm not going down those ladders. It'd be tempting fate.'

She was adamant, in spite of John's wailing, emptying the rucksacks, sipping her glass of dôle, washing her fingertips in a trickle of icy water, handing out the bread and cheese and red meat, and an apple each.

Across the alp they walked in the scorching sun looking in vain for the village, until all their legs ached and John lay flat and refused to move.

'All right, turn back, God bless my soul! Who would have thought I'd be blessed with such a ninny.'

Going back through the desert of dead grass, the line of peaks white with snow shivering like a mirage in the sun, she borrowed Aunt Mat's handkerchief to cover the lower part of her face, and John's, which he never used, to tie round her head with the dash of Lawrence of Arabia, as she had when she was a child. And there at last, as the sun fell behind the peaks, ran the recognisable slope to the ladders.

Tea was laid on the veranda, and the rucksacks lay where they had been dropped. On the road from the mountain, she saw two strangers stop by the village pump. A villager shook his head and pointed to the hut.

'English please?'

With a great effort they stood, a man and a boy, bowing, their boots covered in dust.

'We have no food – no money. Please.'

The boy trembled, dropping his head.

Aunt Mat brought down a lump of cheese, slices of meat and chunks of bread, and made a jug of coffee, all on the Hof table.

Painful it was to see them stuff the food into their mouths while Aunt Mat made up a parcel for her to take down to them. But they had gone. The china was stacked and the table clean.

'German Jews, most likely,' said Aunt Mat, 'going over the frontier into France in the night. God help them.'

It was the image of the refugees that kept her awake in the night, making up adventures as if she were a refugee and convincing herself they had indeed escaped.

But in the morning it was the alp, like a bright light, that was in her mind as she woke with Aunt Mat loudly opening shutters, closing windows and packing boxes.

'Come on, sporty! John! Holidays are over, back to the hard cruel world.'

Leo flicked the mule, but it kept up its steady plod, safe and measured, down, down to the sun.

'Sing, Aunt Mat, please sing!'

Down to the river, down to the land of promise. The singing suddenly stopped. Aunt Mat was looking at the passing vines.

'The vintage'll be early this year,' she said. 'Oswald'll soon be home and the money in the bank.'

And she started to sing again.

Uncle Oswald, back among his men grew taller with pride because he alone had guessed the number of brands. Safe and sound was the money for the bank, which Alois, the wine merchant, would bring in a sack after Uncle Oswald had gone back for the season to St Moritz where he spent the winter as a waiter in one of the big hotels speaking all the four languages he knew. Alois empted the sack of blue and brown notes and the five-franc pieces on to the kitchen table.

Pauli and a group of men, laughing and singing, had come up the hill after them. He led a mule and an empty cart.

'Bonjour, Mamselle!'

He raised his trilby and tilted it back, the sun in his eyes.

'We to a party have been.'

He came up to her, letting the mule go.

'After the picking, everyone happy.'

Laughing, a young man had come shyly near her. She watched him pick up the reins.

'Pietro!'

Out of nowhere, a warm brown face with warm moist lips brushed hers, swirled away by Pauli's hand. She stood still, stunned in confusion, while all the men laughed. She took out her handkerchief and wiped her mouth. Hot and sticky he was, smelling of wine. Pauli turned to her, blocking the others out.

'I am sorry, very sorry.'

He stood close so that she knew he was with her.

'May I walk with you?'

The confusion fell away and her face cooled. Breathing deeply, she slowly began to walk and the trembling stopped. Like a soldier, he had stood by her. When her fists clenched against the young man, all the men laughed again, but Pauli was angry for her.

Now they were real friends. He walked with her through the village under all their eyes while the hay cart rumbled. At the Poste he shook her hand, leaving her to lead the mule and cart into the post office yard under the stone arch. Then she ran up the hill to catch up with Aunt Mat at the top of the steps.

'Before Christmas we'll be in the new house,' said Aunt Mat throwing open the kitchen shutters.

'Are we moving?'

It was so long since anyone had said anything about it she had forgotten. Uncle Oswald would not be back until the spring.

'Oh Lord, give me patience. The child never listens to me.'

Like Heinzelmännchen the men had been. They had fitted on the roof like a dark shining green helmet, and the walls and windows had all been painted correctly. The new house shone in the meadow. 'All we have to do is move into it,' said Aunt Mat.

It was Camille who made it possible. He stood brushing snow off his shoulders in the veranda doorway and shaking it off his black hair.

'Bruno not come – the lorry kaput. It does not madder. I do it. Sure. Sure.'

He found men, he pulled the mule through the snow, he hoisted the sideboard off the cart; he was a fine fellow. She could go anywhere with him and Aunt Mat never minded.

Christmas was coming. Parcels came from home. John slung his boots on the new wooden floor and pushed his books about – history, geography. All over Europe, Christmas was coming.

'I want to go home, Aunt Mat!'

'Just when you like. I know what homesickness is,' Aunt Mat said, but her eyes through the thick spectacles blinked. 'You could stay for the skiing, only a few weeks. Do you nothing but good.'

It made her ashamed to want to go.

It was John who made Christmas real, sitting in silence as stiff as the chair he sat on, his eyes flicking away from his books, listening. Suddenly, he sprang up and ran outside shouting.

'I can hear him!'

The sleigh bells rang through the dark.

As he ran, Aunt Mat slid the parcels on to his bed before tiptoeing back to the stove. Breathless he flung open the kitchen door.

'He's been! Santa's been!'

His voice dropping softly, as if in a fairy tale.

'My bed is covered with presents,' he said in wonder.

She must stay until the spring, her mother said in every letter, which was just as well because the snow had closed them in. Within two weeks everyone would be skiing. She stole John's skis and practised round the house while he was at school.

After dark, with the pulley light low, she could read and Aunt Mat had no reason to shout at her. She read Shakespeare just for the stories, not always asking Aunt Mat what the words meant. With John in his room and not there to argue, she told Aunt Mat one night how Macbeth had killed Duncan because Lady Macbeth forced him to, but she then went mad, and Macbeth went on to kill Banquo and had Lady Macduff and her children killed, and Malcolm's soldiers had carried boughs so that Birnam Wood had marched to the castle.

'Enough!' shouted Aunt Mat. 'Cocoa and bed for you, *mein Gott*! Tomorrow we'll go to Sion and buy you some skates. They're cheaper than skis and the egg money'll just cover that.'

It was a little shop at the end of Sion, down two steps, with tools in every corner, and skis and skates on the walls and shelves. Steel pincers held the soles of her boots, the little key square on square fitted exactly. Tough leather straps held the boots tight, and a buckle fastened them firmly. They were a gift. She could take them home and go skating in London.

Every night the snow froze and in the morning the sun shone on the surface to make it flat. It was like skating on the moon. In a day she could balance on the blade.

'I can skate! I can really skate!'

'Not as well as John, or Leo. They fly like eagles.'

They could fly like eagles only because they had skated since they were little boys. Aunt Mat was unkind to say that. She wanted to see her mother. She wanted to say it now, to tell Aunt Mat, but just then Pauli came up with the post, a letter from home. Her mother had been in hospital. They were going to move back into the old house now the tenant had gone and have a girl to live in to help as they used to.

She saw Aunt Mat pick up the letter and put it down again.

'You must go. I'll get the money tomorrow.'

Aunt Mat, bright-eyed behind her spectacles, gave her a quick hug and let her go.

'What a good thing we got the skates when we did.'

Camille came, towering in the doorway.

'Sure. Sure. I come to say goodbye, so long, huh?'

He placed a packet on the table.

'Chocolate for the journey. *Komm weider, nicht?*'

Awkwardly he bowed, threading the rim of his trilby round in his hands. Heavy footed on the steps, he had gone.

'Ah well,' said Aunt Mat. 'Good things never last forever.'

The snow melted from underneath on the station roof, water dripping in the sun. Her small case was stuffed with food for the day, the evening, then breakfast.

'And don't forget to send a telegram when you get there.'

Aunt Mat turned away and called out, a shrill note in her voice, 'Pauli!'

Pauli came, treading over the railway lines, his head a little on one side, his voice quiet. He was a real friend, but there had been no time for French, and very little English.

'Bon voyage! Adieu! Au revoir!'

He smiled, the tiny piece of gold in his tooth shining.

'The next time you come we speak more English, *n'est-*

ce-pas?'

'Leaving us,' said Aunt Mat. 'Her mother needs her.'

All the way to Brig she received messages for the family. 'Tell Julie to marry Tim if she wants to. Tell Aunt Rebecca...' Her eyes were on the mountains turning like scenery on the stage as the train passed.

Houses came round the train. People were crossing the lines in front of it. Its bell rang to clear the way. On the platform crowds of people in gaily coloured scarves and woollen hats sat on sand bins and on trucks – skiers going home!

'Only English people break their limbs for fun,' said Aunt Mat, proud as Queen Victoria to be one of the mad.

A board stopped in front of her. MILAN – DOMODOSSOLA – BRIG – PARIS. A porter slung the cases up on to the rack. Far below the window on the platform was Aunt Mat's pale face and John's pinched and wet. John's eyes were on the massive steam engine, Aunt Mat's on her.

Like small statues they stood, huddled together on the moving platform.

'I'll be back – write to me!'

They were lost in the reds and whites and blues of the skiers waving out of the windows of the carriages behind.

Chapter Five

'She's six inches taller!' Amanda yelled, measuring her shoulder alongside Corinna's.

Laughing, she planted quick kisses on both cheeks.

'Corie!'

Her mother made a quiet pool in the smutty platform chaos. Corinna hugged her, tight-throated. She forgot the toffs laughing at her. Why should she care if they called her shy? They were loud and posh. She forgot the sea crashing over the deck soaking her where she sat by the steps as the deck tipped sideways.

She took a deep breath and stood still. Everything was different from the world she had left behind, bigger and brighter, more exciting.

All the family had surged up the platform. Cousin Rachel pushed her mother in the chair at the head of an army of love, her mother's hands clenched and banging impatiently on the chair arms. The aunts with their dead fox legs dangling and wet.

'One week and I shall have a job,' she said to show them she had grown out of all those wild ideas of old.

Out to the station road they all traipsed to the tube and the taxi – the roadster had gone the way of all good things – to be taken through London in the rain.

'Times're bad,' said her father. 'Better go back to see Miss whatever it is.'

'Aunt Mat said I should be on a paper.'

'Office workers're two a penny nowadays.'

'Well, well, well,' said Miss Letts. 'Never have I seen anyone change so much in a year.'

Down the stairs and inside the old shop, which had stood in the square for 200 years, was an angel. Beth. Fair with blue eyes, and a mouth like a child's, innocent and sleeping.

'My name's Beth. What's yours?'

The noise was tight around them, the bare long wooden tables covered with plates and bottles and cutlery. Long queues of girls talked and laughed.

'This is Jane,' Beth said. 'Jane and I pretend we're in a different country everyday. Today we're in Paris – don't feel you're intruding.'

Corinna carried the plates over to where Jane sat – cabbage and a pile of boiled potatoes, a thin piece of meat, oceans of gravy. Beth carried a plate with slices of bread and butter on it.

'I've just come home from Switzerland,' Corinna started, and stopped.

They didn't notice. They were talking.

'I can see you later,' Beth said. 'On the old stone staircase. I'll show you.'

Beth knew all about boyfriends and sweethearts.

'What does sweetheart mean?'

'Oh, you know,' said the angel. 'Now, the window dresser's just a boy – White – over there – that one with tight curly hair.'

Corinna thought he looked a common little boy. He winked at Beth, but Beth pretended not to see. Corinna felt her fist in his face. Jane didn't like him either, she sniggered when he met them at the exit after closing.

'Keep away from him,' Jane said, letting the door bang.

Alongside the railway lines, the bridge bore a footbridge gripped in iron rods that dropped shadows in the light from the lampposts. Jane stopped under a lamp.

'Look – the city in the water. Paris is like that,' she said, 'the city in the Seine. Beth and I often go there.'

Jane said it in such a matter-of-fact way it was hard to know if she was teasing. Whatever it was. Corinna felt it like a cut. She felt something rise in herself against Jane, coming between them just as she felt another wish – a desire to kiss.

Jane rested her head on the lamppost. Her neck was as white as a seagull's, feather soft. Strange lights were in her eyes. She was very close.

Then the hand under her own had gone, snatched away as Jane flung herself free and strode off calling out, 'You'll miss your train.'

Corinna watched her vanish into the dark, her heart recoiling. Never would she go back to the shop. She could hear the laughter. She walked slowly on to the tube, but before she caught the train, she knew she would have to go back or she would never see Beth again.

Nothing had happened. By the next morning, all signs of last night had gone. She showed Beth a brooch Miss Dubois, head of the jewellery department, had given her.

'Antique – over one hundred years old.'

She kept her eyes on Beth's angel face, dreamed in Beth's delicate perfume.

'You can keep it if you like.'

'No… no… really.'

Beth walked ahead of her across the shop floor, past the girls staring through space, seeing nothing.

Now she was in the heart of the forest. All the wild creatures were watching her, all unknown enemies. She broke her rifle and slung it over her shoulder, walking forward, alert. She opened the door of the little stone cottage. The white table was laid under the lamp. She stood her rifle in the corner of the kitchen and dropped the dead rabbit into the sink. They ate and laughed, Beth's eyes shining on her, Corinna. The meal over, she knelt by Beth's side and took her in her arms.

Beth had reached her department and said in a whisper, 'See you at lunch.'

'Beth – will you come home with me one weekend?'

'I'd like to do that, yes please,' Beth said.

The caterpillar train stopped. Air as fresh as mountain air rushed in and swept Beth out on to the platform.

'The country!'

Beth, in navy and white, with a tiny feather in her hat and the field of buttercups behind her, was standing in the sun on the station.

'Tell me all about it, living in the country.'

'That's easy! We went to school over those fields – and I fought all the boys – I bit my tongue in half fighting in the playground. I can feel it now.'

Her mother held the darner between the edge of the table and her chair and took no notice when they walked in until she dropped her hands into her lap.

'So you're Beth.'

Her mother said it shyly because she couldn't stand up.

'Corie, I think you should take Beth straight upstairs – the meal'll be ready in a minute.'

Beth stood at the dressing table looking into the centre mirror at her.

'You didn't tell me your mother was a cripple.'

'She's not a cripple. It's just that she can't walk. She's very strong in herself and she knows where everything is in the house—'

She stopped short.

'I'm sorry but... I didn't mean a cripple,' Beth said. She had tears in her eyes.

'I'm sorry too. I shouldn't have been cross. It's just that she wanted to be a stewardess when she was a girl, and she's still full of courage and laughing.'

A shout came from below and the sound of feet in the

hall, and the mood broke.

'They're in! Dinner'll be ready. Race you down!'

The table was laid in the dining room in the front. A stew with dumplings and suet pudding with syrup afterwards, all nice and filling awaiting them. Her mother was in charge, but Mary Ann had been indispensable since the day when her mother had dropped a boiling hot rice pudding while getting it out of the oven. Her father would be in later.

The meal was attacked and eaten in a storm of noise and laughter, the only trouble being it was too rowdy to talk. When it was over each one of them had to take their own plate into the kitchen to help Mary Ann. Benjamin stood up from the table and went to the fire, standing on the rug with his hands in his blazer pockets, his new Oxford bags making him look like a drunken sailor and he still only a little boy.

'What about the washing up?' she demanded.

'We can't all do it. I'm doing the table tennis.'

He went away scowling and he was still scowling when, after much laughing and teasing, the washing up had been done and everyone was out in the garden. He was scowling then because she had taken a bat and knocked his ball off the table so often he had lost his conviction that he was destined to win and had still not accepted that he never did. He flung down his bat.

'Girls can't bat anyway!' he shouted.

Everyone was unhappy that she had beaten him, but Beth teased him and made him laugh, pandering to him because he was a boy.

After the sunshine and the laughing, and the big slices of fruitcake, came the long night. Every time she woke in the night she looked across at Beth sleeping like an angel in Amanda's bed. When she woke in the daylight, Beth moved her head. If she ran across to her, what would happen then? She lay looking at her, wanting to touch her, drinking in every item from her golden hair to her toes lost in the blankets. The sleepy figure stirred.

'What time is it?'

The bedclothes flew apart, cold lino hit her feet. She flew over the floor and slipped into the bed, and lay stiff and cold, waiting. It seemed to her that a second heart was beating in her throat, excitement racing through her. Beth lay stone still. Did she suspect the longing to kiss her? All she had to do now was turn her head. She raised herself on one arm so that she could look down on Beth's sleeping face and saw every bit of it, the tiny laughter lines, the pucker in the corner of her mouth.

'Kiss me, Beth!'

The pucker deepened. Beth turned her head away.

'Do you kiss Amanda?'

'Of course not.'

'Why not?'

'Because she's my sister.'

She had a funny feeling that was the wrong answer. Beth's soft body next to her stiffened, then relaxed.

'You're a strange mixture, half girl, half boy.'

'I feel like a boy inside.'

She stretched out in the bed.

'I can fight, climb trees, make toys with a penknife, things like that. I have to be a boy.'

'But you can't be a boy!'

Beth's voice whined.

'Oh, your poor mother, she must worry about you.'

'Why? There's no need for her to worry over me.'

'But people like that are never happy.'

'Like what?'

A soft finger ran down her nose and along her brows.

'You're pretty too, fine hair and straight—'

A loud scream rose in her head she was a boy inside. She was an animal caught in a net and the terrible urge to get

84

out would send her mad. Words hung in the air.

'Kiss me.'

With a shock, she remembered her father was sleeping across the hall.

She would rather die than have him hear those words because it was wrong to say them. In silence, she washed and dressed.

'Not like that.'

The dining room echoed with laughter. All around her the noise burst. She sat next to Beth, her eyes on her mother's pale thoughtful face, a cold spot in her heart.

'Like what?' she wanted to ask.

It was something that could not be said.

'Do you like Beth?' she asked her mother.

Beth had gone. The house was quiet again, a strange emptiness everywhere. She sat on the floor by her mother's bed and watched the nightlight flicker.

'Of course I do. She's quite a nice girl, very pretty.'

Because it was wrong to want to kiss a girl, her mother's voice sounded as if the question was unimportant.

Edward made all the difference. A tall handsome young man whom Amanda had met with Phil at the cricket club when she helped with the tea. He stood in the open doorway with Phil, Amanda's latest dream boy, Edward's straight blond hair flopping on his forehead contrasting with Phil's dark upright cut. He must be six feet tall.

She tied up the curtains and ran across the lawn, past the table laid on the terrace for a buffet tea – all cakes and no bread, ice cream and strawberries, and fruitcake, like a wedding reception – and past her father as he dragged the box of fireworks out of the shed.

'Hallo!'

They were nice boys, young men really. Their faces shone with smiles as she ran up and sat next to Amanda on the grass bank under the oak. But they were behaving like guests, keeping their trouser creases in order by refusing to sit, and towering over Amanda, looking down now on her as well. She drew the skirt of her dress tight round her knees and hugged them to her chest.

'I hate these clothes. One day women will wear slacks and things. They do in America now, and in Paris someone said.'

'Like the Chinese you mean?' Phil asked down his nose.

He stood out on the grass in front of them both, his wide eyes on Amanda who scowled at him, tossing her head and looking past him into space. Amanda who had known all about boys since she was six.

'Femme fatale,' said Phil.

She was kissing him, kissing the solemn Alex, captain of the team, whenever she could.

Edward laughed and sat heavily on the grass next to her, leaning on the tree and stretching out his long legs.

'He's better on politics, a communist and a catholic too. I don't know how he does it.'

'If he's a communist, I'd like him to write it all out for me, what communism means. D'you think he would?'

'Music!'

Edward sprang to his feet.

'Come on, let's go in.'

Her mother sat by the open doors drinking tea, the sounds of the cello around her with the smell of resin, the strumming of violin strings and cousin Rachel trilling on the piano. Edward plunged into the room. When she reached him he was drumming on the piano top with his fingertips, looking as if he would burst if no one noticed he wanted to play.

She had glanced back to see where the others were when something queer moved in the garden. A tray of glasses dithered round the table tennis table and sailed away. Head down, Mary Ann darted across to the kitchen and her father darted out of the shadows to follow her, a queer self-consciousness in his movements.

'Peter Pan, ladies' man,' said voices in her head.

'What do you expect, Evelyn?' Aunt Rebecca asked her mother. 'A girl living in – it'll be like the others.'

She sat still, trying to bring her mind back to the music, trying to eat a sandwich, struggling not to run after them. The pounding in her chest was choking her. She pulled up a stool to sit closer to her mother.

'Fireworks!'

'Why do the men do the fireworks?' she asked everyone. No one answered.

The musicians strummed and trilled, trying short refrains and laughing as they argued about keys and strings, letting the music die away. Her mother had noticed nothing of her father and Mary Ann and sat peacefully watching from the terrace shade. Suddenly it was quiet, the garden deserted and everyone was gathering gloves, packing instruments and sauntering out of the front door.

'Hallo and goodbye,' said Edward.

He looked pale in the hall light, his skin full of tiny spots, his hair over one eye. His hand felt hot and limp.

'Could I meet you one evening?'

He sounded breathless.

Edward came on Tuesdays because on Wednesdays his master did not ask for prep. That was homework, Latin, the tales of Troy.

'Boys want to jump over the moon,' he said. 'Girls never feel like that. That's why girls are so different.'

'Well, I do – often,' she answered. 'And I can run the hundred faster than anyone—'

But he didn't want to listen.

'It's not the same for girls. They don't feel the same – just different, that's all.'

He sounded as if he didn't like girls very much. She felt

humiliated and angry.

He lived in a big Victorian villa, very dull and grey. She sat on the sofa with his mother and father while he played, watching the rise and fall of his hands on the keyboard. She felt she was conspiring with his parents to make a famous pianist of him. There was no wireless in the house and no papers, only music books.

The best thing about Edward was his bicycle, the way he took the inner tube of a tyre and mended the puncture, even if he did wear gloves to save his hands.

He waited outside the shop, standing under a lamppost, looking very romantic, her boyfriend. He was better looking than the boyfriends of the other girls. Under the trees they walked, kicking up piles of leaves in cool, evening air, sweet smelling after the stuffiness of the shop. He talked about lessons, exams.

She thought of telling him about home, about her mother, but suddenly it all looked uninteresting, her life against his adventures, the poems he knew, his French. She was always too tired to go for German lessons. She was a year younger than him and he was still at school, it made her soul writhe. He went to school, he played his music and he forgot her, but she could not forget him. His life was so different from hers.

One night under a lamp inside the park gates, he bent down and she felt his mouth, moist and warm on hers. She wanted to wipe her hand across her mouth, but he had come too close.

'It's no good kissing, I could never marry a Roman Catholic,' she said.

It sprang out of her and she was free, out in the centre of the path, tingling with sudden courage and boldness.

'Why not?'

His head had sunk into his raincoat collar.

'Because you have a priest. You can't talk to God. And

you say you love God above everyone, even your mother and father.'

'But if I didn't love God first, my love for them would be worth nothing,' he said, irritation rising in his voice.

'And for a woman?'

He said nothing. He believed that women could not love God directly, but only through a man. Probably, like the Moslems, he thanked God everyday for not making him a woman. He walked on with his head down in stony silence, the smile gone from the corners of his mouth.

'I think it is wrong to have the priest between man and God and man between woman and God. Even if He does not exist.'

She felt satisfied with that. He said nothing. He walked with her, but on the other side of the path.

They had come to the gates when he came nearer.

'Don't let's talk about all that.'

He stood close to her and tried to put his arms around her. She pushed him away gently, so as not to offend him, and he stood rigid.

'I suppose you've been thinking about all this – going over it – learning the words,' he said.

She had beaten him. He was spoiled and spiteful. She wanted to hurt him because she was a girl and God should have made her a boy. He was far bigger than her. If she hit him, he would look down at her. Girls don't fight, he would say. She hated him. He was tall and big and had bristles round his mouth. She would never let him kiss her. And that was that.

He thought he was so superior with his lessons and his music and being six feet tall. He was no better than White the window dresser, five feet high with smoky breath and a rough voice, saying, 'Hold that end, I'll take the other – I'll take over.'

All horrid.

She ran for the train, her mother's voice far away and useless – you mustn't take it too seriously. Mr Right'll come along. And her father's, all chaps are the same – marry the one with the money. None of them had anything to do with her.

Chapter Six

Now she was determined more than ever to learn and learn. Latin. Well, she could learn Latin, but first it must be German.

'Bavarian Lady will teach German. 1/6d a lesson.'

She wrote down the address from the card in the shop window. It was the first floor of an old house, the landing lined with books and chairs for a waiting room.

Fräulein Bosch wrote her name in the register with a white slender hand, her dark hair scooped back like Granny's, but black. It was to be one evening a week, a one hour individual lesson.

Fräulein gave her an old grammar book. She took the book in her hands. Green leather leaves climbed the edges and indented over the surface of the spine was 'Dr Otto' in gold. Switzerland! Aunt Mat! The balcony. It was all there, the mountains and the sun, this very minute. It was a sign. She must write to Aunt Mat and tell her, tell her she was learning German with Dr Otto.

'Your essays are very good. In English excellent, but you must learn to think in German.'

She read *Die Leiden Des Jungen Werthers* with Fräulein and the agony of his suicide followed her through the meadows walking home. She suffered with Werther and dreamed of Beth who was Lotte. But she told the tale to Jane.

'Are the Germans really cruel?' she asked her mother.

'Of course not. They're God's creatures like the rest of us. Ask Daddy, he knew lots of Germans in the war in the prison camp.' She would tell Jane that too.

'I saw a line of those men sleeping on a rope last night,' she told Jane. 'They looked like sacks of flour, you know, all bulging at each end and empty in the middle, outside the Labour Exchange.' Jane shifted on the cold stone step.

'But why did the police hit them?'

'They were in the way and shouting and throwing stones. You couldn't blame them for that.'

'What can we do?'

Jane's face had the look of desperation.

'Read, talk, fight. Join the communists and fight for freedom and equality.'

Jane looked doubtful. There was the sound of a footstep, then another, many heavy footsteps coming down the stone steps, breaking into their secret hideaway.

'Well, now you've put the world right, I'll have your names. Out here.'

The manager, the ogre himself, scribbled their names on the back of a file, staring at them with hatred. She hated him back. He said nothing more and left them exposed to the stares of the first floor staff.

'It's the sack,' Jane wailed. 'Oh, my poor mum!'

That was why his kind were bayoneted by the Russians, his beautiful shirt torn and filthy, his fine coat soaked in blood.

'We're cutting down on staff.'

They never tell the truth. She kept her eyes on Miss Lett's face, watching her make notes on a pad, all her friendliness gone.

She dropped down the stairs saying aloud, 'I don't care,' on every step. At the bottom, she stopped. It was a disgrace to get the sack. What would her mother say? She would go through the store smiling at everyone. No one would know, but she had to tell Miss Dubois.

Tears shot into the old lady's eyes.

'He had no right, not without asking me first.'

Her sensitive face was red with anger and hurt.

'I'll speak to the office but...'

Her tears hurt more than the firing that had caused them.

All the way home in the tube Corinna thought of Miss Dubois and her thin fluttering hands. She was a little birdlike person, gentle as a dove. She would keep the antique brooch forever, but what would happen to Miss Dubois when she was really old? That was the sadness of being a worker however sweet and kind.

'That's why we must fight,' Phil had said.

'I got the sack today!'

She stood in the sitting-room doorway. It struck her as she spoke that her father should not be at home and that everyone was talking as the door opened, and it was very hot.

'That's all right, ducky, you'll never get the sack again. We're going into business.'

Her father was dancing round the room, waving a piece of paper over his head.

'Uncle Herbert wants us to take over a new shop, how's that?'

When her father was happy, things were dangerous.

'And Benjamin?'

If he was going, she would refuse to go. Breathless she waited, turning to her mother.

'No, just you and Amanda and Daddy. Benjamin's going on the Stock Exchange.'

How pale her mother's face was. Her eyes were down. A soft smile enveloped the words because he would be a gentleman, when whatever he did he would be a stupid little boy. Better by far to be free.

It was like waking up from a nightmare. Everything was going to be all right. In letters as big as the universe, she could see the word FREEDOM. They would all be free! Her father might be Peter Pan, but she was strong and responsible and her mother had faith in her and was happy. It would be a new life, open as the sky.

'In three months, we shall sell up and go,' her mother said. 'You've got time to get a job in a shop and learn all about the trade.'

A great shout of happiness rent the air.

'We shall all be free!'

There was a card in the sweet shop window: JUNIOR SHOP ASSISTANT WANTED.

'Having worked in town, you will get the job over anyone else,' her mother said.

The job was hers and she started on Monday. It was much easier than getting an apprenticeship in town.

It was an old shop. Theirs would be brand new. She determined to learn the name of the sweets, tobacco and stationery paraphernalia. She bought a notebook and filled it in the first week. It was the easiest job in the world. The other girls chattered and giggled all day, then were bold and cheerful when a customer came. And then there was Monica.

'Close that door, please! The draught up here's murd'rous.'

Straight through the sunshine Corinna walked, shutting the street door as she passed, to the foot of the ladder. A hand came out of the shadows and dropped a box to the floor. Monica, her hair dark and her skin pale, the cream lace ruff under her chin, slim as a moonbeam in her silver grey costume, landed on the floor not two feet away, a miracle of freshness and vivacity.

How did she do it? There was not a sign of dust. Her make-up was as fresh as a flower. Her head bent over a pad of paper on a board, and all round them were the sounds of the other girls slamming drawers, moving bottles on shelves and tapping the broom against the counter walls as it skimmed the floor.

'You skate, don't you?' Monica asked, raising her eyes, mocking and fully conscious of being petite and the boss. 'I'm going with some friends. I could see you there.'

Her spirits rose, and fell. Monica was going skating, but with a crowd of young men pushing, taking over, spoiling everything. But she could skate and speed with the best. For Monica's admiring eyes on her as she came down the rink she would suffer all that.

Her voice came out flat with excitement, 'I'll look out for you.'

She had thought skating would be like a little piece of Switzerland, but the ice here was polished, swept by a dozen men with long brooms, permitting speed unimaginable and the feel of the double edge of the blade which was impossible on mountain ice with ridges like frozen waves. Like magic she could do eights on the beautiful blades Aunt Mat had bought her, and spin, jump and land like a wizard, conscious every moment of Monica.

A London voice boomed across the glass roof.

'Dancers only. Skaters clear the ice, please.'

Couples spun out into the centre. Monica swept past hand in hand with the tall, fair-headed instructor, her head back, advancing in the dance until it sent her to circle back again, away and near, away and near, a fragrant touch of her perfume as she passed. If only she did not have to look so happy, so utterly absorbed in the dance, in the steps set by her partner, his hand firm on her back and his magnificent strides sweeping her with him.

She forced her eyes over the ice, over the band, across the high darkening windows, away, away from the torment. But they drew back, searching the rink, finding Monica being led through the gap in the opposite barrier, lost now in the rise of row on row of seats suddenly crowded by people coming in.

In anguish, she changed her boots, forced herself out into the car park, heaved her bicycle from the cycle stand and thrust down the pedals, crushing out every glance, every touch, every false act she had made, forcing the metal monster under her to carry her home.

He looked like that, a dancer and a prince in his tight black suit, because he was far off and a professional skater. Close at hand his skin was pockmarked and scurf fell over his shoulders. He spoke in the slipped syllables of London cockney and smelt of tobacco and sweat. How could Monica like him!

Her resolve not to speak to Monica in the morning, to refuse to let her dominate every thought, foundered the moment she met her in the parlour of the shop. Her mind fell into chaos.

'What happened to you last night, Corie?'

She watched Monica's face in the mirror, the edge of the lipstick to her lips, looking painfully concerned.

'I'm having a party on Christmas Eve, will you come?'

She was sorry! It had all been a mistake. Monica was smiling at her, giving her courage once more. She still had to explain to Monica that women should not surrender everything to be a wife and mother. Monica, who had never heard of Edith Summerskill or Vera Brittain, had her head full of dreams of handsome young men and having babies.

'Women have to fight for their rights, my mother says. They have to fight for the sake of human dignity.'

'Unnatural,' said Monica, tossing her head. 'As for you,' she said, her head on one side, scorn in her eyes, 'you should've been a boy!'

Words that made her heart sing and time pass.

'How'll you get home? It'll be dark cycling all that way.'

At first, her mother had not minded about the party. Now she was full of anger.

'I'll whiz. I can see perfectly well in the dark anyway.'

She tried not to see the washing-up. She hadn't thought about cycling home late and it didn't matter.

'It's Christmas Eve. The others'll soon be in.'

'Don't be late then. Leave the tea things and go along. It's just that she sounds a bit flighty to me, this Monica.'

Flighty! Monica!

The kiss her mother gave her was brief and reproving. The pedals dragged down the bumpy lane. She pulled the skirt of her dress tight to keep it off the chain. Her legs ached long before she reached the main road. She should have washed up, Benjamin and Amanda would both be in late. All the evening her mother would be sitting by the fire alone. Neither of them would remember to give her a hot drink at nine, sitting there, worrying about them all.

She stood up on the pedals to reach the top of the hill, crested the hump, and flew over it. This was different, going to Monica's. She was a woman of the world. Sophisticated. There were butterflies in her stomach. She reached the shop and, stopping at the yard gate, saw the lights in the whole building go out. In a frenzy, she flung the bicycle into the yard and her feet clumped up the iron steps.

'That you, Corie?' came Monica's voice in the dark. 'I've got a torch here, if you can.'

On her knees in the pool of torchlight, screwdriver in her hand she loosened the wires, reconnected them carefully and neatly replaced the fuse – satisfied she pulled down the brake. A shot of light, and a bang hit her hand. Stony silence fell in the dark. The air tasted charred. Someone shouted. Everyone was laughing, or singing. She held the circle of light on the fuse box. She had crossed the wires.

'Don't you touch a thing!'

Monica snatched the torch out of her hand and punished her by going off to fetch Alan, leaving her in the dark.

He knelt in the pool of light.

'You crossed the wires!'

'I'll fix it,' said he, lord of creation. He doubled up his six-foot length, the spots in his face showing up in the light.

Monica laughed.

'Better hold the torch and watch, and learn for another time.'

She watched, hating him with all her soul, handing him screwdriver, wire-cutters and pliers, seething with contempt.

Alan thrust back the fuse and pulled the brake. Light filled the universe. Everything and everyone sparkled with fun, even the low red coal slumbering in the grate blazed into merry flames. He looked pleased with himself, brushed down his trouser legs and shook back his hair.

'Coming?' he asked, his hand on Monica's arm.

Her eyes riveted on that face until she felt faint and in that moment Monica turned and smiled at her as if she knew she was there. She was forgiven! It was all right! She wanted to run into the crowd to be close to her, but instantly Monica had followed Alan into the dance and a young man stood in front of her ready to join in. There was no escape – her spirit quailed.

'Name's Jim,' he said. 'I know yours – Corie. Monica told me.'

He held her so tightly she could hardly stand on her feet.

'Saw you with Monica at the ice rink.'

He had a soft drawl like a country boy, but his face was bristly, like Edward's, and his shirt front was hard on her face. She determined to be normal, to be herself.

'The truth is that I can't dance,' she said boldly, relieved that he slowed down and stopped trying to whirl her over the floor.

'I'm no good either. Let's just finish this one and go and eat.'

She was still trying to think of an escape when the music stopped. Monica was nowhere to be seen. Jim really did want to talk and eat. He sat on a stool next to her in the alcove where the trestles were with the food at one end of the room, eagerly eating cream pastry, brushing away crumbs as they fell down his waistcoat.

In a pause, she took a chance.

'I'd just like to go outside, please.'

She found Monica at the dressing table in a tiny bedroom for one, flicking a powder puff over her nose, the white cloud falling over a dozen pots and bowls on the dressing table top and on the pile of coats on the bed. Out of a huge white china ashtray with WORTHINGTON in large black letters on the rim rose a fine column of blue smoke.

'D'you like Alan?'

Monica looked up at her.

'Like Alan? Of course, I do. Why, does it matter?'

There was defiance in her voice; defending that shallow male.

Monica had pushed back her chair and was standing close, her soft mouth laughing, so near that the sweetness of her breath with a tinge of the smell of tobacco in it was irresistibly there. Two soft fingertips pressed on Corinna's mouth, the dark eyes taunted, narrowed and laughed.

'That will do, Corinna!'

The slender shadow of her body passed out of the door. Bread and bread – the mark of Cain. Would it show, the mark of Cain on her lips? The devil's hoof? Was it evil, the touch of a slender body brushing past?

'Thought I'd lost you!'

A glass of beer in his hand, Jim blocked the door, a peculiar brightness in his eyes. He grabbed her by the hand and pulled her into the passage, all his boyishness gone. He smelt of beer, of rough male dryness, and there was a peculiar strained look in his eyes.

'Let me go!' a strange wild voice broke out of her.

She pulled away, but he swept her against his body to the outside door, trying to open it, thrusting his mouth close to hers, kissing her with his body tight against hers. With all her strength, she pushed him, seeing the surprise on his stupid face, hearing his voice saying, 'But you kissed Monica! I saw you!' before she tore herself free and ran through the door and down the steps.

The thumping in her chest turned to a mad flutter. She stood by the shed in the dark until the door above slammed. The long black road dragged forward, her legs ached and her head teeming with their faces – Jim, Alan, Monica. She opened her mouth to the cold wind.

How she hated her clothes and having to hold the skirt of her dress away from the wheel. She wanted to wear a dark suit, a striped tie and have her hair cropped – it wasn't fair. She was nearly home without a car on the road, and no one about. Her body ached all over. Exhausted, she slung the bike into the shed and crept indoors, closing the street door and leaning on it hard.

The light from the upper hall fell like a blade across the side of her mother's bed. She fell on her knees to kiss her cheek.

'Where're the others?' she whispered.

'In bed,' her mother's gentle voice said. 'Get yourself a hot drink and come and tell me all about it.'

'It was very hot there. Crowds in a tiny flat. Terribly noisy music and dancing.'

Suddenly she felt flat, and tired.

'You should eat something.'

'I had lots of sandwiches. I'm not hungry.'

'Off to bed then.'

'You all right? Anything I can get you?'

'No. Now you're home, I shall go to sleep. Christmas day tomorrow.'

She woke with a pain in her eyes that lasted all the week. The New Year church bells at last roused her. It was a cowardly thing to do to get her father to telephone the shop.

'We're moving,' he said. 'She wont be coming back.'

In fact, she would be doing nothing but read – finish the story about Tess, read the poems in the *Deutsches Lesebuch*, every word, and read the piece on Goethe's merrily throwing all the pots and pans from the kitchen into the street to the cheers of his neighbours, showing them how rich his parents were. She would read it all in German.

It was quiet all day. She watched her mother's pale tired face, noticing for the first time the dull rumble of the new chair, her mother's fingers awkwardly moving the great wheel. The hospital had known they had made a mistake when the leech had touched a nerve. She would never walk again.

'We'll manage,' her father had said. 'It'll be all right. I promise you.'

He had a gift, Aunt Rebecca had said, of holding everything together.

'Ivor Novello's just opening a new play. That'll make you feel better, duckie.'

Down the aisle he'd carried her in her black velvet cape, his face burning red under the thousand eyes looking at him.

'A good man, your father,' Aunt Alice had said, 'considering the lack of God in his background.'

'What did Aunt Alice mean. She's an admirer of Russia where God is taboo?'

Her mother moved her chair close to the table where a *Woman's Weekly* lay ready for her when she woke. She was never very strong on religious matters and she spoke doubtfully.

'I think she means he doesn't go to Church – which isn't the same. You can still believe in God. In Russia, they don't have churches like ours, but they still believe in God, I'm quite sure.'

'Aunt Mat doesn't believe in God because of the church in the village, but she says without the priest some men like Leo's father would be ungovernable. The priest can put the fear of God into evil people.'

The new shop and the flat over it were ready. They had to move and leave their childhood behind them. The memories would be with them all their all their lives – the oak tree, the wooden steps at the kitchen door, the little rose trees up to the front door.

'The best is yet to come,' Grandpa said.

He said all those things because he read books, rows and rows of books in his old house. That was what she would do in the new business. It would be theirs and they would be free and she would read and read and know more than any of the boys, but first she was going to learn to drive.

Chapter Seven

Gay with sweet papers, yellow, red, brown and cream, bottles of sweets and jars of tobacco stood on the old table next to the pile of *Evening News*. Like a shower of gold the straw packing fell and he caught it up in the broom and shot it out into the yard in front of the taxi office.

He was happy, king of all he surveyed, looking as if he had found the gold he had gone to find in Buenos Aires when he was a boy.

'It's going to be all right – it's going to be all right.'

Should she ask him now? She carried a pile of outers into the shop, stacking them on one of the new counters. He wanted to put them away so that he could put his hand on them 'quick as knife'.

'What are outers?' she asked.

'The outside packing of twenty or ten cigarette packets,' he said chirpily, having just learned it. He sounded happy.

'May I have a lesson today?' she asked.

She stood in the doorway, breathless. As soon as she could drive, she would be allowed to move the taxis in the yard.

'After they've gone, just for half an hour,' he said, still choking, fumbling in his waistcoat pocket for another Woodbine.

Through the long hours of Sunday dinner, the roast beef, the Yorkshire pudding, through the long battle over the washing up, the excitement carried her. She flew up the stairs to put on the light blue dress and dropped down on her heels to find the flat full of people, the family, including Aunt Alice with her collecting box.

'Give for Spain!'

Brilliant blue eyes withered the room with scorn.

'They die for our freedom.'

Nun's hands trundled her little wheelbarrow of propaganda across the world as Confucius had done.

His bright eyes laughing, Grandpa held his cigar like a revolver aimed at Aunt Alice.

'Oh, put it on the mantelshelf, Sarah Bernhardt, and stop being dramatic.'

Aunt Alice turned her back on him and sat behind the door.

'So you call this freedom, this shop, Corinna? Open at seven in the morning, closing at ten at night. My God!'

She opened her great blue eyes in scorn. 'You could do something better than this!'

She looked down her nose at Corinna over her teacup.

'See that you study and learn! That's what Lincoln said. Don't leave it to the men.'

'I've just joined the Communist Party.'

Aunt Alice threw back her head and laughed, smothering Benjamin's caustic remark.

'Women are too emotional for politics. Look at you and Aunt Alice.'

'It is immoral,' said Aunt Alice, standing up and casting words ice-cold over the tittering in the room. 'It is immoral to live on the labour of others.'

She tossed back her Lloyd George mane.

'Alice,' said Grandpa, drawing hard on his cigar, 'you have given this young lady wild ideas. She used to be a nice—'

Corinna sprang to her feet.

'It's true what Aunt Alice says! We need women in power. Look at the mess the men have made of the world!'

Her mother looked white, shocked at all the hate and anger. Aunt Muriel stopped in her wanderings with cups of tea to bend over her.

'Quiet, my dear Corinna, you're upsetting your mother.'

She put a plate with a slice of fruitcake on it into her hand.

'Music! – no more politics, please.'

Fuming she sat in the chair behind the door and listened to Aunt Muriel quietly touching keys on the baby grand while Aunt Alice suffered silently, sitting between her and Aunt Muriel, eating chocolates, thinking revolutionary thoughts and fuming with her.

By the fire sat Grandpa – the tower of knowledge in an ignorant world.

'Lenin,' he said. 'Lenin had the right idea.'

When they had gone, long cool silences filled all the rooms. Debris lay everywhere. Why did people get so angry about politics? Because it is all about having and not having, said Grandpa.

'Why can't I go to university, Mummy?'

It was so cruel and unfair.

'Because we can't have all we want in life.'

The weariness coming back into her mother's voice made her feel mean.

She sat at the piano and banged the *Red Flag* into the dull old room, burning with new anger. It was because she was a girl. Benjamin could go, but they wouldn't have him – and he didn't want to go anyway. And it was no good getting into a temper just when her mother had been so happy.

Sitting now with her head down, trying to move her chair, she was saying quietly, 'When you can drive, you can go to London for night school. London's best, as Grandpa would tell you.'

The road flew under the bonnet, the little eight sign on the car nose bravely leading on.

'Both feet down! Down! Hooter!'

Paralysis seized her hands and feet. People were running on to the grass bank and jumping into the ditches. Through the potholes the car bounced like a wild thing, heading for the main road. It turned itself with a sickening lurch left on to the tarmac and petered gently to a halt. Silence fell.

Her father said, '*Mein Gott!*'

That was all.

Day after day, he took her. It was incredible.

'After all,' he said, 'I came through the war.'

A few weeks later, she followed him into the kitchen on their return and he was saying to her mother, 'She'll do it – better than any fellow I ever taught – all she needs now is experience.'

It was the Buick that passed her the test. Uncle was no-where to be seen. The keys dangling in the switch made the temptation irresistible. She was out on the road, sunspots spinning over the gigantic black nose, cruising through the orchard road into the wide world to the first village at the end of the lane, a straggling line of houses and lamp posts. On and on the engine purred, through the long lanes of open country, the bird's-eye at the end of the tunnel of trees at last opening wide to streets and houses. She would have to go back. She reversed straight into a ditch. The cold shock of the soft plunge shot her out of the car to run for help.

A milk cart with an old horse, his back dipping, miraculously stood at the roadside, the milkman loudly dumping crates aboard the cart.

'The car's in the ditch – I don't suppose the horse…'

She drifted to a stop. He was a young man. She kept her eyes on the back of his hand, the red mat of hairs and the stubby fingers scribbling in his order book.

'What, old George?'

He looked doubtfully at her.

'Could try I suppose.'

He tucked his pencil behind his ear and rummaged in his toolbox for a rope.

The horse looked so wobbly her heart ached to see how old he was and tired. He could never pull a car that size, even she could see that.

Corinna obeyed orders as if under fire, willing George on with all her might as the rope went taut, until with a violent lurch and a great sucking sound the car was free and George was being led back to his cart, patted and praised.

She had no tip to give the young man but grateful thanks, which made him smile, and call out after her as she sped off, 'Better have that axle checked—'

The idea of the axle collapsing any minute, or even worse, collapsing when Uncle drove home over the downs in the dead of night, pursued her down the long lanes. She was tormented by the thought that he who was so kind to the family might be killed by her silence.

She ran the car behind the line of taxis and left the key as it had been. It had needed only courage and control.

The day had come. She had a headache and felt sick. The examiner was as old as Grandpa, without the laughter in his eyes, with a trilby low over a long sad face.

'Off we go!' Smooth and easy.

'The first one I've passed today.'

He almost smiled, but for her it was the greatest moment in her life.

'He said I'd been well taught – would you believe it! Thank you, thank you, Daddy!'

She felt embarrassed to thank him so much; the joy in his face, the pride, would stay in her mind forever.

Like a fleet of ships she organised the taxis in the yard, so that she was the one to take the telephone calls in the tiny office and telephone the drivers with the messages.

'A nice little side line,' her father said, 'and doing a good turn to a pal or two.'

She didn't mind how much there was to do as long as she was boss. He could go to the dogs every evening, except that he took a wad of notes out of the till to go with. That she did not tell her mother.

'Excuse me! D'you think I might phone from here?'

It was a young man, an airman, waving his pipe in mid-air. With a pal. They had run out of petrol. He telephoned and came back.

'I say, I cant lose you like this! I shall be down again in two weeks' time – is there any chance that I could see you?'

He seemed quite solid and real, although the words he spoke came out of another country, weird and shocking.

'We live upstairs. You could call—'

'At three. I know its very irregular and all that, but I'm booked for a posting.'

She watched him go, closed the doors and bolted them. Switching off the lights, she stepped into the parlour into another world.

'It needs great courage,' Phil was saying, 'to believe in nothing.'

His long dark-haired fingers opened and balanced the stepladder top to sit on it.

'Marx was a religious fanatic, we have to accept that. What we have to decide is if there is war with Nazi Germany is it finer to fight or to refuse? The Nazis make the case for pacifism difficult to pursue.'

Alex was standing square in the frame of the stockroom door, looking down from his six feet at Amanda, his eyes adoring, watching her messing about with cups and saucers.

'Well, I'm a pacifist and that's it,' said Bill, sitting on the floor by the ladder, eyes on Phil. Ronald, their classmate, hunched up on the floor by the stove, concurred. Only Stephen kept quiet, dreaming, his lanky body sitting on the floor against the wall next to Ronald. Both were going up to Cambridge. Stephen wants both you girls, her father had said. He had leaned on the lamp post outside Sadler's Wells.

'Don't want me to kiss you, do you?' he had said and almost shrugged. 'Waiting for Prince Charming and I'm not he.'

She dropped the bag of money into the bottom drawer of the desk, determined to equal them all.

'The enemy is Nazi Germany, not the Germany of Carlyle and George Eliot.'

But they were now speaking in Latin – *Dulce et decorum est pro patria mori*.

'For you,' said Phil, 'that means, sweet and honourable it is to die for one's country.'

They would all go – none of them would be pacifists if it came to war. Only girls could be free to go or not and she would have to battle to be able to go. Phil understood that. He would be the first to go. He defended the communists for their bravery in Spain and in Germany, and he defended the rights of women.

How could she not want to live and die like a hero with them all? Who wouldn't live ignominiously under a mosquito net and write wonderful words like, 'the rough kiss of blankets' or die at sea and be cremated on the shore?

'Tea's ready.' Amanda called. 'Not you, Ronald,' she added quickly laying the cup and saucer on the floor like an offering at his feet.

No one expected Ronald to fetch his own tea. He remained hunched up with his eyes shut like that between the wall and the stove, thinking. He was going to Cambridge, though his father was a drunk and his mother was lost in the squalor of poverty. His was a poet's soul, ready to starve in an attic.

'I bought a desk today,' Corinna said to the room. 'Coming up to see it?'

Behind the piano it stood against the window at this end of the room to get the light. Everything about it was quiet and still. Hands in pockets they all walked round it, faces lit up with faint smiles, pressing panels in search of secret sections, running fingertips over the shining oak, opening books and closing them again.

'You'll need to be up at six to read Karl Marx,' said Phil, spreading his fingers over the small grey cover of *Das Kapital*. 'It'll take you a year to get through volume one I'd say, one hour a day – in English.'

'Eerr,' said Amanda, starting to giggle. 'I'm glad she's the one with the brains.'

The spell was broken; the boys melted away. Down the passage, Phil had his arm round Amanda, his head bent over her. Alex his brow as black as a Benjamin scowl, put down the book he held and strode away, pain staring out of his shoulder blades. She watched him go and slowly went in to her mother, throwing herself on the rug in front of the fire to lean against the chair.

'A young man came into the shop just as we were closing,' she said in a careless rush. 'He said he'll come on Sunday, not the next one but the one after, to see if I can go out with him. His name is Tom Bramwell.'

Her mother laughed, a small light laugh.

'That should be all right. Daddy's day on duty, I think.'

She lingered for more. That was all her mother said, but in her silence was a humming sound.

He stood there all stiff and military dressed in a grey striped suit, thrusting a bunch of flowers at her, tall and golden, speaking firmly and clearly. Her mother was absorbed, a pucker in the corners of her mouth.

He laughed a lot, a soft friendly laugh which spread to his eyes under fair straight brows.

'Would you come home to see Mother?' he asked, but by good luck the bus stopped just then right in front of them.

'Richmond,' she replied, 'let's go there – a long bus ride with plenty of time to talk.'

She led him up to the open deck and, because she was practically speechless, she began to chatter and couldn't stop, all about Phil and Alex and the others, about Morley College and Professor Joad, about German literature and Karl Marx. Of course, he was a conservative, she had guessed, with not a question in his head.

'Yes, but surely you've heard of Marx!'

'Well,' he said sounding glum. 'I have heard of him, yes.'

'I'll find you a short version – no, I'll write one out for you as Phil has for me.'

He would be a socialist, she resolved, as soon as she had explained it all. For now, he chuckled and said nothing.

Together they stood watching a flotilla of mallards cruising past on the wash from a passing rower close to the water's edge. After tea, she made up her mind they would resume their climb on the hill and talk politics.

'You mustn't laugh at me over politics,' she said, determined to clear up the matter before it ran into trouble. 'I think it the most important thing in the world – that and God.'

'Oh, but I didn't!' he rushed in. 'But tell me about yourself.'

He made that easy, about Phil and Alex fighting over Amanda and her father teaching Benjamin to gamble. It led to God and justice and the sins of the fathers and her mother's suffering.

'It makes it hard to believe in God even if you want to,' she said.

She told him of the day when she had said at the top of her voice in the hall, 'I don't believe in God any more.'

The house had fallen silent, her mother and father poised, waiting for retribution from above. Seventeen she had been, the time in life when conscience is born, someone had said.

She wondered what he would say, but his eyes were still laughing – the hurdle of God had been taken. On the rights of women he sounded like father – women could not become like men, that was all there was to say.

'Yet they are inferior because they are not like men.'

'Ah,' he drew back. 'Men need women, but not, surely not half-women half-men as mates, like Amy Johnson. Her skin's like leather.'

The sound of his voice struck a quiet street. It was quite dark, the river far over the hill. Her mother would be worried sick. She refused to accept to herself that in the lamplight his face showed any of the anxiety she felt.

'I'll get a taxi, don't worry.'

He became vibrant with confidence as if he could flick a finger and a taxi would come.

'I've got a motorbike at camp,' he said, taking her arm as if they were setting off on a great adventure. 'I'll sell it and buy a car.'

She had determined never to do this again when out of the dim lamplight a little black ship came cruising towards them. Sheer luck.

Neither in the taxi nor here in the shadows of the door-way did he try to kiss her. He merely turned to drop softly down the iron steps with a low, 'Goodnight!'

She watched him go full of envy of his life, his imminent posting and the world that was his to conquer, but she liked him. In his sudden going, his disappearance into the night, she was surprised to feel a void.

Before the end of the week he came, his motorcycle roaring like thunder.

'Been posted – Malta, then India. It means three years.'

He unexpectedly pulled her towards him and held on to her.

'I've slipped out to say goodbye – all leave's cancelled.'

Envy at his going filled her – he had everything before him, sands of deserts, dark-skinned people in long white robes with their long slow tread and gaily coloured clothes.

'Imagine what you will see!'

'But you can't wait for three years for me!'

She smiled to calm her conscience.

'I'll come to see you. It's not goodbye, silly.'

He had gone, out into a life of action, mathematics and machines, a masculine life – yet he had signed away his freedom.

'A one-class steamer, indeed!'

His mother, Mrs Bramwell sniffed.

'I'd've paid the difference.'

But she smiled, her soft blue eyes shining. All they had to do was wait five months, read the books Tom had sent and set sail in October.

'Malta,' she read out to her mother, 'has a history older than Greece or Rome.'

Over tea, she told her more, that in medieval times the knights of St John of Jerusalem lived there for over two hundred years, teaching Christianity to the Turks, until her hero Napoleon came and plundered the churches. Later on, he was defeated by Nelson.

'We use it as a fortress to defend the empire – and we use the Maltese people like serfs. It actually says so here.'

It seemed a most suitable place for a revolution, a fact that added importance to her going.

She came home from Morley College one evening to find Amanda in tears, her father pacing the floor and Doctor Ashley standing in front of her mother, his stethoscope swinging on his chest. He smiled at her mother, one of his gotta-be-cheerful smiles.

'Nothing to worry about – you need a change. What about Switzerland and that sister of yours?'

Late at night he came slipping in at the door left on the latch for when his calls were done, to chat with her mother about life, the days of their youth, the Battle of Jutland and the navy, and operating with a penknife in the Great War. He stood looking down at her, clicking the catches on his case.

'Switzerland! What about Malta?'

Amanda's voice rang out aloud with indignation.

Malta! It was done. The power of a doctor was amazing – breathless excitement was left behind him. A letter to Tom followed a call to his mother, then an eternal eight days' wait for Tom's reply.

'Whereas October is cooler, healthier and mosquitoless,' he wrote, 'and better for sleeping and driving round the island and July too hot and the place full of Italians, it is most beautiful in July with flowers and fruits in abundance. The swimming is perfect, the Mediterranean as clear and blue as the sky.'

Mrs Bramwell altered the date on her calendar. The Jervis Bay booking was changed. The six new dresses Corinna had already ordered were hastened; none had the modern tight skirt – they were all full-skirted, waisted and had elbow-length sleeves. There were rocks to climb and beaches to roam. Clothes were the very bane of her life. Her treasured Daks hidden from her mother at the bottom of her case to avoid shocking her with the dazzling white slacks of the future world.

Chapter Eight

A light-hearted friendship was exciting. It raised Corinna to a new life of emotional joy. She had a relationship with a young man out of the sky. Nothing common or dull. She found it impossible to think what she did feel for Tom, certainly not anything like the passion Amanda had for Phil or Alex. But she felt emancipated, a modern young woman, free and equal.

'When you're married,' said Amanda as a preface to every remark. Since Corinna didn't have boyfriends or sweethearts, this must be serious. After all, everyone had to get married.

'How could I marry Tom? I hardly know him.'

It was in her mother's face too every time she went to see Tom.

'I'm going to Malta to see Tom – a friend of mine.'

It was made easy by her mother's obvious happiness and Mrs Bramwell's obvious devotion to her mother.

The rooftops of Valetta gleamed in the sun. Salt whipped into her face off the seawater in the harbour. Her mother radiated courage as she was held high in the hands of a dozen sailors descending the ladder to the longboat. And Mrs Bramwell tossed pennies for the boys to find in the water because seeing such courage brought tears to her eyes.

A stone's throw from the sea was the villa with railings, pillars and a Victorian bath geyser. Tom pushed the chair and carried her mother up the great staircase to wash in the great white bowl of warm water kept on the wicker table. Later, he left Corinna to help her mother while he lit the Calor gas stove and Mrs Bramwell fastened the shutters and opened the windows wide.

Tom glanced at her shyly and away.

'He's good-looking and he's rich – his people have that lovely house by the church,' Amanda said.

Amanda, always in love, was now in love with Tom. He did things, he didn't stand about like Benjamin, he struck the match, lit the wick, balanced the kettle on the flame and made the tea.

After sundown, waiters in the restaurant on the way to Valetta neatly whipped away the white cloths laid on the lines of pineapples, figs, olives, cream, broken bread and glasses for the bottles of Italian wines. Her mother's eyes lit with delight on Tom as he stood up to serve her. Yes. She was happy sleeping under the mosquito netting as if she always had slept that way.

'I can take care of your mother,' said Mrs Bramwell. 'You two enjoy yourselves.'

They swam and dived off the raft, and Corinna nearly crying over the donkey tied to the wheel in the shade of Musta cathedral. Tom shrugged over the donkey. He was a man's man. Though kind he was too firm, almost hard on animals. He sucked a pipe, laughed with a glimpse of fine white teeth at her witticisms.

'The car – she goes!' he said.

The car, the woman.

'How can you say that – Phil would laugh at you.'

She tried but failed to think out her feelings for him. He was six years older than her. When she zipped with the sheer fever of being alive, he was solemn, considerate, and laughed quietly. He never forced himself on her.

The four weeks fled by.

Malta itself was exciting from the gun turrets over Valetta harbour to the farthest point of the island of Gozo where there was neither a house nor hut in sight. The cartwheel marks in the rock had been there a thousand years.

She was no sailor and was almost ashamed the booking was made for the train. But there was Pisa to see, not to mention Rome for a night and the beauty of Genoa. Though they were stuffed into a train with Italians and Far Eastern travellers, the eruption of Vesuvius as the train made a half circle round it, inspired the entire journey.

As home drew near, her mother became a bit vague, her spirits lifting only when they arrived back.

'There you are – everything just as it was when we left.'

But it was not.

The bronze star left by the kiss of the sun under her mother's chin barely had time to fade before the turmoil.

A door had slammed shut. Voices broke the night. Corinna shot out of bed and ran down. Redder than red, he stood in the centre of the room as guilty as Satan. She knelt by her mother's bed, not able to look at the pain in her face.

'How could you?' she yelled at her father.

It was the affair with his 'lady' friend, Mrs Robinson flaring up again.

He went on as he had before – out at night and home in the early hours. He came into her and Amanda's bedroom, his dark ruddy face over her, tobacco in his breath as well as a faint perfume. Cheap.

'We can manage quite well without you,' she said. Then she held her breath and he started to pummel into her through the bedclothes.

Joy rose in her. Liberated, she let her fury go, striking out with her fists. There was much shouting and fighting, and Amanda shrieking. Corinna held down his head while Benjamin punched him in the back until he wrenched himself free and they all let him go and raced down to their mother.

The crisis was over. They were going to move. Her letters to Tom played down the fight as something shameful, and boasted of the Tudor beams in the new house. They boasted too of the campaign she and Phil were involved in to refuse to tip waiters and all such. They made little cards to hand to the waiters. 'I do not approve of tipping,' it said. 'Like Charlie Chaplin who never tips, I believe you should get a proper wage. Thank you for your service.'

With a sinking heart she watched one particular waiter wearily reading the card. Then he bowed and said, 'Thank you, madam,' and she marched out of Claridges no less with cousin Julie and Amanda mocking her. It was nonsense talk. London was full of politics and the impending inevitable war.

Then, as suddenly as the spring, Tom's letter came. He had asked for a posting. He would be home in two weeks' time. She was shocked into silence. No three years to sort out her feelings. It was now. He was here.

'Coffee?'

He placed a cup in front of her, dunked her a croissant and swivelled round on the bar stool to look at her.

'You look lovely! And I've got three weeks leave due. Shall we go somewhere?'

'Daddy's car – to Switzerland – let's go!'

It was nothing but a dream. Life was zooming by just as it should. Like a shadow Tom walked at her side, talking about nothing and everything. He had booked a hotel. He seized her arm and led her through streets filled with trees and crowds speaking volumes of Parisian French, but he suddenly and urgently had ideas of his own as clearly as if he had spoken them. She had, half closing her eyes with fatigue, only to tell him it was impossible, she could not sleep with him. What would her mother say? But her mother need never know.

He felt her reluctance and drew back, but she felt compelled to say, 'Oh, you don't have to do that!' and her spirits rose. She took his arm and pressed him forward. She was not afraid. It had all been her idea, her great experiment. She was the emancipated modern woman.

Half-drawn plush pink and tasselled curtains hung heavily across the windows at the foot of the huge bed in a sea of green carpet. Silence reigned just as heavily.

She undressed and prepared for bed quickly, feeling sick. Head bursting, she slipped between the cool sheets and drew the bedclothes up to her chin. Her head was full of weird shapes, new sensations and glimpses of a white page hidden in a book. She lay still. The door opened.

He was standing by the bed, not beautiful, rather flushed and clumsy and between his legs a protrusion. She felt him throw back the bedclothes, felt his body warm against hers.

He kissed all over her face, murmuring, 'I'll take care, promise.'

'You did say not—'

She stretched away from him. Even so she was taken unawares, overwhelmed. She felt his penis hard and ready as he forced her legs apart. She wanted to scream. She stiffened and shrank back. He plunged and plunged again, then lay still. It was over. He lay heavily on her, breathing deeply, his face buried in the pillow. He had had his ejaculation without her.

She saw the ornate plaster light rose spinning back to the centre of the ceiling. Blazing hot, she felt unclean.

'You all right?' he asked, voice in her neck.

'I can't breathe.'

Nothing mattered but that.

'I didn't do anything,' he said.

Without upsetting him, she had to go to wash. She shook with a revulsion so strong in her she could hardly hold herself leaping from the bed.

She felt his breath stop.

'The sheath's broken,' he said.

In a frenzy, she ran the water warm in the bidet, splashing herself, wiping away the humiliation, choked with anger.

'Come on,' he said warily. 'It'll be all right. Just come into bed and sleep – I promise – I promise.'

Corinna stretched in the bed, awoke blinking light as the sun blazed through the shutters. She closed her eyes again and listened – voices below, water flushing, running, kitchen sounds up from the yard. She moved her body piece by piece, feet, legs, back. She turned swiftly and sank flat on her back. She was intact, alive. She slipped off the bed to stand at the window, shudders racing through her and over her skin. She steadied her eyes to see the glasses on the little tables under the awnings below.

She thought, *In the years to come I shall remember – I was twenty-two; Tom burst into my consciousness with images unimagined, fears and revulsions, humiliations, roughness of skin, hair, heat and pain – I was flung into breathless chaos.*

Aware, she listened to Tom moving in the room, clearing his throat, running the bidet, using the basin, pulling on his clothes with precision, dry shaving. All without song, but normal. He was as normal as a man would be.

But she was not normal. She was filled with disgust which she was not allowed to express or understand. It made a tightness in her chest, a small whimper in her mouth and rebellion rose in her against Tom's bourgeois book of rules which laid down black this and white that – men from women, keeping them secure.

Other people in the timber breakfast room scraped their feet in their excitement at being there, talking French, music in every word. She let Tom go, and began to laugh, her feet flying inches above the pavement to reach the garage. She watched Tom and the mechanic sort out the carburettor, slipped into the driving seat under Tom's surprised eyes, and took the long straight road south, talking without pause. The mountains came across the skyline and they stopped to stare into the depths of a roadside waterfall, bending over the wooden rail to catch the spray.

'The frontier is only two kilometres away,' she declared. 'I've got a snap somewhere.' And I had the soul of a little boy then, as now.

Daringly, he kissed her swiftly on the cheek.

The white house shone on the meadow ridge. Uncle Oswald, splitting a block of wood, looked up as they came and shouted for Aunt Mat. It was a moment of pure joy.

Tom slipped into village life without effort, sitting with Uncle Oswald on the bench by the cellar door drinking wine and watching Aunt Mat stirring the raglette on the stove. Striding across the meadow by the house, she led him to see where Napoleon had slept, there by that stove, his horse snorting below the balcony. She introduced him to the wine merchant who stood with his hands over his stomach, his black hair up like a Christmas tree, speaking French. He had two girls and a boy at the French school in Sion. He was proud on the one hand, on the other obsequious.

'*Pour vous*, Mamselle.'

He bowed.

'*Merci*, Monsieur.'

It was a perfect miniature wine barrel, with a shining round belly of dark ridged wood studded with black iron hoops.

'No leaks? No weak spots? Can we keep lemonade in it?'

He shrugged and laughed, his eyes saying, lemonade in a wine barrel, *mon Dieu*! Ten thousand francs he had paid for a new bell in the village church, to ensure his name for a thousand years.

'Tomorrow we go to de alp, *nicht*? Ah hef to see der men,' said Uncle Oswald.

He had a name for being soft with the cows and checking that the men treated them all right.

The hut lay snug at the foot of the incline, a long low slate roof jutting out of the stone wall of the mountain. There was not the remotest possibility of a glimpse of that elusive Matterhorn. Stepping past the men in the shade of the wall smoking their pipes and spitting silently with the sweet liberty of maleness unchecked, she ducked under the roof edge and followed Aunt Mat into a stone cool cave.

'The men like it. They stay all the summer and smoke and drink to their hearts' content. And none too clean. Make the cheese here and bring it down with the milk. The women like it, too.'

'Why do they all wear collars and ties and trilby hats?' Corinna whispered. 'And waistcoats buttoned up all the way.'

'Because,' said Aunt Mat in full voice, shaking her black hair free, 'they don't often get women visitors. And you don't have to whisper. They don't speak English.'

She smiled at the men to beguile them away from any suspicions they may have that the talk was about them.

'This is the real Switzerland – none of that tourist nonsense,' said Aunt Mat.

With that aloof servility proud mountain folk have before people wearing panamas and carrying parasols, the men kept their eyes down, stirred the pile of white wood ash on the stove grate so that the loose column of blue smoke rose up through the roof, or poured out glasses of wine on the hefty bare wood table.

'*Ess'n wollen Sie Fräulein? Schmeckt gut.*'

Gestures brought her to the table and sat her next to Aunt Mat. Dark rope-veined hands brushed hers on the glass stem. The wine soft and glistening pale ran over her fingers.

'Santé!'

Tom had come through the outside door into the cavern puffing his pipe, Uncle Oswald slouching his nailed boots on the stone floor after him.

Accepting a glass, his eyes on the room, Tom stood listening to Uncle Oswald's talk with the men and accepted a plate holding a chunk of bread and cheese put together by the man at the bench. His eyes came round to meet hers for a quick moment with a knowing wink before he turned again to listen to the men, to the Italian lilt of their incomprehensible dialect, as if he were in the mess at camp.

'We must leave,' Uncle Oswald called out in English in a break in negotiations. 'When the sun drops over that tip, over there.'

His pipe pointed.

'Presto – with one and a half hours to get down before dark.'

Quite merry he was in his heavy foreign way, giving them orders, having sold the hay and bought the cheese and brought the vintage news.

'It'll take two,' said Aunt Mat, sober as if she had been drinking tea, standing up and brushing crumbs off her hands. The room had fallen silent. From the hut door, through a piercing ray of sunlight, Corinna saw the track through the trees below had already fallen into shade.

'Let's go, *mach' schnell!*'

Threateningly dark the forest looked, but stepping into it was to enter a world of bird song, the sound of running water and a new lightness in the air. Through the lower trees she could see the valley basking still in full sunlight.

Tom had come behind her. He seized her hand and pulled her faster down and down, calling full-throated yodels, leaving Aunt Mat and Uncle Oswald far behind. They broke into the valley sun and she stood at his side holding the wooden road rail, panting, laughing and watching falling water crashing down from the glacier to the river.

'Look!'

Tom had come close to her pointing. A mass of birds was flying straight at a chasm in the peaks. They circled and swept up the slopes, retreated and circled again – and again, up and over – and away.

'Off to Italy,' he said. 'Beautiful – and gone.'

It was the first time she had felt poetry in him.

'I'll read you some Byron when we get back.'

The final challenge was the Great St Bernard. Hannibal had crossed it, why not they?

Aunt Mat watched them leave standing on the front balcony, as though saluting the troops like Queen Victoria and all that. They had rucksacks full of food, sweaters for the cold, walking sticks and the camera. Don't forget your boots, nor British esprit.

Over Sion the road climbed, winding on and up through the tiny village of Bourg St Pierre where Napoleon had breakfasted before the ascent with thirty thousand men to Marengo, through narrow streets and alleys between houses huddled together against avalanches, wild boar and robbers. Towards the summit, she told the story of Napoleon to Tom, who listened entranced, scoffing at her in his precise manner nonetheless for her painfully imagined details of Napoleon's horses snuffling into the tufts of dry mountain grass before crossing the wilderness of rock. They rose to the glacier and the little inn of Cantine de Proz, and on up to the hospice.

Here a monk rustled up to them in a long robe with a heavy cord dangling low in the folds. His sandals slapped on the stone floor. White hands placed the tray and two small glasses on the shining wood.

'Welcome to the hospice – God be with you.'

His English was good.

Another monk walked slowly out of the mist, his hands crossed into his sleeves; at his side was a great white-footed St Bernard. Without stopping, she put out the back of her hand.

The monk in clear French warned her, '*Ne le touche pas. C'est jeun.*'

He smiled and walked past her, dropping quiet commands into the dog's brain, plodding past the main entrance where Tom came out.

'We have to go down now – or much later. The Poste is coming up.'

'What was he talking about to you?'

'Oh – war – things like that.'

In a flash, she saw her father's face – 'blown to pieces at my side, young Cotton'. She saw him running across no-man's-land, a sniper at his heels. War was inevitable. Everyone knew that. It made her head ring and her heart shut tight with excitement. She wanted to get home to see her mother was all right, to hold the reins, as it were, because some great power was overtaking them all. She felt as if all her life she had been waiting for this catalyst that would transform the world.

Chapter Nine

The old gentleman in striped trousers and spats, who once waved a piece of paper and spoke of 'Peace in our time', had put down the paper and the microphone.

'Our country is at war with Germany.'

The great adventure had burst upon her. Corinna tucked her gas mask under her chin.

'I'll have to go!' she yelled.

Her mother sat still. The words echoed through the house. The bus and tube crawled into London.

'I know – I know – but only one of us has to stay and I have to go! I've got a medical at half past three.'

'Find a café and eat – Mummy says. Eat all you can.'

Amanda let the fuming go and began to giggle.

'It'll be all right, silly.'

Corinna left the telephone booth elated.

The army offices in Tothill Street bulged with women in leather-belted khaki, ties neat and straight, heads over desks, eyes rising alert and calm. Signing a form and taking one deep breath, Corinna ran to the top of the narrow stairs.

'No need to undress – just undo the buttons.'

The stethoscope touch was cold.

'Breathe in – out – how tall? Five foot nine, and a bit.'

The ruler ran across the board. She could read it all. The doctor was the only man on the premises.

'You'll do,' he said.

'Well, at least we know you're fit,' said her mother with that brave Nurse Cavell look.

Days and days it had taken to obtain her mother's acceptance. How else could she go? It meant leaving her mother. But, at last, she won a kiss and a fond sigh.

'Everyone has to do their bit.'

At Waterloo, there was a puddle so vast it completely cut off the trains from the passengers. Rain dropped, trickled or fell in a great soft silver cloud on to the paving stones. Most of the passengers jumped; some pushed their way through the corridors and jumped from the luggage van, their luggage tumbling after. In the centre of the puddle was a tough fortyish woman in uniform with three stripes on her sleeve.

'Sergeant Wright here,' came the voice over the Tannoy. 'A lorry will take us t' *dépôt*.'

'How kind!'

Dry humour, two deep blue eyes that darted away. Shy. The girl stamped her feet through the puddle. Black hair fell over one eye while she tugged at a suitcase and laughed.

'Form fours,' came the voice. 'Halt!'

The girl with the black hair stood still, half a cigarette between two small white fingers. Nicotine curled round her upper lip. Quickly then.

'Who are all these people?'

The eyes laughed. The girl shrugged.

'The hoi polloi.'

Like Phil's, the nonchalance. She had been in Kenya for three years, but was pale as a Londoner. This was fun compared to all that.

A sixpence snapped down on the counter.

'Tea please.'

A pause.

'Call me Stevie – name's Stevenson.'

'Call me Corie – Corinna Eliot.'

Sergeant Wright stood in the pouring rain, her board at her chest, the paper clasped to it like a dog's tongue licking the rain.

'Knight – Eliot—'

Down they dropped to the black road under the tail flap, their cases landing after.

Knight sang as they marched up the first garden and when she sang all the haughtiness of her Swiss boarding school echoed in the raindrops.

'Frère Jacques – *dormez vous – dormez vous – sonner la –* whatever.'

Corinna joined in.

'We're in the army now—'

Abruptly she stopped. They were late. Supper was ready. Leave the cases there. Instructions were shot out at them by a sharp little voice.

'Hazel,' Knight said as the bedroom door closed. 'Can't stand surnames.'

She snatched up a towel and was gone, leaving Corinna time to undress and pull on her pyjamas. She shook with shyness, slipped in between cold sheets and watched the door.

Hazel returned under a cape of golden hair, and marshalled her pots and bottles on the dressing table top.

'To beautify myself.' Perfect vowels.

'Bonsoir Corinna! Water's hot.'

There was a bang. Straight through the crack in the curtains blasted a roar of fire.

'Planes!'

Hazel was sitting up like an Egyptian Mummy.

'Idiot!'

'Social butterfly!'

But Hazel was flat with hysteria, with infectious roaring of laughter. How could they laugh with Tom in a tent and Benjamin in a submarine.

'Idiot!'

There was not a plane in the sky – a rick on fire more likely.

In the morning light, Corinna, half awake, slung off the

blankets, splashed cold water on her face and landed at Hazel's side at the kitchen table for tea and toast.

'How can you drive in that skirt? And in a coat like a spinnaker?'

'I like walking, moi. Reminds me of school, cold water and all that.'

'We didn't have breakfast at our school – but I learnt German in a Swiss mountain village. Hochdeutsch, too.'

'Uck!' said Hazel. 'Uck!'

In the new world, there was a small dark-haired cherub with a cigarette, flicking the ash into a dusty corner. The neat fingers were nicotine stained and touched the driving wheel deftly, the cherub blinking at the 'Double-de-clutch!' of the instructor.

The instructor checked his list – Stevenson, Knight, Eliot – *inter alia*. Passed. How did the working class reach these positions of authority?

The new uniforms came with brass buttons, and baggy trousers for women. The overcoats were big enough to fit a guardsman and Stevie was only five feet tall.

Hazel fell into fits of refusal.

'Can't – I just can't!'

'We just have to.'

Stevie was concentrating massively on buttoning up her greatcoat.

'We have a war to win and five hundred trucks to Aldershot isn't the half of it.'

They were in Oxford for lunch. A postcard of the High perched on the driving wheel.

'Fish paste sandwiches – ugh – if only Hitler knew!'

The quiet ring of her mother's laughter would lift their morale, nothing less.

'Hazel?' asked Stevie at the running board under a khaki bath cap.

'Gone to find coffee and some Scots Guards.'

Corinna jumped out of the truck, a small green book falling with her.

'*The Oxford Book of German Verse*,' read Stevie picking it up. 'I'd hide that if I were you.'

'Byron. I'll bring Byron next time – or a book of socialist songs.'

She slipped the card into the pillar box. Then she was walking through the shadows of the colleges – or the long green lane in Flanders – walking with a comrade at her side. Old dreams; new dreams. She was telling Stevie stories about home, her mother, the new pup and getting married in January, to please her mother you could say.

Outside the *dépôt*, past the guards, the grass bank ran wide and green along the roadside.

'Here I sit down. I'm changing, moi,' said Hazel throwing off her shoes.

Stevie sat on the ridge, quoting to the air between coughs caused by a reluctant cigarette.

'The Spartans on the sea wet rock sat down and combed their hair.'

She relit the cigarette.

'Scotland tomorrow – these shoes, gels.'

Corinna watched her sitting there, brush back her hair under her cap with small square hands.

'May I give you a lift?' he asked.

A short bellicose middle-aged man with a familiar moustache and forelock stood on the kerb, grinning in happy recognition of esprit before him. He opened the door of his two-door Morris Minor and let three shoeless volunteers with bulging rucksacks pile in.

'That's the war et al.'

Scotland. The North Sea wind and the rain. *Nil desperandum*! They talked of the heroes of ancient Greece, of Andromache weeping farewell to Hector, of women and slaves, and of men the heroes. Stevie laughed with raindrops running down her nose.

'Could be like Theban warriors, you and I, back to back unto death. Would that satisfy the romantic soul in you?'

'I'll do that, Stevie, stand back to back with you in the field of battle.'

'Let's simply leave old Agamemnon at rest and go back to baths and grub.'

Her black forelock was flattened with rain.

All that night Hazel tossed and turned in the next bed. Three feet away across the bedhead slept Stevie, her voice coming through the black shadows.

'Goodnight, cherub. Into the darkness rode the six hundred.'

Darkness fell.

Hazel calling woke her. Corinna sat up, staring over a room full of sleeping girls.

'Look at my chest,' Hazel was saying. 'It's covered in spots!'

When they came up from breakfast, Hazel had gone, taken into quarantine with chickenpox. There was no message.

'She'll be back,' Mitchell said. 'Though Scottish hospitals have a shocking name.'

The ghostly quiet in the little house by the river without Hazel was relieved by a letter on the bed. It was from Amanda writing to tell her Skipper had run out of the house into the town and under a bus. It had taken ages to get the police and a vet. She scribbled a note to Stevie and pushed it through next door.

It was their first intimacy, Corinna thought. The intimacy of words. There was no talk of Skipper or of the letter in Stevie's hands. They walked along the river bank and exchanged one glance of sorrow. That was all. Stevie climbed the stile to the fields and sat on it looking down at her.

'Talk to me about socialism.'

Stevie listened, but she was bitter.

'Remember, in this brave new world woman will still have everything – in the child. It's ridiculous for any woman to want to be a man.'

Africa Stevie had travelled, travelling light from the Cape to Cairo. To Corinna it seemed she was full of sorrow, yet brimming with laughter. The talking stopped. The light fell over the river.

'Christmas already – I'm going home, Stevie.'

'And so we tire the sun with talking and send him down the sky, said the poet.'

On the bridge, Stevie's hand touched hers and was away.

There had been a wedding. That was not possible: knowledge that faded into the outer rims of life. Wearing khaki trousers and jackets, they dressed like men but were paid like women – 9/4d a week. Her mother saw it differently – it was marriage that made the world go round, that sketched society. Grandpa with his watch chain, the aunts in their foxes, Doctor Marie Stopes in the clinic. The liberation of the new woman meant she could be all those things, and herself, and make her mother happy as well.

'Eliot? Or…?'

Change your name, but not yourself. It was a shock, like someone you expected to die dying after all. But it was nauseating. His closeness suffocated. He was beyond control. She saw that the cap was safe – that, and she could breathe again. A child was impossible to contemplate.

She, Corinna, lay still on the great double bed, his mother's bed, with chintz curtains over the blackout and sombre flowers down the walls.

She shut her eyes, her mind clenched against him, against the response of her body to the mere act, stiff in herself, suffocating in his closeness. If she rejected it, nothing could happen. Or was that too an old wives' tale?

Ninety-nine per cent, ninety-nine per cent. Why not one hundred? She lay still waiting, fretting over her safety.

She watched him throw back the bedclothes. The bed sank, his legs enveloped her. He was naked. His lips, warm and firm, were on hers, on her forehead, on her neck. His hand lay on her breast, on her stomach holding her down. He moved to raise himself over her, his voice low and tense.

'I want you so much.'

She had felt fear in Paris, but this was different – this was marriage. In Paris, she had felt his fear too, but now he was bold and strong, taking her with him. Urgently he groped to take off her pyjamas, stroked the bare skin of her buttocks, his knee moved her legs apart. His flesh against her and the hardness of his penis shocked her as it tentatively then forcefully found its way into her secret being. He plunged into her – deep, deeper. She shuddered and held on to him. Violently he made love. It began – it was over. She shuddered. She felt sick.

She felt sick with deep revulsion. It was unnatural, this determination that not even God could make her have a baby – *Nothing, not even God, was greater to one than oneself was.*

The whole thing churned in her in one long story – she should have known in Paris, or at home when Tom kissed her goodnight. She should have known at every step of intimacy. And turned away. It had all seemed so exciting – the service, Malta, the Alps, her mother wanting it for her after all the doubts of the years. Was she a girl or a boy inside? She was convinced that she could hide nothing from her mother.

Despair dragged inside her, despair at London's endless harshness and Tom's love for it. Everything he did was to please her, yet nothing did. How could she say she knew him, Stevie had asked. Malta, Switzerland – life was not one long holiday.

The week had gone by and he seemed happy enough, unsuspecting all her inward strife. Crunched up she watched him kick-start his motorcycle, his face as cold as the wind.

'No chance of their going without me,' he yelled above the engine. 'Things are warming up.'

He had gone. She ran for the bus, ran for the train.

Stevie shunned her, refused to speak except in those clipped offhand tones, her eyes smouldering. Like a monk following the Holy Grail, Corinna helplessly followed her. She made sure nonetheless that they were in the same hotel room, eating at the same table.

At last, Stevie's eyes rested on her and it was over – the magic swept back. The air in the dingy Carlisle dining room tasted sweet. Breakfast was demolished – the rack of toast, the tiny pat of butter, the scrambled egg, bacon. *Nil desperandum*!

Life was a rendezvous with Stevie and her Latin tags, her French quips and endless recitations 'Take up the white man's burden, send forth the best ye breed…'

Hazel came up behind them.

'Ah! Kipling – de rigueur at our school.'

Hazel and Mitchell rode; she and Stevie walked by the river or tramped the road to town, talking, talking. In a shop window in the town centre sat a honey bear not twelve inches high, golden as a marigold, great brown eyes full of unshedable tears.

'Let's buy him and make him happy – shame! Sitting with all those starchy dolls.'

Stevie cradled him in her hands as if he were a tender living creature.

'Napoleon – Emperor of bears.'

A honey bear joined in the long discourse on Rudolph Steiner and the need for seven lives to enable us to get things right, 'To mint the coin with which to pay the debt we owe.'

'Do you honestly believe we settle our moral debts in future lives, Stevie? You seem so sane to me.'

'Maurice did,' said Stevie, 'and he was quite brilliant. I lived with Maurice for two years – a long time when you're twenty-two – a Bluecoat boy.'

'Well, I'm a revolutionary – barricades and Karl Marx. Wipe out all those – Hazel, Wilkes, etcetera.'

'Maurice used to talk about Rudolph Steiner much like that – he was just as crazy.'

The Scotland convoys became as hilarious as a day at the seaside when they were young. They teased the young officers of Barnard Castle and watched their more frivolous comrades flirting and getting drunk before the long trip home in the banger of a coach.

'Let's have a song – it's all so bloody boring. Day off tomorrow, sarge says. Coming riding? You, Corinna? Stevie? *N'est pas* bloody boring!'

It was an education, the deep plunge and suck of the hooves in the mud at the bottom of the hill. Hazel, poised like a duchess on the hunt, made teasing irresistible.

'Yes, ma'am, not dogs, hounds. And they bay, for God's sake – they do not bark!'

Upright, Hazel sat like a knight in armour.

'Proud of you,' she said, her voice raised over the clatter of hooves in the yard. 'Coming to tea in the village, Corinna?'

'Sorry – promised Stevie.'

Corinna threw the reins to a stable lad, catching a glimpse of Hazel tossing her head with a smirk.

She ran with her hand in her pocket taking snippets of biscuit and chocolate, eating as she ran. Stevie was not in her digs as she had guessed. Corinna ran on down the road over the bridge into the town. If she simply walked she was convinced fate would lead her to Stevie.

The shops in the town were shuttered, but the cafés were waking up in dim lights. The shining canal was the only brightness. She stood by the water, unbearably tired. The endless streets ran on and on. Stevie's hard independence hurt her. She turned back to the road, and immediately her eyes fell on a small erect figure ahead of her in the dusk, a girl with a peculiar jaunty step purposefully heading into the town. In that walk, that jaunty toss of the head, was a cry for help. She ran to catch up.

'Hallo! Please stop, Stevie. I'm exhausted.'

Stevie stopped and looked at her, then silently walked on. Corinna fell into step, listening fascinated to their footsteps on the empty pavement marching into the town, marching into the first public house and up to the bar.

'Two whiskies, please.'

Side by side, Stevie and she stood to receive the fiery liquid, tossing back the glass. That was the way soldiers of high rank drank their whisky. Two empty glasses landed with a shock on the counter top. The giant door closed behind them.

Footfalls and a thousand poets echoed in her head – because it is she – because it is I. Slowly, they walked down the long road with the sun falling down the sky.

Chapter Ten

White slept the world in ice-keen air. Down the long undulating bootlace road over the Shap Fell the convoy of mountain huts attached to the skidding trucks stopped and slid one by one off the snow crunched tarmac into the gulf of snow.

'What the hell do you think you're doing?'

Mitchell pushed her cap back so that she could yell at the wide-eyed driver in the black saloon car blocking the road.

The entire army, it seemed, had landed on the slope, a hundred hands on the truck walls.

'Stop!'

Lieutenant Wilkes raised her hand and trailed a coil of rope through the snow. The strength of that silly woman was amazing to behold. All was still, watching her sling the rope round and call unintelligible commands.

'Here, over here! Pull – stop! – Pull!'

One by one the huts regained the road and were dragged into position. The engines roared and spat, and wheels turned.

'Next stop, Catterick!' called Mitchell, a veritable Hannibal urging the elephants across the Alps to Catterick barracks and on to Stranraer.

High echoes rose over the trawling trucks, high voices with guts:

When we get to Berlin
The Kaiser he will say
Louder!
Och Och mein Gott
Vot a bloomin' fine lot
Are the Tenth Rifle Brigade.

On the bridge, the convoy stopped, for Stranraer bridge was the unknown the secret entrance to fairyland. Tiny lights surrounded the harbour water like jewels in the folds of the night.

Stevie stood entranced, certainly not in the mood to listen to a brief summary of the theory of Henry George, however brief, but saying, 'Look at the lights or you'll miss the end of the rainbow.'

'Volunteers!'

Wilkes walked into the light of a lamppost, her uniform as immaculate as when it was new, lolloping with none of the grace of the monocled dandies who led men to their deaths in thousands in the Great War. Her boy's voice pierced the dusk.

'You, Eliot, and Stevenson, Mitchell and Montgomery. Get the trailers aboard.'

The chosen, that made them grin.

Gangplanks groaned under the truck wheels. Into the dark hold the trailers thundered. Trailer after trailer was wedged into the narrow coffin-like lines, the trucks thundering out again over the gangplanks back to terra firma. Robert Louis could not have devised a more eerie scene.

Out of Stranraer bumped a lorry full of timber planks. It stopped, and their feet struck the road. The weary face of the driver smiled. He waved, and the lorry gathered speed. Loch Lomond sparkled in the pale sunlight.

Corinna tried to move, but there was something wrong with her legs, Stevie staggered about the road like a broken windmill; both were weak with laughter. Over the bank could be seen the waves rising and falling menacingly under a suddenly darkening sky.

'You said the bonnie banks and braes!'

'It's February. What do you expect?'

'February! That's winter!'

For one second, Stevie's white face filled with doubt. But they were here for adventure.

'Come on, I'm the great rower – all you have to do is take over the rudder.'

Corinna grinned, adding, 'And recite to me.'

The boatman mumbled, but he took his shilling and handed over the rope. Stevie lurched aboard, gripped the sides so that her knuckles shone white and sat petrified in the short rear seat. The strength of one would have to do.

Free, the boat circled out into the water as if pulled by evil forces, sharp little waves hitting the side.

Tugging the oars into the rowlocks Corinna pulled, shouting over the wind, 'Pull the rudder straight.'

Louder.

'Straight!'

Her voice dropped into a wail.

'Stevie, why are you so funny!'

'I'm not, it's you!'

Or both of us, the one reflecting the other. Stevie had recovered. Her face was radiant like the face of a little boy, now brave, now frowning, whom someone had saved from disaster. Sitting with her eyes on the water, head down, she recited into the wind that took the words and brought them back an echo.

> Now who be ye would cross Lochgyle
> This dark and stormy water?
> O, I'm the chief of Ulva's Isle,
> And *this* Lord Ullin's daughter!

Stevie had started and nothing could stop her – the murder of Polonius behind the arras, the curfew tolling the knell of parting day, Lycidas who must not float upon his water bier unwept and welter to the parching wind, and St Agnes' Eve, ah, bitter chill it was! The owl for all his feathers was a-cold.

Wandering away over the waves, her voice lost itself in the mist, her black shining eyes peered after it.

She stopped in her recital to ask quietly, 'Where're we going?'

'I don't know. I thought you were steering.'

Their laughter had a hollow ring to it, and died away. The lake had become a sea and they were in a cloud of pelting rain.

'Turn back,' said Stevie, grim as the snarling waves.

By sheer force of will, her heart a beating drum, Corinna plunged in the oars and, half rising from the seat, pulled with all her might. Stevie sat motionless, poised on the boat end, and catching her eyes at last, burst into laughter as if it were the greatest joke in the world, Focusing her eyes the distance, she opened them in surprise.

'I can see the boathouse!'

Stamping their feet on the gravel path, their hearts rang with joy. Stevie stood staring dreamily back over the water cap in hand. Her black hair was lank, her uniform as trim as Wilkes could wish it on a half drowned soldier.

'I forgot to ask you, Stevie. Can you swim?'

'Hardly a stroke.'

'I can't drown. I was born with a caul. I'd have saved you.'

All through the night she lay half awake in the narrow bed, the room full of sleeping girls, tormented by what might have been if the boat had gone over in the icy water. She would have saved them both, of course. In every scene plaguing her, she saved them in the end, laughing, and they stood on dry land with Stevie laughing and reciting, 'Hero of Loch Lomond!'

Something had happened at Loch Lomond.

The aura of Loch Lomond lasted for the long run home with enough daylight left over for a walk by the river. There were a million things to say to Stevie, but they had slipped away and inevitable it was that, Stevie at her side, they should stop on the old bridge and lean on the stone wall, the dreams drifting by.

What was it, Corinna? The desire to touch that small hand clenched on the bridge wall. Maurice was it? Making her heart bang. Stevie talking about Maurice. He had asked her to marry him, she said, but only on the night she had come to say goodbye, the ticket to Mombasa in her pocket. He had taught her not to duck the truth. She refused him and left him standing there in Victoria Street in the rain. Her heart died. But there was something else heavy in Stevie's voice – jealousy of Corinna with Tom.

'And now? Hero of Loch Lomond,' Stevie said, laughing.

Pull the rudder straight. Not guilt about Tom – jealousy of Maurice, Corinna saw it clear in her mind.

She saw her own hand move on the bridge wall, grasp the clenched fist, hold it tight – at once she was aware, as if struck by a knife, that the hand had been snatched away. Stevie had gone, dropping down the river bank. Swiftly she dropped down after Stevie, catching her by the shoulders, drawing her close.

'Don't do that – I love you, Stevie.'

She stood holding Stevie in her arms, rocking to and fro to ease the deep moan in her self. This was what was wrong – this was where the truth lay. Where all that was female was but a shell for being a boy. She was destined to love a woman, to love Stevie. Forgetting Maurice, forgetting Tom, she kissed Stevie – kisses without number.

'You have all my heart, Stevie.'

'Not possible – you're a married woman.'

And yet Stevie stood, eyes downcast.

'What shall I do, Stevie?'

Stevie shrugged and walked away.

'Kiss the joy as it flies.'

Going up the slope through the grass and mud, obstinately plodding up, laden with sadness so childlike, it was unbearable.

'Here!'

Stevie held out her hand. Pale yellow starlets in a bed of fleshy leaves, a dark head bent over them, desperate in the need to possess.

'Together we will conquer the world, Stevie.'

'Maybe.'

Her eyes were on Corinna's mouth.

'But we don't have to tell the world, as Wilde did. Much more romantic not to.'

'Squad leave next week. Come home with me to meet my mother, won't you?'

Stevie shook her head with that obstinate indifference she knew so well. It meant long days of argument, Stevie's face dark in wild thoughts, giving in at last with the grace of Pluto so foul it had both of them laughing.

'All right – if I must.'

She was tight-lipped, frowning, as if on the way to her own execution.

This was how it would be forever after the war, walking with Stevie in the London rain, listening to her erudite witticisms, watching the curl of sarcasm on her lips and their sweet repose. The future would be made out of this – the tube train's foul-smelling air, jolting carriages, Coughs and Sneezes Spread Diseases on walls, on platforms, London faces preoccupied in silent resolve.

'This is Stevie, Mummy. I told you about Stevie, remember?'

'Yes, of course I do. Come in.'

Here, there could be no secrets. She fastened her eyes on the stark outlines of the hall furniture, and on the huge velvet cloth over the air-raid shelter.

Silence made the house sound deserted.

'The others in the shop?'

'My word, you both look very smart,' said her father, suddenly there, fresh with racecourse air and forgetting his earlier sarcasm. His and Benjamin's dark maleness brushed aside the darker secrets of the soul. Standoffish, they would all see Stevie, sitting on her hands, her eyes lost in thought. How could they not know the truth there in every glance?

'I mean to study and learn,' Corinna said, the flap of the desk down, revealing notebooks of essays written under the guidance of Phil – the 'History of English Literature', the 'British Working Class'.

'Specialise, that's the way,' Stevie said, like Phil, turning the pages. 'If you go to university, you find your level. If you don't, you spend your life trying to find it.' There were notes in Stevie's voice that hurt, her usual wit dormant.

'I have a fear that because I had no education I shall spend all my life trying to catch up. Grandpa did that.' Silent with anxiety, she let Stevie go up to bed, quietly calling after her, 'I'll be up in a minute.'

'I can't think what you see in her,' her mother said, sadness in her voice.

'She's a wonderful person when you know her.'

Quickly, she smoothed the sheet under her mother's chin.

'Does Doctor Ashley still come in after surgery?'

Her mother stirred, sighing, the white skin of her forehead cool to touch.

'Yes, he's a good man. Reminds me of Tom. Says he will come and he does.'

She sounded tired, dispirited.

'Is there anything you need before the others come in?'

'No, don't worry. I'm all right. You'd better be getting to bed. You need plenty of sleep.'

She lifted her face for a kiss.

'And not too much talking. Goodnight. God bless.'

Stevie was in Amanda's bed. She changed the colour of the world, made it laugh. Words came tumbling out of Corinna bringing to life the family as they really were, like her father, broke and yet taking them all to see *The Dancing Years* to recover, and to dinner at Claridges.

'Why Claridges?'

'No reason, except that he'd been a buttons there as a boy. Mother's the brains and the strength in our family.'

Long after the talking, while Stevie slept, she lay in the dark with her heart aching for her mother, repeating over and over that the old must not win though they love and are strong, though they are loved and love. Because Stevie had brought DHL into her life. But it hurt.

The war had begun again. There were convoys to Scotland, to Colwyn Bay, to the wilds of Wales, to Liverpool where the people loved them, to London where they were ignored, lost and found in strange corners of the great city incredibly far from their destinations, driving round and round Marble Arch, sirens gone, gasmasks under their chins ready, tin helmets on, unable to get out of the panicking traffic, arriving at the docks four hours late.

The next day, it was back to llkfriston with its bookshops and teashops, to the river, the long walk back to the village, and to the trips into the town at every opportunity. Outside the Black Swan that splendid June day, they met Mitchell, cap askew, a dashing Prince Rupert, her eyes bright and bringing news – the British troops were getting out of France and the Channel was full of little boats rescuing them. Only one word could they hear between them – 'Tom'.

There was chaos. Under the opaque high glass roof of the station, there was chaos, doom and a terrible relief. Trainloads of men in a hurry searching for their families – soldiers without caps, rifles, gasmasks, knapsacks or great coats. Dishevelled heroes, grey with fatigue.

He was coming. He needed her. Deserting her husband in the moment of defeat, how could she get a divorce? Her eyes met his mother's, and her life stopped. She riveted her attention on the crowd; she had to be the first to see him.

'Darling!'

He was there in a gap below the wooden platform, his forage cap straight, jacket buttoned, gripping the strap of his knapsack. Dark lines streaked his face, dark trouble in his eyes. For this moment, she had to get it right.

'Tom!'

She slid down the platform steps – he was there. How thin he felt, and cold. Over his shoulder, she could see the tears running freely down his mother's face, Benjamin hesitating with his hand outstretched to Tom's shoulder, Amanda's blue eyes brightly shining as she called, 'Hallo, Tom! You're home,' as if from a holiday, her father patting his arm. Tom held on to her, gripping her to him, speaking through closed lips. There had been no way to contact her, all communications had been jammed.

At the car, he drew himself up.

'Now we'll really fight. All the chaps say that. Now we're fighting for our homes.'

He slumped into the seat.

'The French'd no heart to fight – not after last time – but our farmer helped us to get away. No news of Robert – Mother will go mad with worry.'

He slurred to a stop.

'God, I'm so tired. The Germans were after us for days.'

She felt nothing. She was surprised at the hardness in her. The predominant thought in her brain was that his hands were large and hard whereas Stevie's were warm and small. She was afraid that he might know and pressed his hand more firmly. How fate could let this happen all at once she could not understand. The world was in turmoil, yet her own life had risen like a phoenix out of the flames, bringing her Stevie.

'They're twenty-one miles from England across the water,' Tom said. 'It'll take all we've got to stop them.'

'But we will,' said her father. 'We did the last time.'

It was amazing, the underlying feeling that they would defeat the Germans, and this time utterly. To think otherwise was impossible, was treachery. Tom sat at the table in deep silence, his eyes in sunken darkness, his hand heavy with the cigarette, before blindly obeying her mother's, 'Off to bed now,' and stumbling up the stairs.

The whole house lay awake. All England was waiting. But Tom was fast asleep, the deep swell of his breathing keeping her alive to him where he had thrown himself flat on his back in the narrow bed. Amanda with hardly a thought had gone into the spare room.

She crept into her own bed and lay still. He stirred.

'You didn't say goodnight.'

She sprang out of bed and ran over the cold lino kissed his forehead lightly and felt him slip away.

She lay in bed staring into the grey darkness of the room. Stevie would be asleep. Her heart faltered.

'Dark near shining water,' Tom said, 'is a sure target.'

How could she be tied in this room miles away from Stevie! She had to talk to her. She shivered and listened. No sound. Only a sinister silence. Not only men would have to fight. She would tell sarge they should have pistols, like Tom's under his jacket, his life had depended on it, he said. She had to gather all her strength in secret – she must.

Not until he was leaving did he smile. Standing in front of her mother clean and spruce, thanking her for the care she had taken of him, he brought his face down for a kiss, and stood up smiling down at her, the blue in his eyes bluer.

'It'll be all right, Mrs Eliot. Everything'll be all right.

Somehow I feel it.'

She stood on the platform her eyes on him as the train set off, his fatigue gone. He gave a brief wave as if he were going on holiday. She walked slowly back to the car. He did that for her sake. He thought she was afraid for him when her silence was because all she could think about was how to get back to Stevie.

'I've put the car in the garage,' she said as she opened the house door.

Hiding the truth, she hung about the house, then brought her case down, the sickness in her dragging her under.

'Shall I make some tea before I go?'

Escaping explanations.

'Just half a cup'd be nice.'

Back on the convoys, her mother was with her. Where Stevie had tormented her at home, now her mother's vulnerability on the edge of London plagued her day after day. The war was one step closer – trucks shipped out of battle had to be collected. The forlorn trucks landed at London docks with canvas roofs torn, broken cigarettes in the driving seat, and an old penknife, the stub of a pencil, or a smear of blood on the windscreen.

After two weeks, news came that Stephen had been killed at Dunkirk. Panic seized her – they would all be killed – Alex, Phil, all the boys. What did it mean to be going to Cambridge and to die under a tank?

When Tom's letter came to say he had seven days' leave she held it like fire in her hand, crushed it into her pocket and left it there for four days on convoy, when she blurted it out to Stevie in the coach on the way back. The next morning, pass in her hand, she was on the train.

'I was on convoy, I missed your letter.'

The lie made her heart beat in her throat. She kept her eyes on her coffee. She had to be hard, there was no other way. Stevie had forced her into this.

'Mother,' he said quickly and stopped.

He had looked well when she had met him under the clock. Now she could see red lines round his eyes. He was struggling to speak.

'Robert's been killed,' he said. 'The plane didn't return. Last week he'd been grounded because he was so shaken helping to get his rear-gunner's body out.'

His mouth making strange broken signs.

'They shouldn't let boys do these things.'

She put her hand over his and gripped hard.

'The telegram only said killed in action. It was his twenty-first – all the cards and things were sent back to mother unopened,' he went on, crushing his cigarette end in the ashtray. 'Clive's with mother for a few days. Could we go to your home?' his voice was heavy and dull.

The house was in despair. Robert's death had made a wound in every heart. Only the passing of time would help and in the passing of time came the night. Three days were left of Tom's leave.

Corinna seethed in the deceit. This was home, yet it was a trap. She wanted to get out, leave it all, but supper was ready and her mother's face glowed faintly in the warmth of the room. We have to have courage.

That was what her mother meant when she said, 'Let's light the fire – it'll cheer the room.'

It came in the end, climbing the stairs after all the goodnights, to such a silent frenzy in her that she knew, following him into the bedroom she would have to say something. It was life and death in her.

'I've got an awful headache, Tom.'

With the light off, he talked quietly about Robert, but his grief left her mind on Stevie, on depths he could never know, where Stevie saw the mystic release of pain that healed.

Dull and heavy was the morning, a moist heat without sun. Her case packed and her sandwiches in her pocket, Corinna stood in the dining-room doorway to look back at her mother. Very upright, she sat in her wheelchair, pale and thin, sipping tea now and then from a cup on the swing table. Corinna left her case and walked quickly across to her mother, holding her close for one long minute.

'Got to report before midday.'

'Yes.'

A quiet resignation.

She ran through the door into a cloud of drizzle, the road swimming in her eyes, and jumped on the bus as it started.

From London to llkfriston she sat in the train in growing fear, a fear that pursued her out of the train and down the long road to the village, her eyes fastened on the bend and the cottages.

There she stopped, her hand on the gatepost, conscious of the silence of the river, and Mrs Baker saying Stevie had taken a forty-eight hour pass on Thursday and had not returned.

Chapter Eleven

Stevie, in the dim light with the wind from the sea cutting into the dark hollow of the hall, behind her.

'What a time to arrive! It's nearly eleven.'

'I couldn't get a pass. I'll have to be back for the morning.'

The words floated up the stairs. The curfew along the front meant only Stevie's family could be there.

Snatching her cap off the hallstand, Stevie said, 'Better walk,' and plunged into the darkness and the strong sea breeze. 'I will not be responsible for your marriage going wrong – you lack discipline – you've been spoilt.' Crossing the road to the promenade, she started a long diatribe, 'You're only aping the male. You can have children. That's the way to compete with men.'

These arguments were all exhausting.

'You just don't believe me. I can't go on leave with Tom!' Anger made Corinna blaze, 'And I don't want children! Stevie!'

Stevie stopped and faced her, silently looking up at her out of a small white face, defiant and unapproachable. For a long time, they were locked in angry silence, but reason saved the moment and they began to walk on.

'You and I, Stevie, will have Plato's children, of the mind.'

'But he was jealous of women, can't you see? Children of the mind! Rubbish!'

Stevie's voice shook.

'You must go back. You can't do this to Tom. The war's getting worse. Anything might happen.'

Stevie's voice had shaken. It was all over. Nothing else mattered. Peace had come again between them – because it is she – because it is I. Children of the spirit were born every minute of the day with Stevie.

'I can't live without you, Stevie.'

That firm little voice came back, 'Many people are living without their loved ones at this time.'

Then silence, unity. Her love for Stevie had in it Yeats' pity that lies at the heart of love. It tore her asunder, made her whole again, while they walked every town in England, Scotland and Wales, talking, talking.

They had walked and the pier had risen out of the dark like a seaborne monster crouching on the shore. Long deserted streets rose up the hill before them. She felt odd, sick, seeing bits fall off house walls. She stepped off the kerb and it moved under her foot. She couldn't breathe and something was pulling at her tie.

Stevie said, 'You're hungry – silly kid.'

She was sitting on a step in a doorway, in the light.

'You've chosen a good place,' said Stevie. 'Right outside a café, an all-night one at that.'

Up the narrow staircase they went, Stevie urging her.

She let Stevie order and sat back marvelling that out of the deserted streets they had come into a room full of people eating and talking as if it were lunchtime instead of two o'clock in the morning; and they were all eating eggs and bacon and sausages. By dawn, she and Stevie would be in camp again, back on the milk train that runs up the map of England through the night. Life would go on with Stevie.

The war resumed its spirit of adventure through scorching heat that sent drivers to sleep at the wheel and through teeming rain and gale winds, though they were proud of being soaked and frozen and there was never a whimper. Villagers reporting them as spies, they had to plough their vehicles round roadblocks of old cars, tyres, empty manure drums and farmers' carts at village entrances. Mitchell's arm was ever raised – 'Drive on, chaps!'

'We're going to build a new world, Stevie, where you and I belong.'

She took Stevie home again to see her mother. The battle was still on, there was no way to talk to her mother as she used to. Stevie rescued her, suggesting a play in town. Weak as Stevie's voice was with uncertainty it raised her mother's spirits.

'That's the idea, go to a play, enjoy yourselves.'

Charleston and Streeter – their courage, their defiance was Stevie's and hers. They were looking for the same thing, the new world that they would help to build after the war with no more poverty, no more war, order out of chaos and leisure for the workers to lift their eyes to the stars. In Thunder Rock lighthouse two women would do the work of men, reaching the inside of the inside of each other's minds, she and Stevie. Coming back to camp elated, she was shot into the present by Hazel's vivid face and her voice.

'Don't touch me!'

For a long time, it rang in her head. In the yellow of the electric light, faces looked brilliant white, still and silent. One girl sat with a fork poised rigid in the air, others with cups held to their chins, the eyes of everyone on her own face.

She felt nothing, then there was the desperate effort to speak, bringing out that breathless thinness in her voice.

'Sorry! I didn't mean—'

Her hand smarted from the contact of their hands on the door as she opened it and Hazel swept out, her face blazing, her eyes cold but branding her.

'What is it?' Stevie asked, the frown, the straight question, meaning she had genuinely not heard.

'Shall I get the tea?'

Corinna concentrated on the order, put the tea on the table and sat in the painful silence.

'D'you know,' said a voice close and clear, 'we've rejected Hitler's peace efforts. Got one hell of a war on now.'

Mitchell might look devilish with her tie falling freely through her open jacket and her cap awry, but was beau geste after all, and not far away Ashton's eyes were shyly watching, lingering as if on the brink of words. Voices sprang out of the silence, chairs scraped the floor. Never would she forget that debt to Mitchell and to Ashton to be paid now or in the life to come with the coin minted on this day.

Stevie, however was scowling at Mitchell's retreating figure.

'What happened, did I miss something?'

Inside the inside of another's mind. There was no secret in her from Stevie. It was fate, Stevie said, chance had it that there was a rundown room in the attic at Mrs Baker's along the passage by her own. Mrs Baker would be delighted to get another volunteer.

It was like stepping into heaven. Life off duty was a world of poetry, Plato and Socrates, Wilde and Proust, and of love that found Stevie at dawn, asleep at her side, arm flung over her head, waking softly laughing.

They became conscious of girls in the *dépôt*. Two from the north watched Stevie and her with soft brown eyes, and so did two young officers in another world of their own – classless Mitchell, outrageously libertine with not a dull thought in her egocentric mind, and Ashton. What was it about Ashton? A girl of daring who had had affairs they said, an artist from Paris, with a flat in town, forever in Mitchell's shadow, dreaming, moody and as pensive as Stevie. It was a revelation. Within society there was this secret society like an underground river of joy.

After every spark of political taunt, the world collapsed in laughter because, as their eyes met, that inexplicable abounding joy swept them away from the mundane.

'*Carpe diem et al*,' and Stevie. 'And *contra mundum* if needs be.'

Letters from Tom, anxious and weary, left Corinna untouched, Stevie not. One glimpse of his long white envelope and she was plunged into gloom.

'You've got to go – leave me – or I shall go and never return.'

Corinna could never feel sure if Stevie felt as she did. It made no difference. She would love enough for both of them – it was something she felt in her running blood, something she had to touch, like Lawrence.

Wild fears seized her nonetheless when Stevie blithely said, 'This is madness, Corie, my love, and will pass.'

'That's where you're wrong, Stevie. After the war, we're going to Venice. We'll motorcycle across the world to China and India, you and I.'

And the laughter rang with their feet on the *dépôt* yard.

Letters from Tom were the price she paid for all this – the fear of making Stevie jealous, of hurting, of rousing an anger that might send Stevie away for good, forever ready as she was to pack a bag and go. Opening a letter, the trembling in her hands was as sickening as if life itself were threatened. Waterloo? She had just time to get leave. Seven days. He had worked everything out, the dates and the times. Nothing could break the bond between her and Stevie as long as it was in her hands to preserve it with her life. She could keep secrets, burn at the stake if necessary. Stealthily she read the letter, listening for Stevie, her heart pounding, and then flushed it away.

Hot and uncomfortable in the heat and steam of the kitchen she kept her eyes on her sausages and mash, suddenly aware of the announcer – raids in London. Her mother in danger.

Anxiety over her mother, the shock and pain of the news, covered the guilt running like a fever in her of destroying Tom's letter. In the commotion over the supper table, the children's white faces, the agitation in all their voices over the closeness of the war, Mrs Baker could never ask if she had safely found it. Stevie suspected nothing.

He had come. Smiling, her soft midland voice joyous with the news, Mrs Baker met them at the door.

'Your husband came on his motorbike – he's going into the town and I'm to say he'll soon be back.'

Stevie fled. Corinna kept her eyes on the road and walked steadily towards the town. Of course he would come – what else did she think he would do?

Roaring at her side he came, his hair free and upright in the wind, his eyes distressed.

'Didn't you get my letter?'

Anger and hurt twisted into words.

'I've been waiting at mother's,' he shouted into the wind.

'I've been in Scotland all the week. We got back only late last night.'

The lie fell easily. The thought hit her that he might have been to the *dépôt*. Astride behind him, his scarf flying behind her, she lost her calmness. She wanted to ride, not talk into danger.

'Let me ride it – please!' she shouted.

He stopped with the engine thundering. Not daring to look at him, she knew exactly what to do – thrusting her cap at him, avoiding his eyes, she slipped her trousered legs easily into the enormous saddle, and turned the throttle, sending the machine hurtling over the tarmac.

His voice came after her, 'Careful – it's pretty powerful!'

It was like a meteor, like Pegasus, with no wheels, no road, only space. Nothing existed but the machine under her.

The wind was in her hair, the handle grips vibrated in

her hands. Over eighty the needle flicked. She was free –
gloriously free, charmed by the gods, protected like Achilles
on his Xanthus. Without looking, she could see Tom
standing on the grass edge.

She slowed down, kicked the gear lever free and looked
at him laughing.

'Nearly touched ninety!'

The laughter was cut short. It exposed the guilt she had
meant to conceal and her raw emotion.

His face was grey, his eyes sunk beneath a heavy frown.

'My God! You could've been killed.'

He took the handles. She let the motorcycle go into his
hands, snatching her cap from his fingers and striding off
over the grass.

'Anything,' he was shouting at her side. 'You could've
touched anything – a matchbox, an empty cigarette packet.
At that speed, you wouldn't have had a chance!'

He was gripping her arm. On the kerb the giant black
and silver panther was raring to go. She would have to tell
him. Now.

'I want to be free, Tom.'

He said nothing. Perhaps he had not understood. He
followed her across the grass away from the traffic. She, so
exhausted she could have collapsed.

'What is it?' he asked quietly. 'You don't write to me.
You don't care.'

Corinna shook her head. His caring hurt. He was so
humble, she felt humiliated for him. His hand on her arm
pulled her to him. She let him put his arm round her, draw
her close. The blue of his jacket was that peculiar slate blue
of his eyes. It occurred to her that he might cry – there was
a strange faintheartedness in him. She was wounding him,
but Stevie was in her eyes.

'Come to mother's for the weekend. I'm due back on
Monday. Corie – please!'

She strained away from him. He let her go, slumping against the university wall as if she had hit him. Her courage failed.

'It's the war. All those things,' she said.

'I'll desert.'

He seized on her words.

'We can go to Ireland. I know a chap – we can get away – go to America.'

His voice faded on the rack of duty and honour.

'There's another chap, isn't there?'

She shook her head.

'I just want to be free.'

In the blank silence, she was conscious of a pity for him that drained her. She had married him, given him dreams. It was still incredible that he, a grown man, could love her. The terror of losing her family never left her, but she could not live that other life and she could never let Stevie go. With a strange cool reserve she knew what she had to do.

'Why did you marry me?'

His voice sounded like a sob, dry and flat. He pushed himself off the wall and stood, uncertainly, his legs apart.

'Because…'

She turned away from him over the grass, the dry yellow grass blades crunching under her feet, back to the road, keeping her spirit hard against him. He stepped round in front of her, desperate and white faced.

'I shall wait for you to come back to me.'

He waited, but she could say nothing.

'I'll take you to your billet – if that's what you want.'

She shook her head and put on her cap, tugging at the peak.

'No. A bus goes past the door.'

She stood on the bus step looking back at him. He was lying in the centre of the wide grass verge, raised on one elbow, his face was dark and his hands tearing to pieces a strand of grass.

All night the words said between them repeated in her head. News of the bombing over London had dominated supper, heightening her fears for her mother and the family. Not until walking the three miles to the *dépôt* in the morning, walking with Stevie in cool autumn rain, could she say anything.

'Tom and I talked,' she said. 'Nothing else. He went back to camp.'

The initial relief had left her. Her head was heavy with guilt, and with the accusation there would be in her mother's eyes.

'I'll phone home at the first stop, just to see they're all right.'

By the time they had reached the *dépôt*, rain clouds hung a few feet off the rooftops.

'Tomorrow,' said Stevie with a crooked smile, 'the sun will be shining, winter sunshine worth a guinea a box.'

New recruits filled the hangar.

'Conscripts, quell chagrin!'

Stiff and new they looked, casting glances at them as they headed for the office notice board.

'Eliot. Message for you.'

The lines of the wood panels and glass that made up the office wall broke into pieces. Lieutenant Head stood in the open door, a paper in her hand, her hair a shock of disorder over her pasty face. The room lights behind her threw the desk and the paraphernalia on it into queer shapes. Lieutenant Head's face made loose movements, her high-pitched voice was far away and difficult to hear.

'There's been an accident. Your husband's in Grimsby hospital. You will have to leave at once.'

There was the vast shed full of uniforms and trucks, noise and commotion, and against the office wall Stevie's white face lifted to her, angrily questioning.

'Grimsby! Couldn't you get a vehicle? You'll catch a cold, you're soaking already.'

Her voice trembled.

'Do what you know is right. That's all. I know you will.'

'I've got forty-eight hours and a rail pass. Stevie – I love you.'

'I love you too, cherub.'

One long moment and she tore herself away. Stevie stood alone, her dark eyes following her, at the edge of the frenzied activities of the army, her small figure getting smaller as the concrete space between them grew.

At the great doors, she began to run over the marshalling yard to the road. Her first instinct was to run to the station, her next to stop a passing van, the rain dripping off her cap, making her greatcoat as heavy as if it had been washed and put on wet.

'Hop in,' said the young man after she gasped that her husband was dangerously ill in Grimsby hospital. 'They might've let you have a car or something,' he said.

If he could, she felt, he would have driven her all the way. She jumped out and ran. Water in her shoes and inside her collar.

The train closed round her. She leaned back in the seat and shut her eyes, conscious of a dozen people pressed about her suffocating her, and that the window was closed. She needed courage, the courage she had from her mother. She pulled herself up and looked steadily out of the window at the bleak wet countryside.

She had been in a stupor perhaps. The whole station seemed to be boarded up, full of people in dim light lost in the mist. Someone came running up to her, someone she knew from home.

'Did you know a landmine came down near the river last night?' he asked breathlessly.

'No—'

She found it impossible to say any more than that.

'Thought you were going home. I must catch the train – hope your people are all right.'

He had gone, running through the crowd.

Numb with fear for her mother, a peculiar helplessness crept into her. She took off her cap and shook it, unbuttoned her greatcoat and walked, coughing, down the platform, through the iron gates into the waiting room to sink on to a chair at a trestle table, the icy water in her shoes freezing her feet.

'Would you like some tea?'

A steaming mug of hot tea was being held in front of her. A young woman in black and white uniform leaned over her, turning the mug handle for her to hold.

'There's sugar in it. You ought to see a doctor about that cough.'

The kindness choked her.

'No – no charge.'

She had gone. Sweet and hot, the tea soothed her chest. The young woman was like a young army officer at the *dépôt*, gentle, unconscious of class. It was the common purpose. Why did it have to be only in war?

She had forgotten to ask for money at the *dépôt*. Her fingers found her top pocket. Not much in there. Sipping the tea, she realised she was starving and she would have to wait to eat. That's how it must feel to be hungry and to have no money at all. She took the cup back, glancing her thanks at the trestle table, refusing to see the plates of buns and sandwiches.

All she could feel was a persistent drive to get where she had to go. She climbed aboard the wet train and sat alienated in a line of strangers, waiting for time to bring her to Grimsby and staring out of the window at the fading light. At last she could fling open the carriage door, jump down to the platform and run through the gloomy long wet streets, asking the way as she ran.

The doctor was waiting to see her. He looked very young swinging his stethoscope and frowning at his pad. He was a little distraught, speaking with his eyes glued to her face.

'Mrs – Bramwell—'

Her mind hesitated. That was her name.

'Your husband died five minutes ago. We tried to contact you.'

He moved his hands as if to throw the pad away.

'His head was excessively damaged.'

Her eyes fixed on him, on his eyes and his white face. She stumbled on his words that come to her from far away in a high-pitched voice.

'I'm so sorry.'

He had gone. Nurses ran silently in and out of a cubicle. The sister at her side put a little glass of liquid in her hand.

'You may see him if you like, but—'

Corinna shook her head, following the sister into a small white room.

'Drink it.'

The bitter liquid in her mouth. She felt cold.

'Remember now, life is for the living,' said the sister sharply.

The hospital porter opened the great doors, his eyes downcast.

She stepped past him out of the hospital. The night sky was high and clear with not a sign of rain.

'Look at the stars,' she heard herself say.

She began to walk towards the station, conscious of being cold, remote, untouched, of not being at all.

Her feet began to quicken, faster and faster, her heart beating quicker with them. With every step the revelation grew in her that she was free.

Chapter Twelve

It was over. The tears trembled in her mother's face; the roses lay scattered on the grass. It had all been swift as a knife blade striking through her. Her mind was numb with guilt – she had killed him. No one need ever know, but the truth was there in her forever. The endless hours of the night had passed. It was over, but never would she escape it.

In the morning, waking from that strange non-sleep, her chest was so tight she could hardly stand up. Doctor Ashley's jovial voice thundered in the hall, his stethoscope in his hand.

'No more six-ton lorries for you, young lady.'

He tucked his equipment into his little black bag. She stared at him for one long moment.

'I like it,' she said. 'I like the army.'

'I want you to see a chest specialist, young lady. Nothing to worry about, just a precaution. If Amanda will call at the surgery, I'll give her some tablets.'

'I can't leave just like that. I have to report back,' she said desperately.

She started to cough. They were hemming her in. She had to see Stevie.

The tablets had a bitter taste, but made her feel better. Over a week it had taken for her to be able to stand up in comfort. She dressed, made tea and took it in to her mother.

'I'm better now – I'm going back. I'll be home again soon. Promise. I'll see the specialist and all that later.'

She marched to the window and back and stood by the fire near her mother. With a long sigh, at length the answer came.

'Off you go then – God bless.'

One thought drove her on, in the bus, on the tube and on the train – *Stevie*. She pressed herself back into the corner seat. The tablets gave her a queer hollow feeling. Slithers of fields fenced in with trees flew past the train until she felt dizzy and closed her eyes. When she opened them again, the train was slowing down. The llkfriston station board stopped outside the carriage. She sprang out of her seat, out of the train and ran.

At the *dépôt* gates, the breathlessness returned. The strength drained from her legs. The hangar was empty but for a few girls round the office. One of them was Ashton, coming out with a pass in her hand, saying on seeing her that she was off for three days. She needed more than that, she said. Her mother was ill. All poured out in a rush as she flew.

Corinna stood at the notice board reading the order sheets. Stevie had gone on a convoy and was not expected back for three or four days. Her own name had been moved to Section F. She felt antagonism in the transfer. She would have to go home and Stevie would follow her because she must – *contra mundum*.

Ghost-like in the yellow lights, the girl sat behind the desk. Wilkes was on convoy, Stanton would be on duty later, Head would see her. Heart sinking, she made her way through to the rear office.

Talking to Lieutenant Head was like talking to an impenetrable wall. Extended leave was out of the question. She had had all leave due to her, Head said, out of that unwashed, cold look in her dark eyes that never seemed to be listening.

It was impossible to speak to someone like that. In that moment, she wanted to get out of the army. Forces of destruction were turned on herself and Stevie.

'But I have to go—'

'You've signed a contract. The army's not a job! If you take leave you will be deserting.'

The contempt in that voice!

'You'd have no ration book, no identity card. How would you survive? A girl who breaks her oath can hardly expect her butter ration.'

Head pushed back her chair.

'Come outside. We'll talk out there.'

She led her through the narrow door at the back of the room. Fresh air blew up from long fields reaching to the horizon. Piles of rubbish lay about as if a building had been demolished. Head's voice persisted, penetrating and hard, continuing the diatribe about God and her country, war and duty, walking with her head thrust forward, her hands clasped behind her back. Now and then she sighed, then droned on again. The grit under their feet was the only other sound. Head walked slightly ahead of her, pursuing the bitter sharp argument and following the line of the broken wall down to the end where she swung round on her heel to walk slowly back to the beginning.

Corinna had to escape. She decided to concentrate on the strange fact of the quadrangle being here, behind the *dépôt*, with fields spreading out to the skyline, wild and free. She would say nothing, and go. She was aware suddenly that Head had stopped talking and was looking into her face.

'I think you should see the MO,' she said.

It was a trap. She bit back her instinctive no and followed Head inside, took the form for the MO and stepped across the immense concrete no-man's-land. Her heart pounded, but her step was calm. Her spine tingled with the effort of keeping her stride braked to conceal her desire to run. She passed out of the gates under the unsuspecting glance of the *dépôt* guards.

Rotten luck, she thought, throwing her things into her case, that she should have had to see Head. Her chest was tight, she was exhausted and there were no tablets left. She laid her uniform on the bed, took up a notebook from the dressing table and sat on the bed to write:

> I had to see Head – I've got to get out of the army, Stevie. I shall have to leave before you get back – phone home from London YWCA. I'll come. Stanton won't send the Red Caps.

The squeak and rattle of the pushchair wheels rose like a fire alarm. The sky was extraordinarily light. She held the suitcase steady while Mrs Baker pushed.

After a few minutes, she could see houses, trees, even the paving edge. Not a soul was in sight. How glad she was not to be alone. Moonless, the sky shone with countless stars. One day she would come back to give Mrs Baker a gift to show her gratitude for the pushchair and for the children's feet pattering ahead on the bridge, their little figures like marionettes in the starlight.

'I hope you get back before there's a raid. I wasn't thinking.'

There was so much to think about.

'If anyone comes, just put them off until Stevie's been. Tell them we've gone out, things like that.'

The great shed of the station rang with their feet. On the train steps, she looked down into the children's eyes full of envy and wonderment.

'Goodbye, then.' They watched her climb into the giant toy, hissing into the mountain of the night.

'It'll be all right. Jus' you take care of yourself. Go'bye. God bless you. An' take care of that cough.'

Dear unhappy woman with a husband who was never there. She was as thin as her own mother. She leapt down and gave her a quick hug.

'I'll never forget this, Mrs Baker.'

Leaving them in billows of steam standing like a sad Victorian picture that told a story.

Cautiously she sat in the only vacant seat, trusting her clothes for protection, the silk stockings and the raincoat.

She knew no one. No one moved. The grey of the war and of winter was in all their faces. With awful regret she had laid her uniform on the bed. She tried to breathe calmly, but instantly the thought that she was deserting made her panic. She had broken the law while girls were being parachuted into France, fluent only in basic French. Montgomery would never believe she had deserted.

All the passenger's faces had an eerie bluish glow. How could she sit still for four hours? She closed her eyes. Tom's face was there, broken and bloody. She opened her eyes wide. It would never go that cut and swollen face – so damaged the hospital did not want her to see him.

She stood up and pulled open the corridor door, closed it and stood against it, staring down the corridor running like a silent tunnel, blinds down and doors shut. She pressed her head on the windowpane. She and Stevie would find a new beginning. The train roared and lunged faster as a door opened and a girl in uniform came out.

'Ashton!'

'Hallo!' Out of the black silence in her head Ashton's voice added, 'D'you feel all right?' A moment's hesitation, she said, 'I'm off for three days. Did I say? I'm going home.' She added shyly, 'I had to do some shopping for mother after lunch.'

The shock of Ashton's being there not twenty feet away in the train corridor overcame her. Ashton came nearer.

'You looked pale. Must be the light.'

'I'm all right – just wanted some fresher air, that's all,' Corinna said, and stopped.

Someone shouted down the corridor. Someone else laughed. Ashton's quiet voice was trying to reach her.

'There's more room in my compartment. You could come back with me.'

'Yes please!'

The scene in the canteen flashed into her mind. She pulled her case off the rack and dragged it along the corridor.

Ashton had a way of admiring strength, first Mitchell's, now her own, loco homo. She forced herself to push her case up on the racks and sat down leaning forward to hear what Ashton was saying – something about finishing a picture while she was at home, she always started with tones. She was painting bottles, a landscape of glass. Yes, that was surrealism, if you like. Words. Words.

Ashton was sitting in the corner seat by the window with a magazine in her lap. Trim as a new recruit she looked in her uniform, her fair hair cropped, cap on her suitcase. But all the time Ashton was talking, she felt the sickness in herself. It weighed her down. She kept seeing Tom's mother sobbing and red roses on the grass. All words useless, broken sentences saying nothing.

'Tell me about your flat. It sounds exciting.'

Ashton looked sleepily at her under half-closed lids and smiled.

'It's not a flat precisely, it's the top floor of mother's house, Victorian just one room big enough to take the paintings. I sleep there and make tea and have friends. Mother's easy.'

She spoke hesitantly, conscious perhaps of *dépôt* talk, but going on.

'In normal times I have parties, even now when possible. You and Stevie must come.' She opened clear greenish eyes wide and unfathomable, speaking in a soft clear voice which was a strain to hear over the sounds of the train.

'What shall I call you? Not Ashton.'

'Lisa.'

She cleared her throat.

'And you?'

'Call me Corie – that's short for Corinna.'

'Corie then – I'm so glad I met you. I hate travelling alone.'

She gave a little laugh.

Thank heavens there was no one else on the train but Ashton, now closing her eyes again. She fixed her mind on the picture of the art room at the top of the old house, but it slipped away. She tried to keep her mind off the stale tobacco smell in the carriage and on the sleepy faces of the passengers, but Tom's face, the accusation of his dying, filled her mind. Stevie's voice, Stevie's presence, called her. Urgency rose in her. She unbuttoned her raincoat and jacket and stifled a cough. Lisa was in uniform. She envied her. There would be friends in the art room sitting on the floor, smoking, intelligent people talking all night, a university of artists.

This was the first time she had talked to Ashton. Now it was Lisa. She was glad to have met her and not one of the others. It helped to stop the other pictures in her mind. Drifting, her eyes met Lisa's on her.

'Be in soon,' Corinna said, and minutes later the dark roof was over them, the cases hauled down and the carriage door crashed back. She was out in the push and shove of Londoners, taking gulps of cold soot-tasting air and peering hard into the dimmed lights.

'My address. You and Stevie must come. Any time, stay for a while if you wish.'

A small card was thrust at her, before Lisa vanished into the crowds.

À tout à l'heure!

So she knew about Tom from the *dépôt*.

The escalator groaned and clicked under a million feet. She had to think of something else.

À tout à l'heure!

An artists' retreat. Stevie would never go there. She tried to picture Lisa Ashton in brightly coloured Picasso blocks and romance between artists and poets. No Latin, no Greek, no Theban warriors. Something in the tired grey-green eyes had been inscrutable.

The card was in her pocket. Her pulse raced. Now that she was alone, all the agony came back – she was deserting. She had to get home, and wait for a message from Stevie.

No one mentioned the army. No one mentioned her civilian jacket and tweed skirt. She sank back in the armchair, conscious only that her mother was near and there was peace.

'Drink this!'

It was her old drinking bowl from when she had bitten her tongue at school.

'Egg and milk and brandy,' said Amanda. 'Mummy's concoction. Raw egg, ugh!'

After that they were all quiet, faces downcast, afraid perhaps of what might happen to her. That was the loyalty of the blood. The warm drink flowed into her veins. They condemned her, but they had to love her. She would change into slacks and begin to feel better.

Her mother's love and anxiety took away all the anger at the *dépôt*.

'Sit there quietly. Amanda will go for those pills. You must rest or you'll be ill.'

The fourth day, the call gave her a shock. Stevie was in London, but the line was bad. Stevie's voice sounded far away, but where she had been ill with exhaustion she was now in a frenzy to be gone. She had been depressed, now she was elated. She put down the receiver and stood still, trying not to shout for joy, not to run. Up to now nothing had been said – now it had to be.

She threw open the sitting-room door to a dance band, violins, trills on the piano and the throbbing of drums, and raised her voice.

'I'm going to London to meet Stevie.'

Silent, unable to raise her eyes, she stood still. She and Stevie would be together. Destiny had opened the way.

'I shall be back soon – I promise.'

She had married Tom because she had not understood. She had to leave her mother because her mother did not understand. This agony need not have happened. One day in years to come it wouldn't matter, Stevie would save her.

Trembling she stuffed her bag with things for the night. Later on she would come for the rest. Ready to go, she felt sick.

'I shall see you soon.'

She was not doing this of her own free will. Stevie might leave her, her mother never.

'Take care, God bless.'

The taste of her mother's tears was on her lips.

She held the bony little body close for one moment, then ran for the bus, and the tube for London.

Fires burned on the rooftops, pieces of flak spun on the pavement round her feet, ricocheted and fell like red-hot cinders. She ran convinced she was invincible in a world of fire and chaos, because fate was with her. She ran until the flak ceased. Bells rang, an ambulance skidded round and faced the wrong way, its wheels embedded in a foot of broken glass. People were singing in the dark, defiant, keeping their end up. Her footsteps slowed down.

She could hear Stevie speaking about Lawrence and the depths below depths where love does not belong. Stevie was saying youth must leave the golden maze of immaturity, the coin must be paid, the coin they had minted, their love, their happiness No Stevie could not do that to her.

A resounding thud shook the air, then another. The world splintered into showers of broken glass. She walked across the road into the dim entrance of the hostel, pushing through doors covered with blankets. Inside lights burned. The hall was full of people filing into a narrow doorway.

'Catherine Stevenson?'

The girl at the desk looked as if she were about to run away.

'Number fourteen. The main light's going off. You can come into the basement if you like.'

Corinna shook her head.

Plunged into darkness, the hall revealed a tiny red glowing light, the wide staircase rose in the shadows. The house vibrated and the air tasted of smoke. She ran two-at-a-time up the stairs, her heart racing. Up here, another red lamp glowed. She walked hesitantly along the passage, peering at the numbers on the doors. It was strangely quiet. She stopped in the centre of the line, finding the door at last, conscious of violent apprehension, and threw it open.

The room was empty. The curtains were open. In the shadows the furniture stood out stark and bald. Shining white in a shaft of light, an envelope lay on the table.

She was standing in a world of fire, though cold night air struck her face and overhead a brilliant starlit sky encircling her head.

'Stevie!'

She wanted to die! She couldn't breathe! Her heart opened to let out a great sob. She would go mad – there was a wall in her head. All the people in the square had gone. Through the air a dark swish of metal came close, closer, loud, louder. She flung herself down, feeling the earth vibrate under her, tasting it in her mouth.

She groped along the river wall to sit on the steps, and quickly stood up again to shake off the chill of the water. A massive black stone edifice loomed in the dark and the portals of a square door blacker than black with a circle of iron for a handle. The door groaned a quiet groan, candles flickered in the dark, cold air swept over her. Inside she stood still, terrified, but held by the sound of the heavy intonations of voices in a great vault. The white gown of a priest showed as he passed the candles, chanting prayers.

She felt with her fingers along the edge of a pew and cautiously sat in the dark, unseen, until the thought hit her that someone might speak to her. She stood up, gripping the rail, looking up at the roof beams becoming visible in the gloom, and clearly it came to her that she could speak to any priest who would listen about Tom, but not about Stevie.

'It is a sin,' God would say, 'to be like that, a sin to love as you loved.'

Turning her back on God's candles, treading as quietly as a monk, she crept out of the great door, shrinking at the thought of explaining her love to a priest. She could tell it easier to Spinoza's IT or the Buddha's OM, impersonal gods too remote to condemn. But tell it to a priest and she would be cast out.

She walked on through the night, watching the dawn at last. Gangs of men were sweeping up the debris of the raids. Day and night had rolled into one. Sleepless, she accepted with numbed gratitude the cup of tea at the tea van under the bridge.

'Better be getting home, Miss,' said the bony weather-beaten tea van owner. 'They'll be coming back.'

'I want Cricklewood,' she heard her own voice articulate. 'Could you tell me the way?'

Without thought the words came out. She would go to Ashton, she would be sure to have extended leave, she would find her somewhere to sleep in that big old house.

'Straight on, through the park and straight up the

Edgware Road. You'll never walk it.'

She set off, the cold air keeping her moving. Sirens sounded, died away. But something was going wrong with her legs, her hips cutting into the flesh.

'Cricklewood?' she asked a milkman.

He dropped his horse's rein and yanked down a crate to land it with a clang on the early morning pavement.

'Straight on.'

The boom of his voice stunned her senses. She could no longer feel her legs, but they had to walk on. At last, at last there was the road nameplate, and the house with a dim light in the roof.

Now she knew she must not stop to think. The important thing was not to think. She pressed the bell and leaned on the door jamb, listening. She heard Lisa's voice.

'I thought you would come – eventually.'

Corinna stepped into the darkness.

'Lisa—'

'Up here,' said Lisa, leading her up the long staircase in pitch dark and opening the door at the top.

She stood inside the room, noticing only that it was long with low lights on small tables, conscious of the smell of paint in the air and Lisa's perfume as she walked away to turn off the music playing, and came back to her.

'You need a rest. Look at you! Shoes undone – what a mess you're in. How did you know I was here? I might have returned to camp.'

'Lisa,' she began.

But she was too heavy with fatigue to talk.

'Thank you,' she said over and over, sipping hot milk laced with brandy while sitting at a low table, a plate of fruitcake in front of her. 'I've been walking for days, half-slept in my clothes by the river. I can't sleep – I can't tell you – all night walking.'

Uncontrollable sobs were rising in her voice. It all

needed to be explained, but she was too tired.

She forced her voice enough to say, 'I'm going to get a job – drive an ambulance, something like that.'

'I'll run you a bath,' Lisa said, pulling blankets and sheets into order and preparing a sofa for a bed. 'You can sleep here.'

She stumbled on.

'I must explain – Sophie's here. Mother's been taking care of her, but she's ill.'

'Sophie?'

'Here, come with me.'

Lisa was leading her down the long room, drawing aside a curtain in front of a niche in the wall. And there she was – a sleeping child.

'Nothing disturbs her,' said Lisa softly. 'He's a pest, her father. I joined the army to avoid him.'

She bent over the child possessively.

'Now he's found someone else, fortunately.'

The child had slept on. Silence hung in the sky, now from far off, the siren rose and fell. She sat up, a pale-faced pixie child, her great luminous eyes looking straight at her. Her mother touched her and she lay down again, asleep.

'Why didn't you say?'

Not that it mattered, but it presented an entirely different Lisa from the one she had thought existed.

'Lisa?' she asked, her voice like a stranger's. 'Did you know Stevie wanted a child? That was why—'

It came to her that Stevie was searching for a child like the one she saw before her. She had so much to tell Lisa, if she would listen.

Lisa looked at her with the wondering look of a girl, mature yet innocent, and led her back through the room to the sofa.

'Your bath's ready,' she said. 'I'll make some coffee.'

Corinna could smell the coffee while she bathed. Lisa

was sitting deep in an armchair by the sofa sipping it when she came back into the room. Lisa being there, calmly waiting, brought all the agony of Stevie alive again. Corinna stood slumped against the chair unable to move, in unutterable misery. Lisa's hand came up to touch her.

'Lisa?'

Her throat tightened in pain.

'It's all right about Sophie,' Lisa said. 'You can stay – if you wish. I'd like that.'

It was said in the light way she had with words, and there was an indefinable expression in her eyes.

Her head was full of Stevie. She wanted only to talk about Stevie. But she was too tired, except that she could see Lisa's presence made her feel at home in an odd way, free to be herself, and she was amazed to find herself there, in an attic, the war outside, with Lisa. The difference it made, Lisa's being there, was more than she could grasp. Later she would find a job and make a new start. This awful sickness in her would go.

'Lisa?' she began again, but she was already falling down the dark slopes of sleep, conscious only that Lisa was pulling the blankets over her as she went.

Chapter Thirteen

Five Years Later

The figure of a young man, slight and lithe, slid out of the moonlight into the black of the window. There was a rustle and a gasp and she was in her arms, the sound of kissing in a long sigh.

'It's you.'

There was the sound of a kiss, a humming sound, and a sinking sound.

'Who should it be?'

'I thought it was a young man breaking in…'

'I was – I am.'

They made love on the old wood floor, hands under serge and satin in the dark of touch with the sweet milk of love instead of semen. Here in the dark shadows of the cases, the rucksacks stood like furniture. Lying flat, their hands touched across the floor.

'I'm starving,' she said dramatically.

'Here.'

Stevie scrambled across the floor and dragged back a rucksack, a dark figure moving in silence, stopping to poise over the open bag. She took out a long white loaf against the moonlit window and a packet of food, laying them both on the tea towel on the floor.

'I'm getting used to the dark – look, cheese,' said Stevie.

They stuffed buttered chunks of bread and cheddar into their mouths, laughing and listening to the munching in the silence.

'I had to walk up. Bessie ran out of petrol. Let's make tea

cherub, there's an old gas cooker in the kitchen at the end of the passage.'

Corinna sprang to life and opened the door, peering into the black hole, then stepped back to look at Stevie sitting up in the midst of the chaos of the food, a moonlit picnic.

Stevie smiled up at her with that cockeyed smile, saying, 'Let's just stay here – I'm half asleep.'

She lay down again, nudging the rucksack under her head, closed her eyes and opened them again. Corinna found that she was wide awake.

'D'you realise all the money's gone getting the motorbikes repaired.'

''spect this lot'll be a load of trouble,' Stevie murmured. 'Or a gold mine. Whatever we make it.'

And she fell asleep.

It was the money from her mother that would save them until the house money was settled. A wrench it had been to leave the editor, for all his primitive views on women, and Godfrey and Charles with their printing presses and paraphernalia, needed, they said, to produce the journal et al, (and all that) and their wicked wit. And Stevie had just had to leave that wretched man on his little throne with twenty typists under him and not exactly falling over himself to leave his wife.

Like a child, Stevie slept, mumbling and dreaming on, making Corinna's heart drag in fear or leap in excitement, the pictures vivid in her eyes. The men at the tea van counter had pitched down their scraps of soldiers' pay to fulfil Stevie's dream of independence.

'Sugar?'

'What do you think! Not seen any for years.'

'A shovelful?'

Fleshy young mouths sank their teeth into the shining skin of buns and doughnuts. These were the leftovers from battle. She and Stevie had packed all that money into the

177

Post Office account – out of sight out of mind, Stevie had said, determined not to touch it, not even if they starved, the ghosts of her rich ancestors egging her on.

Softly fell the moonlight on Stevie's face, taking away her animation leaving her defenceless in her care.

'David.'

The name was like a stone in her head.

'David?'

'Yes, David.'

Stevie sat up straight, her face paler than pale in the dim light.

'How could he be here of all places, I dunno?'

'David here?'

'Saw him in the town.'

David! A strange ache throbbed deep in her, icy yet burning, from out of the past. She pressed up against Stevie, pulling her close.

'Don't let's talk about him.'

'Silly,' said Stevie snuggling down. 'We're here just for each other. It's up to us to keep it that way. We shall make a castle out of this old house, you'll see.'

She flicked her lighter and the shadows changed and settled back.

'Nearly midnight – time for sleep to unravel all that care.'

Corinna held Stevie tight and fixed her eyes on the moon edging into the windowpane. Silently, silently as the moon:

> Oh, love let us be true to one another
> Let us live, my Lesbian, and love.
> And let us count not worth a farthing
> The grumbles of glum old men.

And she drifted into sleep.

It must have been the smell of mould and wood damp from rain in the open window. It brought back the flat, the cellar under the road and the stinking mattress. Stevie's hand gripped in hers, she led them out crawling, laughing, feeling along the slimy walls, not buried in the tarmac or drowned in the sewer.

And not a street away, the little shops outside Holborn station were gone. Not one was left. Nothing.

'Just because you wanted to live in Bloomsbury to be near Virginia Woolf we don't have to be killed. She won't be there, I can tell you that.' Stevie laying down laws.

After the raid, he came down to check on the damage. He stood in the door frame, long pale fingers on the door jamb. He had a touch of the theatre, said Stevie, a gentleman, dashing in a wicked sort of way. Like a stick of rock his penis against her as he signed the rent book, determined Stevie said, to take her out to dinner, and all that.

'He made a pass at you and you didn't know it.'

A bitter note somewhere.

'You'll meet a man one day – and you'll fall in love.'

How could Stevie! Outrage boiled in her. Why did Stevie never know it was there, in her blood, not merely in her mind – never could she love a man.

In the big sagging bed she buried her face in Stevie's hair, trembling in anger. Her father had kissed Stevie in the doorway, there in the sun with a box of kitchen utensils in his arms amid all the moving paraphernalia.

'He kissed you!'

'It was nothing. Don't make a fuss. He was only tormenting you.'

She stretched out on the hard wood floor of another old house, far older than in Bloomsbury. She escaped the air raids, the stolen identity cards and ration books, the scribbled lies in her army book No. 64 and Stevie deserting her job in the FO. The things they had done since then – the tea van, renovating old houses, buying and selling shops. Five wonderful years making money, losing it, working for a journal, a lifelong dream. Then back to this – capitalism.

Between half-raised lids, she caught the sunlight trying to pierce the filthy glass. Stevie sat like a Buddha looking down at her.

'I heard little feet in the night in the walls,' Corinna said, stretching.

'Mice,' said Stevie. 'Dad used to catch them sitting on the floor in the dark. You look as if you've seen a ghost – there's sure to be one. Perhaps Uncle Jack peering at us to see we don't make a mess of it all.'

Down the black hole they went to the kitchen. Stevie stumbled, flung open the door as a shadow leapt out of the broken windowpane.

'A cat! Quick, feed him! We need him.'

In daylight, the rooms became long and bare, the ceilings high, and cracks appeared in the ornate plaster. In their sleeping room, there was a chandelier fitted with dead lamps. Dust and soot and mildew made the windows opaque, holes marred the wall plaster, screwed up newspaper filled the fireplace of marble slabs, and there was a burnt-out log in the grate.

'Must've been rich, your uncle.'

'Made it running slaves through the American blockade,' said Stevie dreamily. 'Tomorrow.'

She woke up properly and began to talk.

'I have to see the solicitor at eleven – must find some ideas by then.'

She wandered out on the terrace.

Snatching the leftovers of rolls and cheese and sipping hot tea, she followed Stevie out across the broken terrace slabs, to stand by the sundial plinth and overlook the garden.

'There's a pergola down there – look! Reminds me of home.'

And of her dear mother in her last days.

'Needs weeding though. Must be full of rosebuds.'

'What about a hotel – but who'd come out here?'

'Or flats, how's that? One-roomed self-contained flats for businesswomen. We haven't been upstairs yet—'

Passing through the kitchen, Stevie stopped and brushed a woollen-gloved hand over the windowpane.

'There, now you can see nearly as clear as it was before. Come on, through the portcullis and down to the cellar. You go first because you're bigger.'

The cellar was a duplicate of the ground floor over their heads, except that it smelt stale and dusty and the ceilings were only a few feet above them. They took a quick glance round. Little doors opened into minute rooms lined with switches for electrics, the gas pipes were falling off the walls. In the dim light of day they shuffled back up the stone steps, out of Stevie's portcullis, smacking down their trousers.

It took an hour to explore the rooms and make brief mental notes on decorations, repairs. They counted the black iron fireplaces – all twelve of them.

'Work for a thousand years,' said Stevie.

'No – I can tell. Nothing really bad, only superficial. Needs a builder and an electrician, and a plumber to put a basin in every room. And someone telling them what to do.'

'What we must have is a telephone – *immediatement*!'

From the attic window there appeared to be a dip at the bottom of the garden.

'It's a lane,' said Stevie. 'It's on the deeds. There's a gate there, and shops not far down, a pub too.'

'Lunch perhaps?'

'Let's leave all this and get some food. It's too expensive to eat out.'

By the time they had reached the bottom of the garden, the sun had turned it into a nest of warmth and humming bees, intoxicating after the chill of the house.

A greenhouse had sunk into long seeding grasses. A cautious push and the door to the stable creaked open to a curtain of cobwebs. They both ducked under the lintel, treading on a thick dirty straw carpet, and stood looking up at gaps in the roof tiles, letting in sharp slices of sun.

'A flat and a garage,' said Stevie, officiously. 'And a ladder up into the loft – what jolly larks have gone on up there I wonder.'

'There's a stream down here somewhere – listen.'

Deep under boulders of moss, water trickled right down from the mill, making pools between the mossy banks and a dozen small waterfalls.

'Just like Switzerland. Let's have a sluice in it,' Corinna said, stepping on a flat stone in the middle of the stream.

She stood watching Stevie splash icy water into her face, lifting it to the sun and laughing at the water running down into her collar.

'This garden's big enough. Perhaps we could let it to the local football club!'

'Well, where there's muck there's money – dear old Samuel Smiles,' said Stevie. 'But mud is not muck, of course, it's the antithesis of the stars!'

'You staying in the big house?' the shop owner asked, packing into a paper carrier bag sausages, eggs and bacon and a long loaf big enough to feed a family of six.

'My uncle left it to me,' said Stevie impishly, stalking out of the door, watching his face drop.

Girls, it said, do not inherit manor houses from their uncles, not in his world.

'Wait until we meet the vicar,' said Stevie. 'He's going to call one morning.'

Stevie was laughing, infectious laughter such as they had

not had since the group of little children playing outside the house had asked Corinna if she were a lady or a man.

'A bit of each,' she said, taking a bag of cough sweets and a bar of chocolate out of her pocket and handing them over.

Lisa, at her loveliest in cream and white, came with Dan, back in England after five years in Cairo.

'In Cairo?'

'Entrepreneur, arranging the money. Selling electricity, coal, things like that,' Dan said, wandering off to inspect the garden and saunter back.

Still married, incongruous as that seemed, Lisa sat on a box in front of the lines of books standing up in orange boxes along the wall.

'How many?' asked Lisa.

'How many? Two thousand or so.'

It sounded impressive, but Lisa said nothing.

'How did you and Dan know where we were?'

'Stevie sent us a card every time you moved to keep in touch.'

'Must keep in touch with old friends,' Stevie said, disposing of a pile of wartime copies of *Woman* and *Woman's Weekly* by dropping them into an old tea chest.

'All these magazines'll have to go. The heroes and heroines have changed out of all recognition, in spite of the indisputable fact that it's the women who still make the curtains as always and make the beds.'

Lisa stood up and walked the length of the room to look over the front garden, standing as if in a dream.

> She walks among the loveliness she made,
> Between the apple blossom and the water.

'We're selling the old house,' she said, 'and mother's going into a nursing home. The flat in Baker Street will do nicely. Lovely views over Regent's Park through a minute crack between the houses. And Sophie's in a small weekly private school, being taught by nuns.'

She laughed readily as ever she always did, witty and light in heart. She held the curtain off the floor while Stevie trawled it through the sewing machine. How she could look so cool and virginal made the room spin.

'Dan's on to a new waterproofer. He'll waterproof the cellar if you like. It's sure to need it, all old houses do.'

'Cost much, Dan?' asked Stevie promptly.

Strike while the iron is hot was Stevie's motto.

'For friends – umph.'

Chuckling, Stevie led them in a line up the carved staircase, up one floor then two, the final flight narrowing to ladder width and leading into a short passage and a square gap. There were two doors to the left, and one to the right opening with a thud into a complete room with a slanting roof and a skylight window.

'An atelier!' cried Lisa, standing on her toes, shoulder to shoulder with Stevie, to see the garden below.

'Now for the down under,' said Stevie proudly. 'All these can be rooms, about a dozen I should think.'

The cellar door had jammed. Dan slipped a penknife blade through the lock and hey presto, they all burst into the bowl of foul air.

'Through the portcullis,' said Stevie, choking her way down. 'Mind your heads. All heroes were little chaps – Napoleon, Nelson, and yours truly, et al. It's Corie who knocks herself about.'

Ignorant as Stevie was of the affair in the Cricklewood house with Lisa and the bombs dropping outside, her instinct of possessiveness brought her to Corinna's side.

'I can imagine it all,' Stevie said. 'Can you? This'll make a – something or other – any ideas? Corie says flats for businesswomen.'

'You'll do it if anyone can,' said Lisa, her eyes through

the dusty air falling on Corinna. 'I know someone quite desperate for a flat.'

Corinna's heart stood still. If Lisa betrayed her by look or touch – the air stifled her. Stevie was a foot away on one side, a foot on the other side was Lisa, a faint smell of perfume in the sensual dark.

'Do it for you any time,' said Dan.

He was a long dark form bending down to his rule stretched out across beams and shoals of dust.

'Start when you like, Dan. Someone'll have to clear it up first.'

'Splendid cellar. It'll take a few dozen bottles, unless you want to let it to a little man.'

Gradually the dust settled. Shelves of wood, brick and slabs of stone, ran round the walls of the inner room, stone-floored, beneath land level.

'All it really wants is a good coat of whitewash. My man'll do that for you,' Dan said.

He pushed ahead and another door burst open into the garden, where he stood slapping down his expensive suit shoulders to turn ups, a tall dark aquiline figure blinking in the sun.

Stevie had followed him, leaving Corinna with Lisa close in the dim light. Corinna hesitated and stepped away, her blood rising, willing Lisa to go.

As the door closed behind them, the cat sprang out of the narrowing gap, twining himself round their legs.

Lisa was transformed magically from a sophisticated lady about town to a simple-hearted girl – she knelt on the ground and spoke to him, lifted him and whispered into his ear. She ran her finger tenderly down his back, did remarkable things to make him slide over and tuck under her hands through her diamond-ringed fingers. Then suddenly, self-consciously, she released him, a captive still, twirling round her legs.

'Dan loves Siamese – Sophie too. Ours growls like a dog, sits on my shoulder by the hour.'

'Biffa's a true bred moggy,' Stevie said. 'He's the mouser here. He doesn't sit on shoulders, he sits at the fender ends and waits for the mice to come. He's beautiful, too, you must admit.'

It was a long speech. Her eyes were dark in a subtle tease, with a tinge of envy perhaps at Lisa's easy ways.

'We have to go,' Lisa said, lifting the cat again and kissing him between the eyes. 'Cats are like people, they come and they go.'

Lisa, overshadowing Dan with her loveliness, picked up her cream handbag and the long-handled umbrella.

À tout à l'heure.

She held out a hand to Stevie who gave her a soft maternal hug.

The door closed. Only a faint touch of perfume remained in the hall, and the coil of Dan's cigar.

'What a girl!' said Stevie. 'So pretty, she could choose anyone she wanted – and she chose Dan – ain't life weird!' There were secret dreams, perhaps, in Stevie's heart.

'But Dan's only eccentric, after all.'

The words rang feverishly in Corinna's head, in her head only. Six years ago it must have been. Nothing could harm Stevie and her now. The sensitive innocence of Stevie, her sincerity, the tender circle of their love protecting them.

'Into the breech, dear friend!'

Stevie sipped coffee at the frontline kitchen table.

'First of all, you have to get a book.'

Coffee it was because Stevie did not believe in breakfast, except for others.

'Eat up that egg and toast and you'll catch the little bookshop on the common. They'll have the very thing.'

Your House in Order. A slender red pocket book, two

shillings. It was a mine of information, from tools for making holes in walls, to Keenes cement for filling them up. The difficulty lay not in the filling, but the filler. How to keep it in the hole.

'We are in a new revolution, a wild-headed fellow at the Fabian meeting said – plastic. It will turn our lives upside down. A thousand times more useful than Bakelite.'

Stevie gave the pages a cursory glance.

'Nothing to it. Just elbow grease.'

But Stevie did not have Germanic ancestors insisting on the polishing of bare boards and the abolition of linoleum. The gas meter under the stairs reigned in a sea of tools and pots and paints, marking the exact amount of elbow grease required.

'Stevie, I seem to remember a pledge long ago to find out where we were going and then to get motorcycles and travel the world before we started.'

Said Stevie, 'We just need a holiday. I fancy the Lake District with Wordsworth and all that, Coleridge, *Kubla Khan* et al – which never did get finished.'

'I give in. You're boss. We could do the kitchen first.'

Now that she studied them, the kitchen walls were more like a map of the trenches at Army HQ, picked out in blue and red. She picked up a piece of cardboard and made a list of what to do with one hand holding *Your House in Order* open with the other.

'Tea first, Stevie, please!'

She stood out on the terrace to drink the tea, her eyes closed, the last rays of the sun on her face. It would be better not to see Lisa again, leaving her head full of visions of her face and the sound of her rich soft voice. The sword of Damocles hung over every word.

Tenderly she loved Stevie, knowing she had broken their vow of faith, but Stevie had made it possible by leaving her that night. That could never happen again.

Cricket stumps were on the common. The house shone. In every room the walls were distempered in the nearest thing to pink. The tenants of the first floor and the second were paying up like troopers. These good things were balanced by the top floor splitting up. And there were other danger signs on the horizon to Stevie's experienced eyes.

The beautiful blond young man who stole up the stairs every night left Lisa's friend, Jane, screaming in the bathroom night after night, the other tenants said. It was such a respectable house, they said. The screams went on up to the day the tenant deserted, the mattress bloodied and the basin cracked.

'That's normality for you,' said Stevie counting the cost, reckoning that the mortgage would need boosting from somewhere. 'In future, we'll find our own girls, dull and respectable and as silent as the moon.'

Before the holes in the wall had been filled, Lisa called again, this time alone. She had two friends who wanted a flat – two girls, both absolutely all right.

The kitchen was quickly smoothed over and white-washed. Stevie got busy with a notebook and pencil – two rooms at twenty-five shillings each – top floor, small, but with wonderful views.

The telegram came just as the last flat was let. Stevie's mother was ill and wanted to see her. Stevie had to go.

'It must be urgent. Mother never wires to see me. How will you manage!' she was packing feverishly.

'There's plenty of food. Remember to lock up.'

Stevie stopped short.

'Lisa, I'll call Lisa. She'll come to help.'

Corinna watched it happen, watched Dan bring Lisa to the door, take Stevie to the station. Helplessly she watched, feeling faint, trying to say no.

Chapter Fourteen

Corinna kept her eyes on the Mercedes vanishing down the lane. Behind her she could feel Lisa long before those cool sensuous hands touched her.

She closed the great door and turned as Lisa fell into her arms lips open to hers, teasing and closing tight round her own. She was lost, conscious that Lisa was lying on the sofa, her hands pulling her down to kiss her again. Then Lisa took her hands – time stopped.

'Beautiful hands, like an artist.' Low and deep was Lisa's voice, with the sound in it of the song of the sea. Her maturity was terrifying and exalting, the experience that had taught Lisa the ways of love held her spellbound.

Lisa took her fingers, spaced them out and counted them, bent them as if in torture, feigning to hurt, letting them go, taking them firmly down to enfold her waist, teasing her with the suppleness of her body.

Everything Lisa did roused the male in her to new levels awakening senses never touched before, luring her with kisses of such depth that she was lost utterly, crazed with new limitless desire. She kissed Lisa's lips, her ears, her eyes, with the pent up passion of years.

She wandered with Lisa through the rooms, locking up, giving Biffa his milk. As if drawn by another force in Lisa's slender fingers, she followed her to the bedroom.

Without seeing she knew Lisa was on the bed, clutching a large white pillow, looking as startled as a wild young animal caught. Swiftly she drew on her pyjamas, switched off the bed lamp and shot into bed. Finding Lisa naked, she began tearing off her pyjamas again.

'Can't Lisa – not in this bed—' she gasped, hardly releasing Lisa's lips.

She rolled the bedclothes on to the floor, and in a pile of sheets and pillows she felt Lisa's body against hers, and ran her hand down it trembling at the touch. Incredulous it was that the hair in her eyes was Lisa's, that teasing mouth in hers. A terrifying pleasure swept through her as she kissed Lisa's neck, her shoulders and her body clung to her. Lisa tightened her arms round her as if to bind them together for all time to come. Intimately she broke into this beautiful creature's deepest being, touching the anemone, the mouth of her sex as warm and moist as of a young girl, teased it into undulations, until there was a moan of pleasure and the seizure of the long spasm that engulfed them both.

'Lisa – at last.' One kissed the other until all passion slept. And woke again.

Again and again over the hours of the night the spirit awoke – the movement of hands, of fingers, of the hand in the place of the penis – and sweeter by far with its faint acrid smell. Hands slid over Lisa's body – over her thighs, her breasts – fingers trailed through her hair. The feeling of Lisa's naked body against hers from the shoulders to their feet.

'I love you,' Lisa said breathing deeply, kissing Corinna's mouth with long vibrant kisses. 'I've been waiting so long.'

'And I – I love you,' Corinna whispered, having pushed aside her vow of loyalty to Stevie long ago.

Lisa's arms were tight round her until, moving free, she slid her hands over Lisa's shoulders, down to her thighs, and up and round her breasts. The loveliness of Lisa's fairness, her blonde hair, her fine nostrils and lips, all Corinna could see in the dark as if it were afternoon. A tremendous calmness fell over Corinna and passed into Lisa. Peace enveloped their bodies, kept them snug and warm, at one. She lay in the dark holding Lisa close –

dreaming daydreams. Stevie – oh, my God! No, leave Stevie out of this. This is her philosophy – live to the full. No fault in Stevie. Just that she and Lisa…

Words. How could it be described? The wild flame between them. She had waited all this time – five years. A touch, a glance from Lisa and she trembled, was set on fire, lost all her sense of direction lost her moral certainties, lost her sanity.

The male in her was enthralled. It was proof of the male in her blood, of her masculine blood count, her physical quirks and her father's – long feet, bony hands, and a tendency to cough when she laughed. It all fitted. It was the boy inside, the boy her mother wanted to replace her father if he didn't come back from the war.

Again and again through the night, that night and the next, Lisa was there. A thousand words couldn't tell anything so intimate. It dodged words. Cunt. Fuck. DHL had no idea how to do it. In his poetry, perhaps – if she came to me now. She buried her face in Lisa's hair above her ear. She woke her, loved her sleepy organ, touching, waking, sharper and sharper until with a groan Lisa awoke.

'There? And there? Shall I? Or there.'

Lisa sighed with joy in dark recesses deep in privileged folds of flesh, in the grip of feminine muscle to defend or to open to the crowning.

No words – not from Rilke's *Mein Herz ich will dich tragen* to Lawrence's 'if she would come to me now – while the hay is ripe.' No words could describe that but love.

Now their moment of glory came – with Lisa, with her. Now Lisa knew her lover's ways. The climax leapt between them so that one gave and one received and neither could say which.

'I love you.'

'I love you.'

Love – the only four-lettered word that describes the

loveliness, the inimitable, the arrow striking home.

And between her and Stevie?

Corinna stretched out on the crumpled bed, kissing Lisa's hair where it fell across her mouth. But her heart raced with guilt.

'Try to sleep,' Lisa murmured. 'We shall both feel wretched in the morning.'

At daybreak Corinna awoke with Stevie's face full of pain in her eyes. At her side lay the warm, glowing body of Lisa.

The telephone rang while they ate at the kitchen table. Corinna sprang to her feet.

'Where is it?'

Was that her voice shouting at Lisa!

'Where is the telephone?'

It was not under all the chaos of Lisa's possessions scattered far and wide. A greater chaos was in her own mind. At last, Lisa found it under her coat, picked up the coat, dangling it from her shoulder by the hook and walked swiftly into the garden leaving Corinna holding the receiver.

It was Stevie's voice full of tears. She would have to stay a week or two and leave Corie in charge. Could she manage? Was Lisa a help? It was like a game.

'Yes, everything's all right here. Can't hear very well. You must stay if you have to.'

Stevie had gone. Corinna stood watching Lisa through the kitchen window walking across the terrace, stepping over the uneven paving stones and walking under the trees with the breeze in her hair and early sunlight bathing her in golden light.

A game for two it must be because Stevie need never know. The fear of detection made her feel sick with panic. The thought of hurting Stevie turned the shadow of Lisa, now at the door, into a threat.

And Lisa saw it – she came up to her, took the receiver out of her hand and desperately raised her face as she replaced it.

'Kiss me Corie, kiss me!' she said, her voice demanding.

Knowing Lisa was like knowing all women, their passion and surrender, their gaiety and frivolity. She teased the cat and flirted with any male alive, including the plumber and the electrician on constant call from the ancient services in The Lodge. Her wit and laughter were immediate and subtle, though perhaps not of the level of Stevie's but still not far short.

It was the gaiety when there should be serious thought, Lisa's way of facing life's red lights, that made her mad. Lisa would spring up off the sofa, where she had been lying listening to her latest obsession, Mozart, and lead Biffa out on to the terrace, making him arch his back against her legs until he was drunk with ecstasy.

'Dodging the hurdle,' Stevie called it. 'That much she has in common with Dan.'

When Corinna felt the need for sympathy, for confidences, Lisa was gay and teasing, leaving her irritable, angry even, so that she shouted and Lisa burst into tears, running out into the garden shoeless in her petticoat.

She watched Lisa, fuming because this was the technique of the chase and Lisa knew her well enough to call up the cruelty and dominance of the male in her. And she felt exposed and despised before being triumphant.

She caught up with Lisa under the oak tree down by the gate to the lane, took her roughly by the shoulders and shook her.

'Don't be so hysterical!'

'Take your hands off me!'

'Lisa, please, don't cry. What are you crying for! I need you. I want to talk to you!'

'I don't want you while you love her! Why did you make

love to me?'

'I don't know. I just had to.'

She gently pulled Lisa's coat straight across her shoulders.

'You'll get cold, you're only half dressed.'

'Why did you?'

'You made me.'

'As if anyone could make you do anything.'

The crying reached new levels, sobs and tears shaking the slender figure from head to foot. Corinna knew she had to be calm and strong. She pulled the coat close again and Lisa stood still. Slowly the crying stopped and the sobs slowed down.

She did recognise it was insecurity that made Lisa behave like this. She found it terrifying, but that she would not say. If she condescended, it would all start again. And yet fear did seize her that Lisa would leave her, that she was guilty of failure.

'Let's go in. There's no one about. I think they're all out upstairs, all gone to work probably.'

She took Lisa by the hand and led her back to the house. It now gave her a wicked sense of strength over Lisa, a moment of mastery to pit against all the other moments when she was Lisa's slave.

In the house again, they sat by the open coke stove in the kitchen, sipping coffee, Biffa watching her like a dog, catching her eye to see if she was finding something for him.

'He shakes when we quarrel,' she said. 'For his sake if no other reason we shouldn't.'

Lisa rubbed his head and Biffa arched against her legs. She was laughing again.

That evening Stevie telephoned. Her mother had died. She would have to stay another week.

Full of tears and trouble, Stevie's voice was weak and far

away, but Corinna managed to say the right things, telling her she was missing her, and that everything was all right.

'Love you, little one,' she finished in a low tone, turning her back to Lisa and shutting her eyes in shame.

'And now,' commented Lisa, narrowing her beautiful eyes and looking straight at her from deep in the armchair, 'it's gloomy here. I think it would be in order to have a few friends in – don't you?' That settled she added, 'I'll see Sophie this week instead of next.'

Music travelled freely through the house and out across the garden. The lofty rooms echoed with voices and laughing. Cigarette smoke and strains of Frank Sinatra wafted from the conservatory where the gramophone stood in the centre of the tiled floor with tenuous wires leading back into the drawing room. Lisa's friends were in occupation,

'Look out for the lamps, Julien.' All eyes fell on the slender youth.

Julien shuffled the great wooden ladder across the carpet, trailing a bunch of balloons on string, his long white fingers deftly tying them to the chandelier frame.

Mesmerised, Corinna stood watching him attach the balloons to the centre so that they fell clear of the lighted lamps. A slight dark young man slid across the floor and held up his hand, ineffectually supporting the ladder under his friend.

'Cecil, look what you're doing with the ladder, my dear,' Julien called down.

'Sir, to you up there,' Cecil answered back.

She was fascinated by their gentle ways. They felt quite normal, they said, and Cecil had recently inherited a title and land to go with it.

'Divine here lives in a cottage in a corner of the land and runs a small chicken farm,' said Cecil, stepping back to bow to a young woman in breeches at his elbow. Sotto voce, he said in a clear aside, 'Smashing girl, Corie, don't you think? A name like that, too.'

Divine laughed and held out a well-worn land-loving palm to shake, watching with interest while Cecil detached himself from the ladder and squatted cross-legged to wait for his friend to descend.

Corinna found Lisa in the kitchen placing piles of sandwiches and dishes of little cakes, custard tarts and sausage rolls on to the old wooden trolley.

'Where did you get all that food? Certainly not down the lane.'

'Jemima brought it with her in the van. It's useful to have such friends. She and Andy have a string of snack bars round Soho Street. This is some of the remainders…'

Corinna wandered through the lively chaos of her home. In the bathroom she found a young man sitting on the floor reciting reams of poems – DHL was ringing out.

For he seemed to me again like a king,
like a king in exile.

'Trying to keep sane,' he whispered to Corinna as she peered in to listen.

'Someone's put a spare mattress on the bathroom floor,' Corinna said to Lisa. 'He's reciting *The Snake* – sitting there in the middle of the mattress like Ozymandias in the desert.'

'Sexual undertones,' said Lisa briefly.

'Well, don't fall over the mattress. He must've found it in the cellar. How many people are there?'

'Oh, I don't know – twenty perhaps.'

Lisa's mascara was already smudging. She took out a handkerchief and wiped it off, leaning over the trolley to kiss Corinna lightly on the cheek, then lightly on the lips as Corinna turned to her.

'Don't flirt. I shall be watching you!' Lisa whispered.

By midnight, the great drawing room was stuffy with smoke. She walked over to push up one of the big windows and a long white scarf flew in followed by a young man jumping in out of the night, brushing his jacket straight and pulling on his tie.

'Sorry, I'm Harry, one of Lisa's friends,' he said. 'You must be Corie, Lisa told me about you.'

He put out his hands and started to dance. Someone had cleared the centre of the floor. There were crowds of young faces looking up at her, sitting in tiers, cross-legged, or on chairs, or lying on the divan.

'Do you mind dancing with me?' Harry asked.

Slowly, cumbersomely, he led her, stopping every now and then at a fresh young man to bend possessively and smile over him, before passing on.

'A son of mine,' Harry said. 'My son, let me introduce Corinna, a friend of mine.' In one cross-legged lap he dropped his long silk scarf, drawing a long 'Ah-ha' from the audience.

Couples of young men and of men and girls mooched round the floor, engrossed in talking to each other or holding each other closer than the dance required. Lisa was in the arms of a handsome giant.

'Harry's not my real name,' Harry said intimately. 'Jemima gave me that name.'

He wandered off and came back to her without letting go completely.

'Limber up,' he said, 'let yourself go and you'd make a good dancer. You and I have more in common than you think.'

He smelt of a most delicate perfume. Now that he had discarded his scarf, she could see his shirt was pink and puffed up under an expensive jacket.

'I've never learnt to dance,' she said. 'I'd rather ride a

motorbike or a horse, but…' she hesitated, accepting a drink unexpectedly handed to her in a wide clear glass.

'Punch,' Lisa whispered before turning to Harry. 'And one for you. Vodka-based,' she added.

Harry sauntered off again to breathe over a young fair-mopped boy, speaking low and softly. He came back to Corinna with a shy grin and danced lost in thought, until he let her go and sat down next to the boy.

'Incognito,' said Lisa from behind the punch end of the table where a dozen hands washed glasses and cut cake.

The whole room seemed to be incognito. One fellow was writing constantly and excusing himself by repeating 'a letter to my mother'. He was incognito, too. A famous writer on the loose, said Lisa.

At the kitchen table, Jemima sat telling intensely personal experiences to an avid audience of young girls who seemed as fascinated by her giant whoops of earrings and diamond rings as by what she was telling them, although it released them, no doubt, from the days of innocence. They were tales of sexual antics with a number of nods and winks to fill in the innuendoes. Their eyes were alive with wonder.

'You've had too much to drink,' Corinna whispered to Lisa, who magically appeared sitting behind the door sad as a neglected nymph. 'Lonely?' she asked, kissing her forehead and thinking of the giant.

'Say,' called Jemima, 'it's your party. There's a young Arab out there, dancing with the boys.'

She waved her cigarette making a chimney full of ash.

'He's too beautiful for that lot. And rich too.'

The next time she saw Lisa, she was dancing with the dusky-looking sculptor from Cairo in his white jacket and pale suede shoes with thick silent soles.

She watched them from the alcove leading to the conservatory, spying through her fingers, elbows on knees and sipping coffee laced with schnapps to keep her awake. Jealousy smouldered in her stomach until she found the daring to tap the sculptor on the shoulder, looked up into his swarthy handsome face and led Lisa away out to the terrace. The music followed them.

'Teach me to dance.'

'Of course,' said Lisa, surrendering her waist to Corinna's arm. The garden swirled round them, bushes and trees leading through the dark grass to the old coach house and through whatever remained of the door.

Lisa pressed herself hard against her, her mouth full of kisses meeting kisses. She went down, falling, pulling Corinna to the hard unyielding floor.

Lisa was murmuring quite clearly, 'I love you so much, and I'm not drunk. In fact, I'm remarkably sober – and I still love you.'

It was impossible to reply, her mouth was lost in Lisa's.

A shaft of daylight had fallen over her. Lisa was asleep at her side. She stretched, aching throughout her body. Then she woke.

The house! The tenants! How could she be so reckless! Mad! Stevie must never know. What would she say! 'Call that a party!'

Heart banging, she leapt up from Lisa's side and ran to the house, her head clearing mercilessly – the tenants! Stevie's mother was dead! She might be mad about Lisa, but Stevie was life itself. Keeping the secret from Stevie would kill her.

The house was full of deeply sleeping bodies. Like war refugees they lay on floors, on the divan, two in the bathroom and some flat out every few feet of the passages.

The kitchen door was jammed. She heaved against it and someone groaned. She reached the sink to fill the kettle, getting out a mass of cups and mugs and busting open a new coffee tin while the water boiled.

'Keep calm,' said Lisa, staggering in behind her. 'The loo's free. I'll speak to Jemima, she'll get them going. Black coffee all round – not ours, for God's sake, just strong!'

Lisa must have known her friends. Corinna stood by the stove until the water boiled, calling Lisa back to make it.

'Lisa, you'll have to leave too.'

'All right, all right,' said Lisa, the smudged mascara making her look thoroughly ill with debauchery.

Corinna held on to the table and laughed. It was all so devastating. She knew immediately that Lisa would refuse to go. She steeled herself for battle. Fear made her strong and decisive.

'You've got to go Lisa. I can't cope!'

Everyone, at last, had gone and Lisa stood still, either unable or unwilling to face the train journey. It was difficult to say.

'Just go. Stevie'll be back and I've got to get the place straight!'

'I'll help you first.'

'No, I'll get Mrs Cartwright to come.'

Coffee, coffee, more coffee and two hours later, Lisa could see it had to happen, and she had to go by train since Dan was away on a job.

Corinna heard Lisa telephone for the taxi and collapsed with a migraine, waiting for her to go.

'I'll be all right when you've gone. It's only panic.'

Lisa, in a beige two-piece and tender as a vision, touched her brow, her lips, with cool fingertips and went without a backward glance.

She lay listening to the door close. The taxi pulled away. By evening, the migraine would begin to recede. A pit of despair opened before her, lying to Stevie and cut off from Lisa.

Chapter Fifteen

'Lisa was a great help, but she threw a party on Wednesday and the house is only just recovering. Mrs Cartwright helped.'

That was it. Corinna said it as she carried the case from the gate into the hall and along the passage to the bedroom.

'It was so bleak,' said Stevie, heavily. 'Mum requested no flowers. Why do people do that? Dad was distraught—'

Corinna pulled Stevie against her with a quick intense hug, and turned to heave the cases up on to the bed. The catches released and the clothes tipped out. The bed had a peculiar look as if a stranger had just lain on it, a stranger who shouted guilt.

'What's this about a party.'

'Some silly idea of Lisa's. Made a bit of a noise, but no complaints.' She added spontaneously, 'I've never known a party like that.'

She had thought Stevie was a woman of the world because of her affair with Maurice. Now she had met a true woman of the world who knew all the cunning ways of love, of tormenting with lips and teeth, by tracing her eyebrows, blowing kisses into her ears and teasing her until she seized the slight vital body and crushed it in her arms. In every corner of house and garden there was Lisa.

Days passed in deceptive quietude. The thunder on the main door came as a violent shock. Corinna jumped as if the army had come for her.

Dan stood glowering on the steps, hands in his jacket pockets, Lisa at his side holding her arms across her body, shaking her head and staring at the ground.

He had come to see Stevie. Would she, Corinna, please go and leave him to speak to Stevie. His extreme politeness was riveting.

She stood for a quarter of an hour with her back to Lisa in the vast room, her hands gripping the marble of the mantelshelf, until, scowling black anger, Dan came back with Stevie white to the lips.

Dan walked up to her as if he would strike her, speaking through closed lips.

'You have taken my wife. I should give you a good hiding. I would, but I've promised Stevie. Who do you think you are?'

Corinna didn't dislike Dan. She had seen him with Sophie on his knee telling tales from the Arabian nights and the Russian steppes, their dark eyes laughing in unison and that old storyteller twinkle in his eyes. She kept her eyes on his face, but out of the corner of her eye she was conscious of Lisa's eyes on her and her own terrible desire to take Lisa in her arms.

'Lisa has sworn she does not want to see you any more. I want you to swear you won't see her again.'

'If that would please you—'

'It would!'

He stood there huddled up in the centre of the room, his jacket as crumpled as his male pride to judge by the agony in his face.

She was trembling so much the words in her mouth were stuck. Dan swung round and seized Lisa's arm and pulled her after him.

Corinna and Stevie were alone, the great house as silent as if only they were there.

'Why did you?' Stevie asked. 'I had no idea. I would never have left her here if I had known. I thought she was only interested in men.'

By some means, Stevie was at her side, she had only to

open her arms. She wanted to fall on her knees to beg forgiveness, pleading with everything in her except words, until a few sounds came.

'I'm sorry. I don't know how to say it. I don't know how it happened. I love you Stevie.'

Stevie turned her back and walked ahead of her down the passage to the kitchen. There she turned to face her again.

'But it happened before, Dan says.'

Stevie was looking hard into her face.

'Only in the war – when you didn't come and Dan was away.'

'I've regretted that ever since.'

Stevie's voice rose.

'To think it was Lisa who brought me back to you.'

She lit a cigarette, eyes averted. 'I might've guessed – with Lisa's history of abortions and other women's husbands!'

The spitefulness hurt, coming as it did out of pain, but Stevie did not place sex high on the human scale of values. She believed in lifting life out of the mundane to greater heights. She could never be spiteful for long.

But for now the house was polluted, the bed, the very tea towels. Their puny wine stock was gone, the empty bottles disdainfully tossed out.

After a tempestuous cleaning-up, after Mr Cartwright had redecorated the drawing room and the terrace flower bowls were filled with young begonias, and the grass was cut, Stevie began to smoke less fiercely, sighing still but with a wan smile now and then.

'Let's forget it, cherub, put it behind us.'

Stevie's voice lightened.

'We could build a temple of love, of the spirit, out there in the garden.'

Stevie's self-sacrifice could be unbearable. She bent over

the pansy bed to regenerate by decapitation, it was almost a lesson in stoicism.

'You could go to Lisa for a weekend, just now and then.'

She paused, waiting for the reply.

'I should never want to do that,' Corinna said, because that was the reply Stevie wanted.

Stevie was a wonderful mate – she might not be able to hold a paintbrush, but she cleaned up, swept up, brought food and tea and spun ideas like gossamer threads, sorting out money in her head and building castles on the ground.

'It's high time we bought a car. That garage on the corner has a little two-seater you'd love, Corie, a silver gem.'

Corinna slipped into the deep leather seat, moved the long black gear stick and gripped the wheel.

'Do you realise I learned to drive about twenty years ago – one of the first tests. And this is my first car. Papa'll love it.'

'It's yours. A hundred and twenty pounds can't kill us, but I can't say where from.'

'Borrow it from Amanda. Gave the chap a cheque first then put in the cash. Amanda'll lend it to us.'

The world itself would have to be moved if need be. Her first car, a gift from heaven with headlights on the mudguards, removable side pieces and wing nuts on the hood and windscreen.

'Looks like a bullet or a bumblebee. I don't deserve it, Stevie.'

'Forget it, cherub. Tomorrow a run to the sea, and while we're there we'll get that pup you're always talking about.'

The kennels were part of a big house off the greensward along the seafront. It was a massive house if one counted all the outhouses and stables. The cellars were full of giant Boxers, Boxer families and puppies von Haus Germania.

The kennel man pulled the pups about, measured their

noses pointed out the 'stop', the teeth, and the most likely champion-to-be, a golden-brindled, black faced beast with white paws and feet.

Out on the front at a picnic tea by the roadside, the champion-to-be dived straight under the back wheels and refused to move. Ignominiously, he was yanked out striped in grease, and promptly returned, Stevie having been persuaded by her father that if the dog doesn't take to you, leave it.

But inside the gate his brother waited, eager to take his place, and scrambled up into Stevie's arms. Bill, the dog of a lifetime, noble in his beauty, in nature a defender unto death. All that for fifteen guineas.

Lisa came. Dan had been held up in Cairo. Strange it seemed to Corinna that Stevie had not taken her vow not to see Lisa seriously, sending cards at Christmas and mending bridges in Stevie fashion.

Lisa had come for one thing – to say that she was having an affair with a sculptor.

'You know, Anton. You met him at the party.'

That party, which Stevie knew so little about, tortured her still.

Corinna left Lisa to talk to Stevie and took Bill for a walk. When she returned, Stevie was alone, busy in her beloved borders.

'Don't fret, cherub, she's not worth it.'

Stevie removed the end of her cigarette and tossed her head as if Lisa were settled, finally.

'I've got something to talk to you about.'

Mr Black had been, yes, on his bicycle. Wanted to know if she could translate some Latin for him, from old documents that needed translating. He knew she could because she'd said something about Latin when they were going through the deeds of the house.

'So I said I'd do it, if I can. I'm probably a bit rusty, I'll get the old brain going again. If you can manage here.'

'Of course, you'll like it.'

The lodge had settled down. Twelve flatlets were let, with twelve garages; the office suite for professional use. The stable alone was left for conversion, and the garden plan pinned on the kitchen wall.

But the sickness for Lisa went on – the smell of her hair, the touch of her hands, of her lips. Corinna got lost, abandoned herself in the dream – to wake rigid with guilt.

The card came from St Tropez, wedged by Stevie's unseen hand up against the bowl of hyacinths on the kitchen windowsill. Sweat broke in Corinna's hands as she replaced it, and her chest tightened.

Lisa was still with Dan. No sculptor. Soon to be home again. The colours of the world changed.

It seemed to her as she walked Bill that her afternoons were elastic. If she walked him later, she could find time – three quarters of an hour there, one hour with Lisa, three quarters back.

The tenants were out all day Stevie was engrossed in parchments of long ago, Bill in the back the car slid out. She would walk him later, or there.

Bill had no preferences – mossy banks and lazy streams, the iron legs of the bench in the Queen Mary Rose Garden, the stone rose plinths, or the rose-climbing colonnades.

On the second visit, the miracle occurred. A new perfume was among the roses. Corinna shook her white linen slacks straight, opened and re-buttoned her blue velvet cord jacket, the pockets bulging with chocolate and an apple, and a ball for Bill. She stood and waited.

As in a dream, she came through the roses, a vision in white and gold, the white of a linen dress against the southern sun in her skin, self-conscious in her loveliness. Lisa stopped, her colour rising, her eyes seeking and finding her own.

'I knew one day I'd meet you here,' Lisa said.

Her eyes fell to Lisa's lips, the familiar curves, the sweet freshness. Drawing Lisa to the seat among the colonnades, she trailed her arm across her back, not touching, aching in restraint.

'Butterflies – did you notice? Absolutely everywhere,' Lisa said in that inimitable full voice.

Corinna kept her eyes on Lisa's lips, and said, 'I could tell you a story about the butterflies on the bridge at Leuk. I sat on the stone wall, this spring it was, snowing enormous white snowflakes, and mixed in with them were butterflies – flying flowers, the Chinese call them – flowers of love.'

Lisa touched her own lips with a finger and fleetingly brushed the finger over Corinna's, and stood up in front of her.

'Come back with me, Corie. There's no one there, only Bella.'

It was the beginning of a summer of seeing Lisa, of telling lies to Stevie, of deceits that made the skin taut and grey.

'You look tired, cherub,' Stevie said. 'Let me do it.'

Such care tore at her. Comparisons made Lisa look cheap, flirtatious and sex mad. The madness for sex overwhelmed her – in the car, in the boat on the Serpentine, in the long shallows under the willow trees. In Lisa's flat.

The flat in town turned out to be two flats over two garages, the rooms long and low, the garages for Dan's vehicles and workshop, not a stone's throw from Regent's Park. The whole flat would have fitted into the artist's retreat at the top of the old house in Cricklewood, where she and Lisa had lived that winter before Lisa met Stevie that fateful day in Victoria Street, and brought Corinna and Stevie together again.

The rarity of the atmosphere in the flat made the closeness of Lisa intoxicating. Long low ceilings, the living room with low windows over the old stables, beds for guests tucked into alcoves in the walls, two main bedrooms filling the back of the roof which sloped over the wardrobe and chest of drawers, and a massive dining table in the window space of the long room reaching over the staircase which led down to the cobbled yard.

It was like a ship, every corner compact and used. At one corner of the table, Lisa placed the wine and held out her glass. She lifted her face so close that the bottle slid to the floor. Lisa's mouth was lost in hers, the glass floated in mid-air.

'Let's eat later. Lunch is already prepared.'

Kissing Lisa always led to this – the lights down, the thumping in her head lying on Dan's pillow, listening for him to smash his way in, Stevie's white disbelieving face.

The short hour passed and all the pent-up passion was at last released, but at four thirty on the clock Stevie would be home. At three thirty she had to leave Lisa kneeling on the top stair as Corinna retreated down backwards, calling up, 'I'll cut Bill's walk – he won't mind.'

In a frenzy she drove home, chased by visions of sheer lust. Lust it must be, since she could cast Lisa aside having loved her violently and leave her tearful.

Forever Lisa would remind her of early love, of its shuddering intensity. What did it matter, so long as there is fire in you, in me?

Still absorbed in the longing to feel Lisa in her arms, she slipped the car into the garage, grabbed Bill's lead and let him go, Lisa's mouth never leaving hers. She climbed the steps to the back terrace and found Stevie was in, lights on, the doors open.

'Had a good walk?'

'Lovely.'

She saw Stevie, the way she held her hands, moved them.

'I'm dying for the cup that cheers,' said Stevie.

'I'll make you one.'

It was like living in a double shell. One on the other, the pieces fitted close and inseparable, but it was like living in hell, as Sartre might say. Lisa was nothing to her – Stevie was life itself, and yet, there had been tears in Lisa's eyes when she had left, their fingers meeting up the stairs, parting with agonising reluctance.

Lisa had a passion for Corie quite unlike any other affair she'd had, Dan had told Stevie. And Stevie had told her. Why did Stevie do that? In defiance of fate?

'I saw that solicitor I told you about, David,' Stevie said in a flat tone, laying an armful of folders on the dining table. 'Black's office is to do some work for him, legal work.'

She walked across the room to look out of the window.

'He's rather nice,' she said thoughtfully.

Shocked, Corinna stood still, trying to take it in.

'Don't say that Stevie. It frightens me.'

'You don't have to worry. I love you, cherub. There's nothing alive between David and me – not even quarrels. Remember the joke with God surprised at the kittens coming out of the ark. "Ah," said the male, "You thought we were quarrelling." I remember you and Lisa used to quarrel – over nothing perhaps – over the cat, which was why I was so surprised. Nothing like that between David and me, he's much too sane – and I love you too much.'

The afternoons went on. Stevie translated the Latin, Corinna, vaguely uneasy, extended Bill's walk two or three hours to see Lisa starting out immediately after Stevie left home.

Corinna found herself grumbling when the flat was full of visitors until Lisa cried. She felt ill with the longing to see Lisa alone, developed a headache, groaned to herself and behaved abominably, masculine and rough, in front of them all.

In panic, she suffered the time to pass. Lisa's friend, Rosie, said Dan told everyone about her; the place was full of laughing eyes falling on her. Lisa, cool and seemingly unafraid, introduced her, 'This is Mrs Bramwell.'

Women like Lisa were never at a loss when playing for time. Eventually the company had gone, Lisa was in her arms, and she was worn out with fear that Dan would burst in and almost in a frenzy to be gone herself. Lisa was no danger to Stevie. She would never leave Stevie for Lisa, that was the truth.

Three days later, Corinna was back. Lisa waiting behind the door at the sound of the car below, spontaneous and lovely, and Dan was far away. She wanting more of Lisa than she could have, going home to Stevie as she must.

'I shall have to stop coming here,' she said.

'Why do you sit there saying that?'

'Because I am infatuated, not in love with you, and I just can't leave you because if I do that fellow will come.'

The wail in her voice trailed in the air.

Lisa stamped her foot, the hot tears rising.

'You make me sound so cheap, Corie. Don't be so rotten!'

She pulled Corinna close.

'I don't mean to be rotten, but I can't leave Stevie.'

Corinna let Lisa draw her to the bed.

Lisa's eyes were a cool green as she lost herself in their depths. Her ears, strangely pretty, small, the lobes running into her neck without a break, sensitive. Her nose was small too curving under gently at the tip. Her mouth, lips curved, was ready to laugh, her hair long and blonde tied into a ponytail. When Corinna kissed her, Lisa yielded, sending her mad with passion that reached out of the world of consciousness.

Things changed between them, there was no more playing at being lovers. She was but herself with Lisa, all temper, irritation, clenched fists and dry lips.

One day she told Lisa she didn't have to use make-up for her, and she hadn't used make-up again. Their kisses were free from detection or teasing.

'Say something special to me, something nice.'

'Ah...'

No, Corinna could not say it, that belonged to Stevie.

'Lisa darling—'

'Say it Corie. Say it!'

Bella intervened and Lisa lowered her eyes.

'I love *you* – why can't you say it?'

'Of course I do. I just find it...'

It was time to leave and Lisa pulled her close to kiss her goodbye. She left her at the top of the stairs kissing her fingertips as Corinna descended, kneeling with Bella arching round her. How could she ever stop seeing Lisa even if her conscience was killing her?

That night the gods intervened. Stevie's translating job came to an end. It was a relief. Then came despair. She wanted Lisa as never before, while walking Bill, head down over the hill, while leaning on a tree. She felt Lisa's hand go stealing... over her face and her hair...

Lisa made one brief telephone call to tell Stevie that she was going to Cairo again with Dan. She had been seeing a lot of Anton. Yes. He was going home to Tel Aviv.

Lisa caught Corinna for a moment on the phone.

'You can't expect me to wait, you've made no contact.'

And she had gone.

So much rage welling up in her Corinna thought would kill her. Night and day she saw him with Lisa, her heart hitting her under the chin, and she woke at dawn exhausted. She forced herself to lie still, listen to Stevie's deep breathing, and try to find Stevie's strength.

Where the terrace met the pond Stevie wanted a stone wall – the Bargate stone was discarded. Corinna began to fit stone to stone, cleared the acacia leaves dropping into the water with a net, and rescued hidden shoals of goldfish. She was building Stevie's dream.

'I'm reading Effi Briest, Stevie. Your garden dream reminds me of it. There's a garden with stone bowls, ponds and terraces.'

Stevie stood up from the border to tap her trowel, deep in thought.

'Effi wishes to please her parents and accepts marriage to a Landrat of high esteem, exact and just, as all good bourgeois husbands should be, considerate and responsible.'

'But,' Stevie interpolated as she stood up to light a fresh cigarette and settled down again, 'but lively girls don't like being left alone.'

'No – how did you know? In the narrow society she is permitted to visit, Effi readily meets a military rogue. They meet in the forest and he writes her passionate letters to which she replies. The Landrat is posted. Effi has a little girl. All is well until the child has an accident and in the commotion to find bandages, drawers are forcibly opened and in one a bundle of letters is found.'

'But what's that to do with the garden?' Stevie asked facetiously.

'It broke the pattern. There had to be a duel. The officer lover was killed, Effi banished and her child taken from her. She pined away and died. The garden reflects the orderly rules of their society and the failure to see the tragedy because honour is saved: the rules have been kept. That's the moral. It condemns the rigidly ordered society as inhuman, by implication the garden is unnatural.'

Corinna looked at Stevie in doubt.

'I'm trying to make sense of being me,' she said.

She stood laughing with Stevie, but the hurt and the guilt were there.

'Yes.' Stevie left the cigarette on her lower lip and

returned to her border.

'I see the point – there are moral concepts of greater value than the rules of society. All lovers know that. Love and loyalty, not only duty. But also, you see, the mundane and the spiritual get confused. We tell lies – even to ourselves.'

Wistfully Stevie turned away.

'We are all wayward – if only in our dreams, yes.'

She could never be perfect in the physical sense – nature had seen to that. Stevie was that other self – the life of the imagination, the endless talk that embraced all of life, trying to sort out the problems of the world and the puzzle of being a human in it – rising with the wings of Pegasus over our mundane selves: striving to forgive.

And yet, in the midst of thought, of talk, of walking Bill – there was Lisa. Out of hidden dreams she stood at the door, their eyes met and unutterable secrets stirred in the sand all over the ruddy limbs.

Her mother, Lisa said, had called her boy mad and sex mad. Those were words a twelve-year-old found bewildering. Her mother cut a rope, tied her to the bedpost and shouted at her. She still had tiny white scars on her wrists. Her mother had cut the rope shorter and the knife had flashed. That to threaten her. She knew even then that it was something to do with sex – nothing to do with her. Corinna linked it with Jemima's little box in her luggage, but Jemima was a prostitute. Lisa was innocent. Lisa had that way with her – innocence in knowledge. Not in ignorance. And so Corinna had tied Lisa by the wrist to the bed, and waited, her eyes on Lisa's.

It was part of a love scene loving Lisa, kissing her, kissing her from her mouth to her toes, finding the secret places, the tiny folds of hidden joys, the eager clitoris, the anemone at its heart. Lisa, like a Grecian nymph, dreamed, sinking her mouth into Corinna's hair while with the tips of her fingers Corinna teased the dark entrance with gentle lover ways and drew out the shudders of passion that brought them both to the pinnacle together. She bent over to kiss Lisa again – and stumbled and fell against a tree, feeling the rough bark hit her hands. A dog was barking – Bill was standing his front legs apart and his head up expectantly. She took his ball out of her pocket and hurled it through the treetops, her face wet with tears.

Chapter Sixteen

Stevie pushed the large brown envelope across the kitchen table while she was slipping Bill's lead over his head.

'Would you drop this in at Mr Black's on your way, cherub? Some papers I've done.'

'Yes, I'll do it. Quite an honour really – the Latin courier.'

'Go up the lane next to the office, it leads to the downs.'

It was the girl she met in the lane every evening. Eve. An energetic little Jack Russell crossbreed pulling on the lead. Bill made for and mastered him in one threatening growl. The perky terrier and the noble Bill now pals forever.

'Hallo! I didn't realise! This is for Mr Black, please, translations and the originals. Take care of them, won't you?'

The girl had a way of looking at her that lifted her spirits. The blue eyes were shy and she smiled at her all the time she was in the room.

'See you in the lane later?'

In this moment Corinna again became Orlando, the hero, consciously defiant, striding through the world, knowing much – having been taught by Lisa – longing desperately for the soft folds of a woman who would surrender in swept-away passion. One like Lisa, but free, like Lisa but secret, because Lisa was still her dream woman while she was too tied up with Stevie. One with dark, straight flowing hair rising and falling as she ran from the train on the platform in Sion, Orlando following her through the narrow streets of the town. The hair fell down her back as they mounted the stairs and entered the room where huge oranges tumbled down the wall paper, a small attic window looked down on the Rhône and darkness covered the bed in the corner.

'Talk to me in Engleesh – plees. That's all I want.'

But her hand, dry and rough, stole round his neck, under his shirt collar, driving him into a pile of strangely perfumed blankets.

He was Orlando, playing with girls who sold books in the market, the lower orders, that is those who work for a living. He was attracted towards people who were sharp-witted, and had a cockney accent, feeling he had an innate bond, inarticulated, some sort of cousin-sympathy with women who thought less of cleanliness, say, in their fingernails, than of expressing warmth in the heart by a deep kiss with cherry moist lips. Soon, too, he knew the literary restraints of poverty on the minds of those who work, as well as he did their rough femininity.

His own viciousness in making the girls love him surprised him – the male in him rose, the sadism leaving a bruise, a red mark on the surprisingly soft nut brown neck, under the open necked shirt of the stable girl. To touch a woman – the centre of her being – he found so much greater a joy than touching a man, the female was so secret in nature, her satisfactions so much greater.

Orlando had left Sion and the mountains with a new light in his heart and a spirit of freedom. After Lisa, life with Stevie ran slowly and Orlando slept, to be woken only by his Orlando voice.

'See you in the lane later?'

An office worker she was, living down among the hills, white-skinned, with dark hair in silky curls down her neck and eyes as blue as innocence itself.

The river came into full view from the top of the hill, lying low in shreds of early evening mist. Bill and Jasper nosed their way through mounds of dead leaves squashed into the mud, a ruddy metallic surface shining on the little pools left as the river receded, Orlando's boots and Eve's boots making muffled sounds of peat soil squelching under trees full of birds calling their sharp and sweet goodnight.

All was shattered by the crack of a gun, followed by nature's wild panic of wings and scurrying, and awesome silence.

'A poacher – he was here yesterday,' Orlando called to Eve trying to curb his trembling excitement.

'Move over a bit, will yer!' the man called, waving his gun wildly to take aim.

'What for?' Orlando called back, putting steel into his indignity.

'The wild duck – he's behind you.'

The poacher swung the gun to fire at Orlando.

'Why shoot him?' Orlando shouted.

'To eat, of course.'

The man ploughed about in the dead ferns and raised the gun again.

Orlando turned to Eve.

'You stay here – I'm going to walk across his aim.'

He kicked the mud off his boots and called Bill behind him.

'Blast you,' the man shouted. 'I'll get him, never fear. He'll be there tomorrow.'

Eve was at Orlando's side, as angry as he was, standing in pools of dead wet leaves up to the top of her Wellingtons.

'Let's hope he falls on his gun – or whatever poachers do,' Orlando said, calm and cool, and in control.

The next evening, Eve was with him by the river when there was a shout and a loud bird's cry. The blue and white beauty of the male duck spun out across the water into a flotilla of brown females. Up and over the river he rose, over the trees, the brown flock following.

'Safe for now,' said Eve, standing before Orlando by the

water. 'He won't come back in a hurry that man.'

A light shone in Eve's eyes, together with joy of facing death at his side.

The evenings were drawing in and the chill and the dark brought the dog-walks further up the afternoon, and Eve had two afternoons free. Stevie did not seem to notice.

Orlando, roused by his new conquest, saw nothing but the fine bloom of youth on Eve's face, the graceful bend of her neck, her childlike lips, heard the tremor in her voice. He remembered Lawrence running away with Frieda, a married woman with children. Orlando, too, felt the call of his blood. He felt young again, inspired, and Eve was happy, if painfully impressionable.

No mental debate could stop Corinna being Orlando and using her superior experience with skill, giving Eve books to read, reciting poems to her and watching the changing expressions in her face. He told her the story of Orlando and tales from the German, of the love of Werther for Lotte and the merciless destruction of Effi Briest on the altar of bourgeois respectability. He led where he knew Eve wanted to follow, and accepted Eve's admiration as flattery.

Out of the wind and rain, Orlando and Eve stood under the old stone bridge, watching the dogs on the river banks, talking. He discovered Eve's sense of humour and her imagination. Sometimes he felt guilty, then told himself this was innocent enjoyment. He kept it from Stevie nonetheless. It was innocent, but would Stevie believe that – after Lisa?

It was not a secret from Jack, the young husband.

'I tell Jack everything,' Eve said with the bright light of innocence. 'I told him everything – that is – up to the time you kissed me.'

All this said by lips of rosebud youth.

'There have to be some secrets in life,' Orlando muttered, face burning.

Sometimes it seemed it would be safer to make the situation open so that Stevie would not be hurt, as she had been with Lisa. Corinna arranged for all four of them, including Eve's Jack, to see a new production of *The Cherry Orchard* when it came to the town in six weeks' time.

Between the booking and the night Orlando went one day with Eve to see the cottage over the hill. Here Eve and Jack hoped to raise a family one day. Before Eve had opened the door, in that moment that Orlando stood under the porch, his hand on the lintel over Eve's head, he began to tremble in overwhelming desire.

'Jack's a carpenter, he did all the woodwork in these cottages,' Eve said proudly, smoothing down the doorframe and closing the door.

Eve did not flirt. She had none of Lisa's wilful ways. She was deeper, more thoughtful perhaps, with a world of wistful lights in her startling blue eyes. She had quiet ways and innocent dreams, and obstinately protected her body and her purity of spirit. She often quoted her beloved Paul, founder of all churches and Baptist chapels.

'It was in chapel that I met Jack. He was so ashamed of being a builder he reminded me immediately that Jesus was a carpenter too.'

Eve said these things without criticism, as facts of being, truths. Orlando made no answer to them, but fondled Eve's hair, touched the hair on her shoulder, kissed her lightly on the cheek, and answered vaguely.

'I only know one or two things John said – "Even in laughter the heart is sad" – I think that's true, but only of some of us.'

He recited this while following Eve up to the bedroom, where Eve, eyes on his lips, began to unbutton his shirt, speaking softly, tenderly.

'But John also said, "He that loveth not knoweth not God, for God is love."' She then drew Orlando down to soft opened lips, an agony of passion in her face.

This bedroom belongs to Eve and Jack, Orlando thought, *this haven so small the walls touch the bed on three corners, with a foot on the odd side to get in and out. This is an innocent young girl kissing me, while Jack's rifle stands between the wardrobe and the wall, and a small snap of Jack holding it stands in a frame on the mantelshelf.*

'Hold me close,' Eve's voice pleaded, her fresh young body suddenly naked in his arms, blotting out all thought except that he was kissing her, her neck, her lips and rousing this young girl's body, helpless and groaning in his arms. Her daring held him in awe. His hand between her legs followed the dictates of desire, the urging of pleasure. He felt movement in his fingers, tension gripping, a deep shudder, and a long swim into the delirium that is the uttermost ecstasy, and was raised to orgasm himself with passionate intensity.

'Who taught you how to love, Orlando?'

'Being a woman, being a man.'

He kissed her still with long deep kisses into oblivion, thinking how sweetly desire was gratified.

He watched Eve slide off the bed and begin to dress, shaking out her petticoat and slipping into her briefs, her quaint underclothes as unsophisticated as herself. She was in love with Orlando more than with Blake.

It had been a conquest, not a love affair. Eve was in the agony of love, but Orlando was twisted inside with shame and guilt. It had been an endless intrigue to get Eve to kiss him; now Eve was ensnared in a love never intended, a love of fear and pain, and deceit, and that in a girl who probably had never told a lie in her life before. Orlando was becoming obsessed with her, her true innocence and her passion.

He came. Across the path on Orlando's descent from the cottage with the sun low across the trees, breaking bracken, heavy-footed, came Jack out of the snapshot on the bedroom mantelshelf, rifle across his chest. He raised his eyes and met Orlando's. In a flash, all was clear, as if read in the headlines. Jack's eyes hardened, spake hatred, the glare of the poacher with his gun loaded.

Orlando felt his stomach turn. He had taken aim with that gun across the garden from the bedroom window. He had laughed at Eve's fear of Jack's sudden temper breaking out of that dull frame. In a long stone-cold minute he stood still, watching Jack slowly spit into the bracken and turn into the woodland. He had gone.

Revitalised, Orlando thrust him out of his mind. Lying with Eve on the bed whose sheets were still warm from the night with Jack, his gun against the wall, the daring, the excitement lost none of its intrigue. Talking, talking the afternoon away, making love as the dogs whined and stretched outside the door, and listening to the rain and wind beating on the tiny house, Eve told him tales of her family.

'You should write them down, make them into romances.'

'You show me how.'

'I will – I'll bring pen and paper, and we shall begin.'

It was the most exciting enterprise, but short-lived. Eve was too unhappy to be able to settle to it.

'Only three weeks to the night of the theatre,' Orlando said to make Eve smile, stopping short when he saw the fear on Eve's face, a moment of desperation.

'Don't be afraid. Stevie won't bite you.'

'I could hardly complain if she did,' Eve said, a bitter note in the voice usually so soft it was like a caress. 'I can't go on like this. You don't seem to mind – well I do. I can't stand it.'

Her voice rose with the hysteria of being trapped.

'I told him,' she said, suddenly quiet, her voice low, 'that if he can't touch me as you do – then don't – just don't.'

Now she was sobbing madly.

Seeing Eve's distress overwhelmed him and filled him with terrifying misery. This was not what he had meant, on the bathroom floor Eve kneeling at his feet, her dark glossy hair falling like a black cape on white shoulders.

'I swear you have all my heart, dearest, my love. Take me – just for six months – do as you will with me.'

Day after day that vision stayed in Orlando's eyes as he strode down the hill home with Bill, his heart turning over a thousand times. At home, he brooded and grieved. He felt sick. He had done something that would condemn him for all time, and only to spite Lisa – that was the truth.

One agonising day, he burst into the house, relieved beyond words to find it empty. Stevie was not yet home from shopping, while for him time had run over the edge of the world. He stopped short to snatch up a note on the kitchen table.

YOU WERE LATE, I HAD TO GET SOME SHOPPING – IT'S THE THEATRE NIGHT. I'M SURE YOU'VE FORGOTTEN.

Orlando in a frenzy lit the gas for tea, and began to clear up the lean-to, sweeping through the kitchen as if to cleanse the Aegean stables, out across the terrace, lifting his face to the north wind to cool the fever in his blood, throwing a desultory ball for Bill.

The drive into the town was the beginning of a long night of torture, sitting between Eve and Stevie in the stalls, passing the box of chocolates he had bought Stevie to Eve, to Jack, feeling he would faint if he couldn't escape.

Eve was a child. She had no idea, no knowledge of life, thinking of Corinna as a desperately unhappy Radclyffe Hall and herself as the Lady with the Dog. The fun had gone out of their romance. In sober mood, Orlando had become Corinna again. The Orlando game amounted to this – panic gripping every thought and every movement. Escape was possible only by hurting them all, Eve and Jack, but above all Stevie.

After the theatre they talked about the play, but not a word said could she remember. Her eyes were irresistibly drawn only to Jack's fair head and sturdy figure in the armchair.

'Well, we'd better go. I have to be up at six.'

He looked at last straight at her, in his eyes an expression of utter loss at this inexplicable friendship between her and his wife. When it had been Orlando and Eve, everything between them had been spontaneous and natural, but not when she looked into Jack's bewildered questioning eyes. Then she knew all the wickedness of what she had done. Instead of crowing over the denied husband as she had longed to do, she shook with fear, desperate with regrets, tormented by the hatred she had seen in the woods.

One hundred years ago she would have been killed, and not even in a duel, being a woman. There was nothing romantic about it – death would have been her just deserts. She would need more than a lifetime to blot it out of her memory. She drew back in the armchair, silent and humiliated.

Completely aware as she had become of this drama which she had caused she only now felt the stab, seeing it all in both their faces. When they had gone, she stood by the fire, all her strength gone.

'What is it, cherub? Better tell me.'

'Eve.'

'I know.'

'How?'

'At the theatre. I could tell.'

'It's been a long time, Stevie, help me – I've got to get out of this.'

Someone else's voice was in her mouth.

'I think he'll kill me when he realises – and he should.'

'That my child, is your conscience.'

Stevie picked up the tray of china and thrust it into her hands.

'For a start stop thinking about yourself.'

Her voice grew sharp with bitterness.

'I never did believe you were attending a literary class.'

Stevie's eyes on her smouldered with anger, but also with pain, a pain that would last when the anger was gone. 'I just hoped it would pass…'

Long after Eve had left Black's office, and at last Stevie could look into her eyes again, she asked her why.

'Why did you chase Eve after all the trouble with Lisa?'

'I don't know. It was something I had to prove, that's all.'

She had always found it difficult to believe anyone could love her, yet each time, in the end, she felt wretched to the point of death instead of triumphant, her ego at war with her conscience. Eve had said she would give all she had of herself, her sight or touch, her body, to be with her as Stevie was. Eve's voice still throbbed in her ears.

'I would come even now, tonight. I'd follow you to end of the world.'

Winter passed into spring. She and Stevie waited, living in the hope that the old love would revive with the steadying urge of reading, Stevie's philosophy, Stevie's reciting endless poetry and quoting Lawrence. The old spirit of their army days tried surreptitiously to edge back.

'Remember, cherub, the little room in the roof of that tiny council house. Those were days of innocence and love and happiness beyond measure and not a penny in the bank.'

And they belonged to the days of youth. Love that was, with Stevie, a natural extension of tenderness.

Corinna often stood in the little church in the valley,

cool, silent, breathing the still lifeless air, and talk quietly to the statue on the cross, but Christ was not pleased to forgive so readily, and remained mute and forbidding.

She went on fretting about Eve and torn by Stevie, but none of that could stop the demon of Orlando in her, at least in her dreams. There were many occasions when she needed to take but one step – and an escapade would open up before her – Ann in the library, Esther with an exciting French mother – Adele so painfully learning English – 'You teach me, Corie – *n'est-ce-pas*?'

She had a magic touch. Lisa had taught her too much to be forgotten. It sounded trivial, but she felt sincere, remaining physically remote and fantasising. In long talks with Stevie she tried to explain, skirting the truth, yet seeking Stevie's guidance because no one in the world mattered to her more than Stevie did.

'Daddy had affairs for years and each one broke his heart, and yet he loved our mother. I know it's wrong, but I see he is in me. I have an insatiable desire to be male, and if I'm not, then to act as if I am. By nature I simply fall in love with women, that's all. I'm not concealing wickedness, like Dorian Gray.'

Stevie fidgeted with her cigarette, tapping off the ash, and taking a moment to examine the end.

Corinna said, 'It's a greater desire in me than to see equality for women. I think that's only a tactic to get certain freedoms, like wearing trousers, a tie and a jacket with pockets bulging, so that I can stride over the hill like a panther, and argue politics with any man. It's the only way I can raise my head, Stevie.'

The cigarette was finished. Stevie said nothing until she had lit a new one.

'If you want to know what I think – you're spoilt. You three're all spoilt. I'd like to be sure it's not simply an excuse to do as you like.'

The abyss between them was still too great, but a current of hope there would always be. Time had to pass in days of peace.

'Well,' said Stevie, cigarette puffing away and the spirit of spring again in the early light of dawn. 'We could go down to the sea – take egg and bacon sandwiches and eat them on the shore, as we used to.'

Through the forest to the sand and the sea, the long climb up the sand dunes, salt in the mouth, wind in the hair, Bill running wild through the low silky rollers coming in, that was the power between them, the unbreakable tie. Walking apart, alone, yet never alone.

In the autumn, the deer began to retreat farther in to the ferns. Bill grew more daring and she followed him until she came to the old road cottages not a stone's throw away. Corinna let her curiosity lead her, pressing through the fern until she could see a line of clothes across the side of a cottage and at the end of the line a dress – Eve's! In that moment, the door opened and out came a young man. He shook out his jacket and pulling it on walked swiftly farther down the lane towards the farm. There was no sign of Eve or Jack.

Corinna stood intrigued, her gaze rising from the still open door to the first floor window over it, her eyes meeting Eve's. Eve stretched up her arm and drew the curtain across. Corinna stopped. Everything in her stopped. Then her mind leapt. A thousand words – anger, jealousy – tears pressed her lids, her face burned.

Eve. How could that be? Eve? With that young man?

Corinna listened and strained to grasp it all. Lies and deceit! All those little flirtations, those airs of scorn, they all meant something and not just for her. She had felt so special. The biblical quotes, the holiness of it all, all too good to be true. If she had been able to talk to Stevie it would have been clear from the beginning. Her heart raced.

The sun in the woods fell into shade and Bill snuffled near her feet. She listened. A footfall could be heard through the trees. She could see a man across the brook at the main road. The young man? No. It was Jack, his head down, his gun tight across his chest. He walked over the track bridge towards her, and suddenly came on towards her through the fern like a wild creature after the prey.

'You!'

His face was ablaze with hate. He stopped and raised his gun. Corinna felt her blood rise in defiance. Then she caught her breath – he was taking aim, wavering.

'You swine – I told you – if you come again, I'd get you – but I'll get your bloody dog first.'

The shot blew a cloud of smoke in the air where Bill had been, but through the bracken Bill came hurtling back to her. In flaming anger, Jack ran back over the bridge, jumped into his truck and roared back driving straight at her. Now the blood drained from her head. She shook uncontrollably. This was fear. For herself she rose in defiance – for Bill she would give her life. Fear made her jump into the bushes, grab Bill by the collar in a frenzy and plough up the hill and over and down, home. In the garden, she pulled Bill to her, ran her hands over him to soothe him, tears falling down her face.

'It's over – I shall have to tell – but how.'

At the terrace she sat on the wall and began to laugh. Eve in bed with a farmhand! How could she have been so deceived! So flattered! But before she had reached the rear door to the kitchen, she had realised the moral was just the same – she was still guilty. Stevie would see that. She was still guilty over Eve, and Eve had made a fool of her.

At last Lisa dropped in. She was taking Sophie to a new school to board. It was a contrite Lisa, not one to be trusted.

The flash of dismay at Lisa's entrance in Stevie's eyes was softened by Sophie's being there.

'I'll take Sophie up the hill with Bill – coming with me, Sophie?'

She left Lisa talking to Stevie by the window overlooking the terrace, hearing not a word spoken by the chatty young Sophie in the half hour they were away.

'Lovely out – Sophie will tell you – we saw deer down by the river.'

Sophie, however, took Bill's lead and drew him into the garden through the conservatory, leaving a hush in the room.

Corinna caught Lisa's eyes brushing over her and away. The talk with Stevie seemed to have trailed off and the sound of a gentle tapping of Lisa's foot on the leg of the coffee table dominated the silence.

Absorbed in the regular tap of Lisa's elegant foot, its persistence and its message, she sat silent, lost in a wave of desire rising in her, holding her in a dream. Mentally she shook herself.

Lisa sighed and stood up to go, taking Sophie by the arm with a defiant glance at her, as if to say, 'This is the child you could never have given me, Corinna.' Cool green eyes fixed on hers for one brief moment.

'Àu revoir, tous les deux,' Lisa said, giving a fleeting smile, re-rolling the long umbrella as the bell rang. 'Must be Dan, I think. He said he'd be here at five.'

She had gone. It was Stevie standing at her elbow, holding the tea tray.

'Carry these in for me, there's a dear.'

There was a strain at the rim of her eyes.

'Your Lisa's having lover trouble, as usual. Funny girl.'

The next day, cold rain and wind buffeting the daylights out of the high street, she met Stevie outside Black's office, standing under the arch in her suit with no umbrella and nothing to shield her.

'Had my raincoat stolen,' Stevie said, raindrops falling

off her nose. 'Miserable so-and-so.'

Corinna felt she was rescuing her from a foul hand. It made her think of Stevie long ago, reciting to her there and then in the rain.

'The cold wet winds ever blowing threaten the head that I love, my Stevie. You know the rest.'

Stevie belonged to her, and what hurt Stevie hurt her – because God – if there was a God – had made them as one.

Peace had come, years of peace between them, which was why she came in that day from Bill's walk with such gay nonchalance.

'I saw deer in the valley, in the snow. It was so beautiful.'

She had begun to notice a quiet boredom rising between them just when she felt full of ecstasy. Stevie did not notice. But this was more. Stevie looked pale and flushed at the same time.

'I saw David today,' Stevie said.

Something stopped in Corinna – stopped forever. The sword of revenge had fallen, and she knew it.

'David?'

'He came into Black's office for a legal matter just when I was picking up some more translations.'

'He must have known you were there.'

No answer. She watched Stevie walk about the room.

'It's all right, you don't have to worry,' Stevie laughed, rather coarsely.

She looked so pale it certainly had not made her happy.

'You and I are all right, aren't we, Stevie? As it used to be?'

Stevie looked up at her and said nothing. She felt a shaking in herself in her arms as she hugged Stevie close, an open pit in her stomach.

'I love you, Stevie. What else can I say?'

'There's someone at the door,' Stevie said. 'You go.'

One of the tenants had found a young female cat with a

kitten in the lane. Corinna took the box with the cats in it and carried it through to the kitchen.

'We'll have to take it to the clinic, the PDSA. It's not far. I know it.'

It was a relief to act, to keep fate waiting.

'I'll take them,' she said.

The pure green eyes, captive, tricked into the box, trapped in the car, trapped as we all are by our inherent fate.

'Well, we can't have them. We have Biffa and Bill – can't be done,' said Stevie.

The clinic was brusque and efficient. A tag tied to the box quite honestly said, 'These for destruction.' There was no need to dissimulate.

'Stevie, it made me feel quite sick.'

She held Bill tight and stroked him. She was so tired of being hurt and hurting. Dead tired.

'Come on, let's have a spin. It'll all look better in the open air,' Stevie said, a tremble in her voice.

Out on the road, Stevie's sombre mood persisted. The car was cold, or too hot, and the wind through the window was giving her a headache.

'But you don't have headaches.'

'Well, I have today.'

'We're over Portsmouth, time to eat. Perhaps you're hungry.'

It was a deeply beamed inn for lunch, the kind of place Stevie liked. They drove on through the afternoon until the great crested waves could be seen below the cliff and the sun set in a pool of liquid bronze.

None of the usual quips and repartee came from Stevie, only a quiet and anxious silence. The sea spread out to a dark line under the sky, and there was nothing – no pain, no love, no joy.

Stevie's hand lay on her knee.

'Let's go home. I forgot to tell you I have to see the

doctor in the morning.'

'The doctor – what for? The headaches?'

'It's all too much for me, Corie,' said Stevie in tears, sobbing in her arms.

She watched Stevie go through the narrow door to the surgery while she waited at the car.

'I told her all the story,' said Stevie, breathless and pale. 'She looked down at you standing by the car and said, "Oh, my God." She had, she said, recognised herself in you.'

Corinna listened dumb with misery, waiting for a miracle.

'I want to get married, Corie, and have a baby. The doctor said I could expect it all to be in order.'

Just as Stevie had been doubtful that she was at the literary class when she was seeing Eve, Corinna was right in doubting Stevie had been working at Blacks when she had been seeing David. She leaned on the car for support and found in her head Yeats' words for her own:

O do not love too long!

All through the years of our youth
Neither could have known
Their own thought from the other's,
We were so much at one.

But O, in a minute she changed—
O do not love too long...

Is it possible to love too long, leaving her bloodless and emaciated? In dogged persistence a mute defiance revived her. They would go on, day by day, waiting for the answer.

She stood still, Stevie in front of her, Stevie's indelible words shattering the past and blighting the future.

Chapter Seventeen

Intrigue had scarred the loving of Lisa and Eve. Now it was Stevie's turn to lie and cheat her way through the tangled web.

'I just can't leave you, cherub. I couldn't bear that look in your eyes.'

Summer had passed in a wave of heat under a nucleating sky. The border flowers were drawing back, autumn leaves being tossed about, driven into terrace corners, and hidden in the gutters.

Angela from Suffolk landed and stayed two weeks, disastrously falling in love with Corinna and possibly with Stevie too, but too old a friend from Stevie's school days to be dismissed.

'What could you expect?' Stevie asked. 'A lonely lesbian hidden away in a couple of acres of potatoes with a dozen cats.'

Answering the main door pull bell, Corinna met two pairs of laughing eyes, the two young men from Lisa's party – Julien sitting cross-legged in the porch, and Cecil jumping up the steps to fly past her into the hall, striking the pose of a Sheridan hero and twirling his boater.

'We heard from Angela,' they said, first Julien then Cecil. 'Keep your eyes off that girl, Corinna. Thinks she's a lesbian Mata Hari.'

Umpteen people dropped in for a meal and a walk across the fields by the river that autumn.

'Lovely place you have here, you two. Quite beautiful! Look at that garden!'

The banter and tales of the family, Amanda's secret

lover, Benjamin's adventures in America, swam past as if on a tidal wave, leaving the real life of heartache and mental rage to surge about mercilessly between Stevie and Corinna.

Stevie, weeding, tidying and planting for the spring in the borders, looked up in bewilderment, white to the lips, her dark luminous eyes seeking hers.

There were no thoughts now of Lisa or Eve. Corinna's mind was on Stevie only, translating poems by Goethe, Heine and Rilke because it seemed translating drew utter concentration, and that turning these poets into English calmed the panic in her for a moment.

She browsed through all the books on their shelves, Hardy and Lawrence, Woolf and Proust, searching, searching for solace.

'I've asked David to come here, to talk to you,' came Stevie's voice. 'He could stay for the day – he has some work to do at Black's.'

He came. The unutterable sight of him in the garden, his sleeves rolled up, seeing Stevie's eyes on him, his fleshy body showing naked through his shirt front. He was to have the top flat. It was all a ruse to get him into the house.

Jealousy like a fatal fever scalded every vein in her body. In her head wheeled images of David with Stevie that crazed her. Corinna felt she had never known such agony as when Stevie told her she had never known such love before – his penis, she really meant – or when Stevie ironed his shirts – Stevie who hated domestic life to distraction – and wanted his child.

'But for you I could have loved him,' Stevie said.

It was a trifle consolation, disregarded.

Corinna lay in bed waiting for dawn, waiting for the old Stevie to rise from the visitor's bed, despairing, wanting to smash her arm over Stevie sleeping still. At dawn, Corinna sprang out of bed and walked shivering down the garden.

Pale ivory pink the dawn came over the downs. The

birds sang as if heralding her arrival in paradise. But it all meant nothing to her – nature, too, had lost its power to touch her. When Stevie came after her she spoke through her teeth.

'Go – or I shall kill you!'

And she struck out at Stevie as she came too near. Shocked, Stevie stopped and frowned at her, but made no answer.

'Then I shall go and take Bill – I shall go myself.'

Corinna slammed doors and drove the car as if it were an atomic rocket.

The sea was out at Christchurch. She threw stones for Bill and started to walk after him into the sea, but weakness crept into her. She sat on a rock and Bill pressed himself against her, little whimpers coming from her.

'I love her, Bill, what can I do? I shall have to leave her.' She had to fight not to go straight home to fall on her knees before her. For hours and hours she felt the dragging of hell – she thought she would go mad. With her foot down on the long drive back, she reached home as it grew dark.

'You must go, Stevie, and take him with you.'

'But I can't leave you, I can't bear it!'

She wanted to hit Stevie it hurt so much, God it hurt like a knife in her brain.

'I love you cherub. It'll pass, I swear it will.'

She began to feel nothing, not even when Stevie came down from the top flat and his presence, radiant. Coldly it went through her. She would not go on suffering. She would find a way to win or go mad.

The conservatory window was open when she walked past and she hit her head, half her head going numb. Stevie took off Bill's collar. She called him to her and put it on again. Silently, Stevie looked at her, eyes brimming over, and Bill looked up at both of them, one then the other.

Stevie was in the garden when David came in to speak to

her. He sat upright, his face pale, his lean neck above a stiff collar. Tall and touched with grey, pompous and without emotion, he was erect, every inch a solicitor. The knowledge that he would be terrified of her, Corinna, overcame the burden in her that he was six feet tall.

'Stevie is only fond of me,' he said. 'She feels differently for you.'

'Probably thinks of me as a puppy.'

'Oh, I think not.'

He stood up three times to go and sat down again.

'Well, you won't see me walking about with a glum expression,' he said.

'I hope not to see you walking about at all.'

She was sure he could not possibly understand a woman loving another woman. He looked as bewildered as Eve's Jack.

Stevie stood in front of her demanding she look at her and stop treating her as if she were not there. She put down the stack of books she was rearranging and looked into Stevie's face.

'You're very pale, Stevie. I thought you'd be happy – with David here.'

'David's going. You can relax, cherub. I can't have you like this. You and I can have a run in the country while he's getting his things out. Would you like that?'

'Stevie—'

There were no words to say.

'You look very fine this afternoon.'

'It's my new jacket, velvet cord.'

She climbed, with Stevie close behind, up the sand hill above the water, the summer sun still in the sand. She sat under a pine bush, drew Stevie down beside her and lay back, watching Bill rolling and kicking up his legs in the pine needles. Stevie remained detached but close, lying next to her.

'I'd like to go away for six months, cherub, that's all,' Stevie said, comfortable in the sand and with the late sun and wind in the prickly fern.

The scream started up again in her head, but it didn't prevent an agony of desire rising in her.

'You're making me ill, Stevie. Why don't you just go?'

She was making a whiny sound. The weight of cowardice bowed her down.

Stevie rolled over and lay in her arms, but jealousy leapt up in her and her heart recoiled. No – she didn't want Stevie like that. Not with David leering at her from the shadows.

'My arm's bruised,' Stevie said, rubbing it.

'That was me.'

Yes it was still there – the love and the pain were still there.

Anger and spite overwhelmed her so that she hurt herself banging about in the summerhouse. While fixing a shelf in the growing dark, she hit her hand with the hammer and left it to swell.

'Coming in, dear? Supper's ready. Just look at your hand.'

Stevie stood in the door frame, alone and tender, a cigarette between her fingers.

Silently she followed Stevie in, all the fight gone in fatigue, and with a sickness deep under her ribs. She had put herself right in her mind by having affairs and acting out fantasies – now she had to pay the price.

Sullenly the sun set. Sullenly it rose.

'I'd like to go out tonight, cherub. Be all right, won't you?'

Every time it was the twist of a knife in her heart and in her head.

'Just don't be late. I don't like the dark nights.'

Not since Stevie had asked him to go, driven by her

fierce reaction.

Now Stevie would be bitter and sarcastic, hate her and resent her, but she trying to hold her back, trying to keep her.

She persisted in praying to God, if He was there, to let her and Stevie be together again to the end of life, however rough the way. Why do humans strive for a dream that will vanish as they reach it? The words changed themselves in her head.

'God, give me freedom from loving Stevie.'

There was no rest. Stevie threatened that the result of Corinna's ridiculous behaviour was still unknown – even if she did not see much of David.

Attempts to go to Cornwall for a holiday, to go hundreds of miles by car, or to town by train, all ended in quarrels. Stevie wanted the car to herself, and she ended in talking about babies and her pride at walking with him through the town.

No wonder there were periodic brainstorms. They were effectively valves letting off steam. In them, Corinna felt murderous strength that left her exhausted.

'You'll have to go, Stevie. I can't bear it like this.'

Stevie made no answer. The ground was dead between them. There had always been that one strength in life, the eternal bond with Stevie. Nothing could break it – Stevie had now forgotten it.

And it did grow in her that somehow, if Stevie left, she would survive, still pleading with God not to let Stevie go until she had ceased to love her.

She walked in the garden, bent down to touch Bill's head. The old Lodge, Stevie's inheritance, shared so generously with her, held so much of life's desire, serenity and beauty. 'But where had gone the apple tree, the singing and the gold?'

She had meant not to tell her family, but found herself

driving, Bill in the back seat, to Dorset in a stream of chewed up thought.

One look at Amanda and she burst into tears, and Alex clamped his arm round her shoulders.

'Stevie came yesterday and told us,' Amanda said, looking at Alex silently nodding. 'We're on your side, Corie, don't worry about that.'

'Stevie came! She tried to get you on her side?'

'You can stay here. You could have a home, a room for yourself,' Amanda said. 'Daddy's here only at weekends, all the week he's at Aunt Annabel's.'

'It's lovely to hear you say that. It'll be all right, I'm not going.'

Only then did she know she would fight for The Lodge, even if she did owe it to Stevie for giving her half.

'But I must tell you everything.'

Her voice rose in a flood of tears.

'I love her, Amanda. She's the love of my life. She wants to marry some fellow she met at the office long ago.'

The wonder of what she had said stunned them. She could see them searching for some sense in the words.

'What about the house?' Alex asked, drawing on his pipe. 'Legally, I mean.'

'We share it half and half. She wants me to go and won't leave me.'

Amanda stopped biting her finger and lifted her head.

'So, it's all about the house, the money. In that case, you must dig your heels in.'

'Yes, now I shall.'

That was how they wanted to see it.

'I'll come with you,' Amanda said, turning to Alex. 'Shall I go?'

Somehow, in that moment, the unknown cloud had dispersed.

Alex nodded, 'Of course.'

All the way back she recited what she would say, repeating it to Amanda, talking, talking. The idea grew – she would fight for The Lodge.

'Stevie believes I can't live there without her, that I shall be ill. She's trying to drive me out, Amanda, I can see that now quite clearly.'

Stevie sat deeply immersed in piles of business papers at the dining table, angry now at Amanda's being there, and tense at sitting next to her.

'I can manage, Stevie. Amanda will help me. She'll stay with me. Alex said it would be all right.'

'They didn't say that when I was there. They know I can't leave you.'

'I shall manage.'

Stevie hung her head.

'I wanted to speak to you, Corie, alone. I wanted you to say you couldn't live without me.'

Silence held them all rigid and waiting at the table, waiting.

'All right, I shall go,' said Stevie, choking in her voice.

Corinna looked into Stevie's face, full of unshed tears, white and desperately sad, and gripped the table edge.

'I shall be all right.'

She did not say Amanda had to go home again.

'I shall be all right, Stevie.'

The words felt every time like a whip on her soul, and started off a bout of coughing.

Leaving Stevie and Amanda to talk, to tidy up and arrange some food, she took Bill and walked slowly up the hill to recover.

It was still there, the river and the sun in the sand where they had lain. As soon as Stevie had gone, Amanda would go – she would be alone. Unreal it seemed, like a drama being played and they the actors.

As she came back, she saw Stevie going through the gate,

the taxi waiting and the driver lifting the luggage into the boot.

She ran to the taxi, catching Stevie at the door.

'Come back one day, Stevie. Come back to me – with your heart.'

Watching the taxi fade into the mist, she heard words Stevie had said still ringing through the treetops.

'You can't marry me, Corie. You can't give me a child.'

Corinna still heard the words hours later when the telephone rang. It was Stevie. David had asked her to marry him.

She put down the receiver and went up the great stairs in pale moonlight from the staircase window, and opened the cupboard door.

For a long time, she stood leaning on the open door, using her torch before kneeling down to look at the electricity cables. The men had left them unguarded, she had noticed it earlier. She had only to put out her hand, there. Six inches away.

She hesitated, and in that second she remembered for the rest of her life, she thought of Bill – no one knew he was alone. She could see, vividly see, the kettle burning dry and Bill in danger. She stood back and went down to him.

It was a living nightmare – wide-awake. The divan bed in the bay window was big enough for Bill to lie at her side while she counted the hours.

Time slid away, day and night. She could say she hadn't slept. She ate in the kitchen with Bill, sharing with him the chicken, sometimes with bread and fruit and drinking tea. It was possible after all to live, for time to pass.

She wanted more than anything to write it all down for someone else to read – for sympathy. Not for Lisa, who wanted her to be a male not a namby-pamby who had to tell when it hurt. Strangely remote Lisa seemed, lost at parties, pursued by dark-haired young men with wives and families in Israel and beyond.

It was Eve she wrote to, pouring out her agony, and it was a note from Eve that made her drop everything to drive to Plymouth, and stop on the cliff top. No – that she could not do. She knew it all already, the false and the trite. Never let anyone hurt you, Jack had written at the foot of Eve's note, keep something of yourself apart. She turned the car and drove home. Jack was a better guide than she.

Corinna knew the truth without seeing Eve, feeling the closeness of Eve there across the green, and what facing the truth meant. Eve belonged to a different sphere of life from her own. Corinna knew she had committed a crime, had taken advantage of innocence and used it. Self-disgust and shame engulfed her. And now cowardice too. She would rather kill herself than kill David. And even that she could not do.

Chapter Eighteen

A telephone call from Stevie woke her from days of mental agonising.

'I thought I should tell you – David and I are married. I hope to see you soon, my dear.'

Was there something else in her voice, a touch of regret?

When the telephone rang next it was Lisa. She had had an invitation to Stevie's wedding. She had tried to ring before, but there had been no answer. Yes. She and Dan had gone. She hoped it didn't matter.

'We're having a party at the end of the month. Would you like to come? All the old crowd. Bring the dog with you.'

The dog!

Three weeks to go. Other people always seem so happy. Loneliness and unhappiness bring out their sympathy, whether from her family, or from all their friends who knew nothing at all about her, the real Corinna. Even Dan seemed boisterously happy and Lisa, who had no idea of what she felt for Stevie, or for Eve, and didn't want to know. She redrafted her will garnering much pleasure from her own memento mori.

Lisa opened the door to a burst of Dan's voice upstairs over a sea of talk and laughter.

'The jet set,' said Lisa, 'or simply the young and jazzy.'

Light-hearted banter was exchanged across the floor. Everyone was sitting cross-legged, smoking, or walking about with glasses and coffee cups. Sinatra was still on the gramophone.

'Lisa, tea please, it's my birthday!'

'I remembered.' Lisa bent over her where she sat on the floor, leaning against the wall.

'I've something for you.'

It was a copy of *Under Milk Wood*, and everyone sang, 'Happy birthday to you, Corinna, happy birthday to you!'

Lovely Lisa looked, quite adorable in the way she used her hands. She was immersed in the affair with Anton again, but he'd be back in Israel next week, according to Dan. Did Dan know what was going on?

They talked sex, Rosie and Jemima.

'It's not the size,' Jemima said. 'It's the way it's done!'

Uproarious laughter. This was better than the livid tales of Lisa's last party at The Lodge.

'Oh, Corinna,' said Rosie in her deep rough voice, and kissed her quickly full on the mouth.

Rosie reminded her of Billy Burke with a boy's voice, the silly billy of the stage, and made her light-hearted and light-headed.

'Would you be jealous?' Corinna asked Lisa.

'Like hell I would,' said Lisa, and kissed her and kept on kissing her because she was slightly drunk.

It was wonderful to be accepted for what she was – everyone knew what had happened. Years and years and then deserted! Everyone there showed affection to her as one of them, which meant every kind of association under the sun.

'I'm afraid for all that you'd take Stevie back at the drop of a hat,' said Lisa.

'I'm beginning to doubt it, Lisa.'

'What about that other girl?'

'She's got children.'

'I've got Sophie.'

Sipping vodka, she watched Lisa dancing with Anton through her fingertips, elbows on knees, and two guitars that seemed intent on tearing down the rafters until midnight.

She threw off the tight feeling round her eyes and grabbed a chance to dance with Lisa. She kissed her bare shoulder, and Lisa bit her arm under the cuff.

'Gorgeous jacket, but you should take it off, good as you look in it.'

Lisa glanced at Anton standing silent, remote and absorbed in himself, his dark hair falling forward like Byron in a love pursuit.

'May I?' asked Ralph, a small-time actor who became homosexual at twenty.

'Why?' Corinna asked, his profession arousing doubts.

'Don't know!' he shouted at her while they danced. 'But mind my banana!' there was a distinct slur in his mouth.

When she turned round, Lisa was dancing again with the sculptor, one arm round her waist, the other hand playing with her fingers, short strong fingers pressing hers.

Corinna was uncannily aware of being watched. It was Anton's wife, a painter, Lisa had said, with a shining name in London art circles. Her eyes lit on her with a smile, and she lowered them as if caught spying. That was because of the kiss on Lisa's shoulder. She felt one of the sophisticated elite, but her heart pounded only for Lisa and she tried to catch her eye, distracted by stirrings deep inside of Orlando.

She slept in the roof with Bill at her feet, under the rafters which spanned the sitting room and kitchen, the stale smell of cigarettes and drink swimming in the tiles overhead.

'Wake me at six, Dan, please. I must get back. The house may be burnt down and I haven't renewed the insurance!'

'I will. I don't want you too near my wife for too long.'

But he forgot.

Never did a weekend so revolutionise a life. But what was the good of loving Lisa again. She would never leave Dan, for all his doubtfully acquired money and the doubtful

244

prestige, much as Lisa might long for romance.

She had not been able to take her eyes off Lisa that night nor could she think of anything else during the long drive home the next.

'Thank God for you, Bill,' she said to the trees, and took him in to sleep with her on the divan.

Eve telephoned the next morning. It was all Corinna could do to concentrate on what Eve was saying. She could hardly collect herself from Lisa's dizzy heights. Eve, so good, so true, but unable to kiss at all. Oh, God, how Lisa could kiss.

'I've got a bit of a headache this morning,' Corinna grunted.

'I'll ring again. Take care of yourself, my love.'

She staggered into the kitchen, took out bread and eggs and bacon. She was starving. The kitchen was a mess, the table without space because of all the dirty china that should have been in the sink. She ate walking about the rooms. Dust was everywhere. Outside on the first border there were dead chrysanthemums, the hydrangeas were dying not of autumn but of thirst, in the drawing room the clothes horse was laden with washed underwear in the bay.

'Marvellous place for a party,' Lisa had said.

'Much more like a morgue,' she said, satisfied that it was beautiful indeed, if a bit of a shambles now and then.

One thing Corinna couldn't bear was pity. She told everyone she liked to be alone. What lies she had told Stevie years ago to save her from all this, the aloneness and the hurt.

She made a list of jobs to be done – borders to clear, plants to tie up, manure to find and digging to be done. She had a sneaking feeling, there in the border cutting dead flowers, that one day Stevie would come back to her. The sensitivity between them would never die. *Doch alles – was uns anruhrt, dich und mich – nimmt uns zusammen wie ein*

Bogenstrich.

Lisa was so poor a friend she forgot to come that day as she had promised. Lisa imagined parties in this room, here with every show of comfort, the eastern carpets, the books, Stevie's family's coat of arms on a windowpane, a French revolutionary's gun on the mantelshelf – all things she and Stevie had collected. And Eve with nothing, her home sparsely furnished, PEP on walls and ceilings, but her spirit flooding it with sunlight and children.

She came. Lisa came with Sophie, Jemima, Rosie and a Land Rover full of children, Dan was en route for Winchester to put down a waterproof cellar floor with his man on board. They brought a hamper full of chocolate cakes and ice cream for late autumn tea on the terrace.

Josephine from the Cumbrian wilds came to stay a weekend. She arrived at the same time as the others, looking for plots for short stories.

'She's no flirt,' said Jemima, sotto voce. 'Not like you, Corinna.'

Josephine was in love with a girl called Imogen, weighed down with immoral longings, as Stevie would say. Corinna remembered how she had taken Josephine to meet Imogen, a tall sweeping blonde, down from another sphere. One glance at her and Josephine had burst into tears. Imogen stared down Oxford Street, biting her lip either from sorrow or laughter, it could have been either, Josephine, tall and gaunt, like herself looked faintly ridiculous in tears.

'I could live with you here, Corinna,' Josephine said. 'We'd get along all right. I could sell up and share. Think about it.'

'I shall have to wait to see what happens with Stevie.'

'The woods,' the children were shrieking. 'Let's go up to the woods – please – please.'

Sophie's and all the other children's faces were shining in anticipation. Rosie and Jemima joined in, Jemima removing her earrings for the occasion.

Up the hill they went with the car bursting to capacity, and out again in the open space at the top.

Lisa whispered as they watched the party scramble out, 'See you afterwards.'

'Careful, children have ears.'

The children raced away with Bill following them. Lisa bent over to kiss her. Josephine was in the seat behind, her stiff presence embarrassing.

'Don't mind Josephine, do you?' Lisa asked.

'It only hurts,' said Josephine.

'I knew it – that's why you should have gone—'

Lisa had her own way of putting things right. She turned round in her seat and kissed Josephine lightly but full on the lips and Josephine fell for Lisa on the spot.

'I can see you two are ideally suited, lucky you,' Josephine said.

'What does she mean,' Lisa asked. 'And me a married woman.'

She looked pensive this afternoon, with shadows of no-sleep under her eyes and downcast lines by her enticing lips, probably due to Jemima's dropping the name Anton.

'That's all over,' Lisa said, unexpectedly softening and rallying herself to tease. 'Rosie's in love with you, Corie.'

'Don't talk such rot!'

Jemima was a sport, but her sex life had a terrifying air about it and Rosie was her closest friend. The thought of being approached by either of them was hideous. Jemima was on her way back, having given up pursuing the children.

'In any case,' said Lisa, 'I told her you have a lover already.'

'Dan's suspicious,' Jemima announced gravely. 'Anyone can see you two are at it. You'll pay the price if you don't take care.'

Jemima deep down was an angel in disguise, even if she did whip men's clothes off their backs.

They had gone, Lisa with only a brief backward glance as Dan took the Land Rover round the corner in the lane, all the children singing until the car disappeared and took the singing with it.

Corinna waited for Josephine to go, followed her about talking, already longing to be alone.

'You're like me in so many ways,' Josephine said. 'I can see myself in you.'

It was a bitter sort of compliment and beyond an answer.

Corinna thought it was rather bad luck that the only lesbian she really knew was so boring, a good sort but no fun. In some ways, Josephine nearly drove her mad, taking the best of the food, eating too much and getting indigestion. The care she took of herself in the rain, or cold, and against infection of the remotest kind was amazing, a lesson in what not to be, save for that gift with her pen.

It did seem that the girl was getting the flu. It put Corinna in a panic in case she really did get it and had to stay. Patiently and politely, she urged her to catch the next train, remembering that once, long ago, Josephine had put her arm round her in the car and told her she loved her. That left an obligation.

With Josephine safely on board the train, calmness fell on Corinna. She sat at her desk in the corner of the drawing room, Bill on the fire rug. There was no time for loneliness. It was the first of the month. She had rents to collect and tenants to see. Never did a business get so neglected as this one.

When the bell rang it would be Miss Maclean, with that debonair attribute and Roedean voice.

'Ah, the old trusted,' she would say, touching Bill softly.

'How did it go today?'

'Still arguing – but we shall win – but we're fighting to

get a Chair for Nurses at Oxford.'

Next would come Erica, a Hungarian escapee.

'I haf a job in zee haus mit zee spitze top.'

Erica, in her effort to erase the past, scrubbed the paint off her room until she reached bare wood and washed that with strong bleach. And Julie, still carrying the sorrows of the war as a prisoner in Japanese camp, was forever knitting socks, scarves and berets for her newly found family. Celia in number eleven was about to take over a boarding school for delinquent girls, and dear old Miss Thorn, proudly boasted a nightly bottle of whisky – corsetière, not above making a corset for the dog next door after his operation.

Overall, they were a happy lot, but some wore sorrow on their sleeves, others Shakespearean tragedy in their eyes. Erica employed her dramatic gestures to support her incomprehensible English – 'I boi a bitsi chicken – zee brest – ça' – and made great swoops to describe chicken breast by laying her hand on her own.

Yes. For some it should indeed be zilch in the brave new world to come. Stevie, now hard up and eager for financial help, took the rent books from people leaving and tore out the spare pages for shopping lists. A truly capitalist enterprise.

How could it be otherwise? Socialism had been abandoned – communal living rejected. Even in the garden, tiny groups separated and were not to be intruded upon. Some were under the orchard trees, others in corners of the grass – even Bill was kept in, while Biffa was left on the shed roof. Not one was it possible to ask down for coffee.

Strange how she felt lonely in a house full of women, all up there in little rooms, on their own. That was their choice, to be independent, not caring for mother into her old age, not living for the highlights of the big city, all twelve here in a great stone house on the edge of a small country town, with that dicey wooden staircase.

Loneliness, that aloneness in the midst of people who were just as lonely. Loneliness because of the secret self, longing to speak to the softness of a woman's heart, but prevented by fear of an unacceptable gesture, an unacceptable glance.

A soft wet breath blew on her hand on the table edge, backed by two great dark brown eyes brimming with appeal. She remembered Chekhov's cab driver talking to his horse, and opened her heart to Bill, sipping tea, giving him snippets of biscuit, and watching the dusk follow the sun as darkness came.

The first week of the month she saw Stevie, meeting her outside her office under the street lamp. Bill was in the back of the car looking down the road resolute and loyal, his little heart banging no doubt with love for them both.

'I do love David,' Stevie said. 'But I still love you, Corie. He's jealous of you, unbearably.'

Stevie was pale, a livid light in her skin. She couldn't sleep, she said, thinking she was with her still.

'No, he will never understand.'

She watched Stevie's face, its dark and pale outline in the lamplight, and turned her eyes away to look down the long black road studded with lights. Sick she felt, the strangeness of their new relationship still hurting and helpless where she was once the one to care for Stevie.

'I'm terribly unhappy. I knew I'd be sorry. Well, I am. But it had to be, because I had never known such love.'

Stevie looked down at her hands soft in her lap, holding them as she always did, in soft appeal.

Corinna kept her hands on the steering wheel.

'I can't do anything, I can't help, Stevie. I couldn't have you home, not yet. Something inside me has died. It's my pride perhaps. I can't.'

'You'll get over it, Corie. I never will. But I do feel, one day—'

'Isn't it strange, Stevie, that two people of one sex can love more than a man and a woman?'

'But it's true,' Stevie said. 'And nothing can break it.'

She thought of Lisa, that if she would come to her she would make her happy. Of Stevie she was afraid. Afraid that she would open her arms to Stevie, and Stevie would bring him in.

'Let's sort out the rents, Stevie, then I must go. I have to sort out the fire insurance.'

The money, she found, was a great simplifier – it was unemotional. Immersed in the house's books, she found hours of peace. The sheer simplicity of minor accountancy cooled her blood and soothed her mind.

'I make my own fate, Stevie. It's not all your fault, angel. I can say that at last.'

For which Stevie pressed her hand, tears falling.

'When I was with you, I was boss. I'm no longer master of my fate – as you may be – and I hope you are for all the time to come. It's a nice feeling.'

'Goodnight, Stevie.'

She drove home, letting Stevie go and thinking of Lisa. If Lisa came.

Lisa telephoned. She had seen her solicitor, a friend of Dan's. He thought Dan would fight for Sophie. That would be his revenge, knowing Dan.

'Corie, I'm afraid.'

'You wouldn't feel afraid if you met people you know. They're all with you, Lisa. Let's have a gathering at The Lodge, a sort of party, to talk about it all. Get Dan to see sense, perhaps.' In fact an act of bravado to throw off doubts and fears.

The rooms were full of people who hardly knew each other, but all knew Lisa, laughed and sang together, drinking, eating the endless supply of refreshments passing out of the kitchen. Talking, talking, and walking about eating. They forgot entirely they were supposed to be discussing Dan and all that. Dan was telling jokes, as usual, as if nothing was happening.

She had felt sick for Dan, but when in the flat she had seen Lisa secretly packing she had seen her relief to be leaving. It revealed Dan's true nature, helped her to brave whatever was coming.

'I'm leaving him, Corie,' Lisa said at the gate. 'No more dithering.'

She followed Dan out, leaving Corinna in a world of promise, treading through bright bronze leaves of autumn to watch the Land Rover like a little bus vanish down the lane.

Would it come true? Like a dream coming true after years of sleep. And if it did, would it be as beautiful as the dream?

Yes.

Long into the next day, she brooded about the rooms tidying up, tormented by thoughts of Lisa. At three o'clock, Dan phoned.

'Is Lisa there? That's all I want to know.'

Someone had spoken out, Ralph, she guessed, that actor-cum-homosexual, the little boy next door reported as calling out, 'Why are they filling up that van next door, Mummy?'

'No,' she said. 'She isn't here, I swear.'

At least she could do that. Lisa was by now at Jemima's, a ruse, Corinna guessed, to delay Dan until Sophie and she could escape. It sounded like Anna Karenina. She could imagine Dan dejected, furrowed, grey and crumpled, as he was a day or two ago. Now rage was adding to his misery.

'Don't worry over Dan,' Jemima had said. 'He has women everywhere – even in Cairo.'

'My God,' Corinna had said to Lisa. 'I hope you never do this to me!'

'I can do it because I feel nothing for him after all these years, that's enough.'

'If I lose Sophie, I shall have you,' Lisa had said, her mouth weakening.

'I shall take care of Sophie too, I promise.'

She was relieved that she had made that promise. It gave her extra strength, as if she were defending the child from an evil fate.

'We will win,' she said. 'You shall win, and I will be with you.'

Outside the little church in Paddington they had made their vow. Lisa promised her and she promised Lisa no one else, not to touch or kiss while they had each other.

'That's our marriage vow,' Lisa said. 'Don't forget it.'

Sealed with a kiss it was and with the diamond ring her mother had left her placed on Lisa's finger.

'But you're an atheist and I'm an agnostic!'

'Oh, it's the spirit that counts,' said Lisa. 'You're just terrific, Corie,' she whispered, kissing her out of her mind.

Lisa was proud of her, proud to walk in public places filled with a thousand eyes. She was never in slacks, and now outside the little church she wore a beautiful dress, and a gaily-coloured scarf. Lisa was not like Stevie, who never could make her feel free in company, and hid their relationship possessively, ashamed perhaps.

She shut Bill in the kitchen and was standing glancing round the hall, the car keys in her hand, when the main doorbell rang, and the telephone.

She opened the door and Lisa walked in, walked to the telephone and took off the receiver.

'Hallo. No, Corie's taken the dog for a walk. Yes. I'll tell her.'

She turned, putting down the receiver.

'Someone called Eve,' she said.

'How could you! I must talk to her!'

Lisa ignored that.

'I've just left Sophie in a new school on the other side of London, weekly boarding to keep her safe from Dan. Jemima brought me down and is waiting outside.'

Lisa took off her gloves and her loose beige coat, and came towards her with hands outstretched while she stood rooted, seeing that lovely face distorted with tears, conscious only that something important was happening before her eyes.

Lisa stopped coming forward, choking with exasperation.

'Don't just stand there, Corie! Do something!'

One step towards her, and Lisa was in her arms.

Chapter Nineteen

'The home is yours,' Stevie had said. 'And the car.'

Because she felt guilty, her old voice was coming back. What would she say now?

The home had changed subtly and refreshingly. She bore down on a momentary flare of anger that this home bought by Stevie and her had been vandalised. She saw it now as it was completed, and looked again.

Regency had come creeping in, bringing elegance and lightness, the rich but somewhat fussy and sombre Victorian velvet curtains replaced by the red regency stripe running from ceiling to floor, and cushion covers in the same cream and red and gold brocade. The old oak furniture – with relief she recognised it – was still in possession on the eastern carpets.

'When did you—?'

'Piece by piece,' said Lisa with satisfaction. 'D'you like it? I made it mine, yours and mine. I used up all the money I had.'

'It's quite beautiful. How can you let anyone touch it.'

And here they were.

All Lisa's friends had this peculiar way of settling into a room tilting the antique chairs back and sitting cross-legged on the floor watching columns of cigarette smoke rise and fade round the chandeliers. While the log fire shed ash, they talked – talked against Bing Crosby and Judy Garland. They talked about Dan, who was not there to defend himself.

'He's only after the child to spite Lisa,' Ralph said sober at last and quite sane, tapping his cigarette vaguely behind him towards the fire as all real Hamlets do. 'Not that he wants young Sophie. And,' he emphasised, 'the case is against Lisa as a lesbian not suitable to have a child. That's not on.'

Corinna walked slowly past spreadeagled feet and hands on the floor and sat near Lisa in the arch where Jemima held another court.

'Dan says he's lost before it begins if Corie wants Lisa. Corie's far stronger than he is, he says.'

Jemima tilted her gold earrings with a flourish of a long white well-ringed hand.

'Lisa's searching for something, he says, something she's found in Corie there. Hear that, Lisa?'

Corinna had been searching, she remembered, for Stevie, but part of her had also searched for Lisa. To Lisa she now gave her loyalty because she had come.

Eve telephoned.

Lisa, walking past the instrument, lifted it out of Corinna's hand, and put it back on the shelf saying, 'The girl's in tears, said she was just about to leave Jack. I don't think she will now.'

'Poor bugger,' someone said.

Lisa kissed her cheek and left her there staring at the telephone, trying to send telepathic sympathy to Eve, helpless with shame.

The next time the telephone rang, it was Dan. Corinna answered it herself.

'No, Dan. We're not having an affair.'

She put down the receiver stunned with disbelief that she could be so calm and cruel.

'I'll take that in,' said Rosie, putting out a hand in a cloud of smoke and looking boldly up at her before watching her cut the cake. 'I like the way you do things, Corie. Are you sure you love Lisa?'

'Yes. Quite sure.'

'But I like you,' she said with a big sigh. 'I have since I

met you at Lisa's!'

Rosie came closer, lifting her breasts and touching her arm.

'Kiss me Corie.'

'And tell Lisa if I did? I like you Rosie but,' she gave Rosie a light peck on her cheek, 'I belong to Lisa.'

'Good.'

Rosie stepped back, apparently satisfied.

'Don't get involved with me. I don't want to get hurt again. I've only just got over Harry.'

A girl who could love men and women, both. And in-between.

She watched Rosie go, carrying the plate of sliced fruit-cake down the passage. She belonged to Lisa, but still Stevie was the love of her life. She would never know another love like that. It hurt like a wound in the flesh which only time could heal.

And yes, she loved Lisa. She passed her now sitting on the floor. Lisa put out a hand to her as she passed, drawing her down making her heart race. How could she have lived all these years with Lisa in the world outside?

'Stay here with me,' Lisa whispered, tracing with her finger a line on the carpet. 'You might find a fantastic girl, not just me – but your difficulty is that I can't think of one who would do.'

She narrowed her eyes peering through the room of slightly tipsy faces.

'So long as you want me, I shall want you, Lisa,' Corinna assured her, kissing her swiftly.

Dull it was after last week at Ralph's when Lisa danced with that young Arabic actor wearing a black and white shirt over tight black trousers, red socks and black shoes. She was all of boy, all of woman, of child, of mistress. They sat sitting close on the long drive home through the long tunnel of trees, Surrey, Hampshire, over the downs, safely into the dark little shell that shielded them from the world, and Dan.

'I love you,' Lisa whispered, breaking into the reverie, 'Why do you sit there writing it down in your head?'

'Because this is supposed to be a serious meeting to prepare for the fight with Dan. No one seems to remember that. I've got to get Stevie on my side, Lisa. That's important. And I have to see her about the money.'

'Well,' Lisa said grudgingly at last when the flat was theirs again. 'You'd better go to see her. I needn't.'

The bungalow stood in a line of bungalows on a small estate by the river. Stevie, who loved old houses like The Lodge, turned up her nose with a cockeyed smile, and picked up the envelope on the polished table.

'Don't dash off again, Corie. Stay and talk to me, please.'

'First of all – Lisa – she sent me to tell you that Dan's suing for Sophie.'

'I know, Dan telephoned me. He told me she had gone to you.'

Pale she looked, ethereal.

'You're free to do as you wish, Corie.'

At last, at last, here was Stevie saying she would never be happy again without her, saying she had never fought for Corie's love. It had just come and she had failed to value it, only now seeing how truly they had fulfilled all of life that mattered together.

'I know, Stevie. I know it all, and I found Lisa.'

She sat with Stevie in the quiet of the afternoon, without tense emotion, it was more a deep suppurating wound.

'I'm so terribly lonely,' Stevie said. 'Even when he's at home.'

'We're sure to be lonely for each other after so long.'

She was conscious immediately of not wanting to get involved in that emotion.

'Lisa is lovely,' Corinna said. 'I can't hurt her now.'

She deliberately looked out of the bungalow window at the newly cut lawn, cut by David.

'Yes,' Stevie said. 'It must be a joy just to see her about the place.'

She looked at Stevie sitting there, dejected, just across the room, and she was unable to speak, a thousand dreams rushed into her head, tugging at her heart.

'I still love you,' she said, trembling, and all the love she had ever had welled up in her.

'But I would come back to you,' Stevie said. 'Freely.'

She meant it. Her voice choked, tears were not far off.

'But I can't lose Lisa now. Besides, she needs me.'

'And you want her to be there.'

She kissed Stevie's hand where it rested on the open window of the car, drew her down and kissed her cheek softly.

'It isn't sex,' she said. 'It's nothing to do with sex, but I shall never love anyone as I loved you, Stevie.'

Stevie's eyes fell on the ring Lisa had given her outside the little church.

She looked at Stevie with her old self stirring deep in her, as Stevie said they belonged to each other still. But she thought of Lisa, knowing that so long as Lisa wanted her she would want Lisa, a different kind of love.

'Stevie's so sad, Lisa. I wonder if she's ill.'

There was heaviness in her voice, but Lisa made no answer with deliberate unconcern.

Lisa. Loving Lisa, she went as man to woman, dominant, free yet enslaved. She touched Lisa and her hands were quick as fire, every nerve leapt between them. Life was driven by fear of losing her. Adoring Lisa.

Lisa stood in front of her and said fiercely, 'Rosie had someone take a snap of you talking to her, flirting. Idiot you are! In court it could sound dramatic. Dan's suing for Sophie was only to be expected, you don't know him. He's charming to everyone, but vindictive. He can't wait to get his own back, as Ralph said. We need help – better ask Stevie and David to tea.'

'Permission granted, that's what I like,' said Stevie on the telephone, a buoyancy in her voice that had long been missing.

It was amazing that Stevie said nothing about the new décor in the drawing room. She sat in silence waiting for the disturbance she made in the air to settle down, thinking. Nothing was lost on Stevie.

'Of course I shall help, of course.'

Over tea Stevie said she would go into the box and swear that in the years they had lived together, there had been no sign of Corie being a lesbian. She casted a swift glance at David and away. She added, her eyes on Corinna, 'I can be strong only about you, Corie.'

David sat immobile, tapping his polished shoe in the air. Daringly Corinna spoke to him.

'I had visions of myself on the front page, as Dan said, you know, the front page of every national paper in the country, as you said. You and Dan must read the same newspapers.'

Stevie frowned. David remained mute. Such daring was not *comme il faut*. Then he laughed in his begrudging way.

'I'm not committing myself at this stage,' he said, dry and clear. 'It could take another six months to come to court.'

She caught Stevie in the hall on the way out, saying a simple thank you, realising immediately that it put Stevie right with David.

Six months left plenty of time to prepare, and Sophie's Christmas holidays starting that weekend brought Sophie home, inevitably with friends.

They were growing up, Sophie and her friends, but still there would be tantrums, shouting fits, scenes of teenage young ladies one minute and hooligans the next.

'To think,' said Sophie loftily, 'that I used to want to marry you. I didn't know I couldn't, because you're not a man!'

She strutted off, the provocative femme fatale of time to come.

In the morning Sophie, her uninhibited self again, wandered after her through the garden, notebook in hand, and round the house, stopping to do a twist and turn on the terrace, exuding intelligence.

'Corie, did you have this entire house, always? Do all these people pay money?'

She didn't wait for answers, as her brain was teeming with questions.

'Why doesn't Mummy pay?'

She smiled as if she knew the answer to that one.

'Why don't I have to pay?'

'Because I like you and Mummy living with me.'

Sophie was a pest. Sophie was a joy, which she refused to see because she was encroaching on Dan's share of a child's love, a domain not her own. But she wanted it to be so, the fear that held her back, the fear of loving and losing, exorcised. Her only justification was the knowledge that Dan was not to be trusted with his own child.

On the last night, Sophie wandered about the study, probably to see if it was allowed.

'Who did that drawing?' she asked, sliding up to the desk.

'A friend of Mr Cartwright's, a surveyor.'

'What is it?'

'A new studio for Mummy.'

'A funny studio – it has a clothesline right through it.'

'Well, you'll be able to check it next time you're home, it'll probably be finished by then.'

A telling sigh escaped. Sophie was not pleased.

'I want to leave school, I hate it. Miss Beal's always hitting us.'

'Mummy'll speak to her about it when you go back tomorrow. You've got to work harder this term, remember.'

'Work!'

The little face collapsed, the child choked, screamed.

'I only said work – schoolwork, reading, things like that.'

'You're so silly, Corie,' Lisa said coming to the rescue. 'Talking to a child like that!'

The hysterics ceased and the child was asleep. Christmas was over.

Days there were when Lisa became the dark woman, straight out of the book, raging, slamming doors, beating carpets and banishing Bill into the garden. They were whirling days of chaos. Spring was coming and this was apparently spring-cleaning. Stevie never did that. Mrs Cartwright would be pleased.

She found Lisa on the telephone speaking to Stevie, asking what to do with Corie who was driving her crazy, accusing her of an endless list of acts of mental cruelty.

'Imagine! – Asking help from Stevie!'

Taking the receiver, she listened to Stevie advising her – in all good conscience – to be nice to Lisa.

'Dammit, Corie, she came to you. You'll have to take care of her. You're older than she is anyway.'

She listened for the tongue in cheek, but it wasn't there.

With Sophie at school, and all her mates with her, the house gradually resumed some order. Sophie's room was tidied and decorated ready for the next holiday.

'You've been doing too much, Lisa.'

'I love Sophie, Corie, but I love to be alone with you.'

They walked through the gardens, across the terraces where with secateurs and shears Corinna practised topiary on the hundred-year-old privet box hedge, strode through the orchard hand in hand where the apple blossom flowered, and stood by the pond watching the fish under the reeds.

'We could do with a dash to the sea and back.'

It needed no more than that.

The sea rushed through the pebbles. Bill was asleep in a hollow by the breakwater, lying with Lisa shielded from the wind, open to the sun and the sky.

'I look at you sometimes, Corie, and feel I can't have enough of you. It's too much, too big to bear.'

Her tone rose.

'And don't lie there thinking of a thousand other things – look at me.'

Laughter ran through Corinna like a shout of joy. She rolled off her back on to her elbow, laughing outright.

'What are you thinking?' Lisa asked.

'I can't tease you. I was thinking I wish I could go back in my life – with you. It isn't being forty that makes us look back. I did that when I was twenty-five. I felt then, if only I were young. You've made me young again.'

A letter from Dan's solicitor waited for Lisa on their return officially announcing that Dan was suing for Sophie, the time and place and orders to be there were below.

'Better get Mr Black. He's the best, and you can see him easily as often as necessary.'

Corinna be bold – have courage enough and to spare. She held Lisa close to her in the big bed in the moonlight, the windows open, the late evening birds calling, and a light breeze of spring soughing round the great stone house. Lisa shivered in fear of losing her child.

Chapter Twenty

Dan's shouting woke her – 'Lisa was corrupted by her lesbian lover!'

The rising sun in golden blades cut across the ceiling.

'What have I done to know such highs and lows, Lisa, as I have with you? It sings in my blood, as Lawrence would say.'

'I was thinking,' Lisa's voice came, softly strained. 'Whatever Dan says in court, remember, won't you, remember that I love you.'

Secret lovers haunting it must be.

'Worse than that, Lisa. D'you realise there's only one way if I go into the box – I have to deny myself.'

It hit her like an electric shock.

'I can't do that, Lisa.'

'You'll have to, Corie. It'll depend altogether on that.'

'No – I can't do it.'

Her whole self revolted against it, standing up in the box and denying her true self. The idea set something in her on fire – why should she do that to support a child she didn't even want!

And Dan would reveal all Lisa's past, her affair with Anton, with the others.

'Why did you, Lisa?'

'I didn't have you then.'

'I shall always feel sick at the thought of you with Anton especially, because I know him.'

Jealousy would always be half her love for Lisa. Day and night it raged in the house, over and over, sometimes with reason, often with none.

Fear of losing Lisa plagued her. Lisa had only to put out her hand and she was crazy with desire, painfully conscious that she could never be truly sure of Lisa, save in that moment that is lost as it comes.

In the square, high-windowed bedroom, where Lisa had insisted on a navy blue ceiling, she put her arms round Lisa and saw her hands on Lisa's back in the wardrobe mirror.

'You're all male, Corie,' Lisa said, and she knew in that instant precisely that had happened before. 'I've never loved like this,' Lisa said. 'I've never been deeply, truly happy – until now. No one can take that away.'

Oh God, let it be like this for ever, her hands on Lisa's shoulders, possessing her, shutting out other loves, other lovers.

She and Lisa walked over the fields in the winter sun, the broom red in the bushes, the valley full of winter smoke and the wood burning. Lisa's shoes filled with gravel bits lifting plates of chalk at every step.

They walked frantic with worry – over headlines, Rosie's evidence, reports from every corner – and tried to toss it all aside, laughing and walking hand in hand searching the ice-blue sky for flying geese – and finding a handful of crows homeward flying.

In the dark came Sophie's face – a dark Jewish beauty, starlit – and Sophie's voice that through the years gathered her mother's rich tones.

'Who do I belong to, Mummy?'

'To me, you belong to me,' Lisa said.

'And to Corie – to Corie as well!'

In the dark, too, came the guilt of stealing Dan's fatherhood.

Corinna looked into Lisa's eyes and saw all the mature woman loving her. No one in the world outside knew Lisa belonged to her, thinking in the way of the world that Lisa was free for romance. That was the cost, the danger, of homosexual love. It was isolated, cut off from men who resented it, and cut off from women who found homosexual friendship too close to love.

'Why did Lisa leave her husband?' Amanda asked.

Corinna started, 'Because she's in love with me—' No. That could not be said. She shrugged, said she didn't know. All this court case was quite beyond her family's comprehension.

All that had happened was that Stevie had broken her heart, and Lisa had put life back into it. She put out her hands and Lisa came to fulfil, to break the sadness in her, bringing promise of sun and laughter.

'Six weeks to go,' said Lisa, and although the day ended in love, everyday there was quarrelling from morning to night. Over nothing, or the money of which there was never enough, over Stevie, over Sophie, over where the lettuces should go, how to cut the grass edges, over her sulks, over Lisa's superiority.

'Kosher cooking! Where did you learn that? Not from Dan, he didn't like it.'

Head high, scorn in her spine, Lisa walked out and round the entire house and back with no shoes on. Hearing Lisa return, she went into the kitchen to find her sitting at the table, an old newspaper propped up against the coffee pot upside down. She left her like that, laughing and noisily striding off down the passage to her desk, looking back to see Bill in the hall, put out to grass, bewildered, and the kitchen door barricaded.

'I'll make an end of it,' Lisa shouted, passion raging high, struggling in her arms, and dropping the aspirin bottle, sobbing.

'What is it? Do you want Sophie home?'

'No, I just want you – you, just as you used to be!'

'Lisa—'

She was holding her tight, feeling the sobs die away.

'I love you angel. I'd go mad if I lost you.'

'Then you'll have to tell lies – for me.'

'Of course I will, if you'll let me have Stevie to help, not my family who know nothing!'

'It's the way she looks at you I can't stand, but you'll have to see her, yes.'

After that, the atmosphere seemed calmer, and warm sun flooded the house and garden. There was little to laugh at, but there was new resolve.

How could Lisa love her? She was full of tension and irritability, tired, tired, tired, full of resentment and jealousy, aching for love. But the die was cast and she would be called as the chief witness to tell lies.

It took Stevie an hour to talk her into a better mood over Sophie. There were no personal emotions, later would do for that. For now, the idea of being put into the witness box dominated every thought.

That and the fact that Stevie was going into hospital for a major operation. The doctors admitted the pills had been an error. They changed a woman's personality and ruined many lives. At the depths, Stevie said, she had seriously contemplated suicide.

'But I'll make the best of it, don't worry. You have only one task – to defend Lisa, I can see that. You know what you have to do. You have to deny all you are, all about us, all about you and Lisa. Deny it.'

She spoke with a certain satisfaction, perhaps, that since she could not have Corie in this scenario, neither could anyone else.

'I shall do it – for Lisa,' Corinna said.

As she drove away, it was the black morbidity over Stevie that seized her mind, tossed it and turned it in fear.

'Stevie's ill,' she burst out to Lisa. 'We'll have to be friends with her. We must. Not just for the court case. Although she says she'll speak for the years with me.'

Lisa shuddered visibly. She looked fifty years older at once.

'It's for Sophie, Lisa. For Sophie and for you.'

And it opened a small gate to Stevie, gave her freedom to see her with a clear conscience.

Stevie looked at her over the tea and the papers on the table.

'There's no one like you,' she said, tapping cigarette ash into her saucer. 'Just no one. You look like one of those crazy scientists at work. They wear their hair falling over their eyes too.'

Stevie still loved her, thank God, as she loved Stevie still, and now she was glad, glad to have loved Stevie all those years. It hadn't changed. It was only that now Lisa was with her and she could never let Lisa go. She could be straight with Stevie – and with Lisa. Love has to forgive, even if it cannot forget. If Stevie needed help, she had to give it, just as she needed Stevie's help to defend Lisa.

When she arrived back at The Lodge, the conservatory lights were on and the upper garden was flooded with light.

She walked up the garden in warm damp air through the conservatory, calling 'Lisa!' Bill and Biffa came to greet her through the drawing-room door. She stood still in the vast empty room, listening to the silence, holding her breath in fear, in love, in doubt.

'I'm paying for what I did to you,' Stevie had said. 'When I've paid enough, it'll be all right again. If you can't have me, I'll have to be nicer to David or I'll have no home at all.'

That made her feel lighter – it meant Stevie would survive, it meant she was committed to David. The burden Stevie had placed on her was lifted.

If Lisa could see all this, she would never feel Stevie as a threat, as David had suddenly realised. He would no longer try to keep them from each other, he said he even agreed that Stevie could go to court to defend Corinna's character.

Lisa was so jealous that it was one long fight just to get her to allow Stevie's presence.

'Five days to go, Corie.'

'Everyday we'll go somewhere, like a holiday.'

Brighton it could be, or the long shores of Hastings. But it was all talk. There was no escape. The desire to drive away and forget grew less as the days passed and time demanded action, the gathering of support, and planning practicalities like transport and food on the day.

If she and Dan had been able to talk, if some of Stevie's wisdom could have come through, there would never have been the coldness that had crept in. Solicitors letters built impenetrable and unrecognisable stone walls topped by broken glass and barbed wire between them all.

Dan came, putting his foot in the door yelling for Sophie, for Lisa, for that swine Corie! He tore through the door and straight up to Lisa and hit her across the face, as she stood stiff as a soldier in front of Corinna to defend her from the assault.

In a flash, fists were everywhere. Dan's hand was round Corinna's neck, choking her. She shot out a fist and struck him, her knuckles turning red and swelling on the spot. She felt nothing and drove him back through the door.

'I'll get you – I'll sue you…' he was shouting down the path. 'You filthy depraved bugger! I will sue you for alienation, for taking my wife and child.'

He would have done that in all probability, but he had a severe black eye, and his solicitor refused to take up the case as so denigrating to manhood.

They feared more violence from Dan, or from an underling he might send to break in to find letters, diaries, anything to incriminate either of them, and this raised the tension and tempers.

'Don't let him in again, or anyone else,' Lisa ordered, pleaded, and demanded, terrifying everyone who heard with tales of Dan's ways of dealing with his enemies.

It roused all the male in Corinna, that newborn defender of women and little children, her fist bandaged, and she laughed at a glimpse in the town of Dan's black eye. She walked round the house, round the garden, watching the trees and bushes bend in the wind, waiting for a knife in her back, or a bullet. If he killed her, it would be said that she had deserved it.

Lisa came up to her in the hall, silently, questioningly, all their nerves strung high, the meal burning on the stove.

She caught Lisa in her arms and held her, laughing, kissing her, teasing.

'There's no one anywhere! You're even making Bill frightened.'

'All I really want is to keep Sophie from him,' Lisa said, collapsing exhausted on a chair at the kitchen table, the eternal female protecting her young.

'She's safe at your mother's. All we have to do is be there tomorrow at nine even if we've had no sleep for a week.'

The thing that angered her most, as she rested her eyes on the shadows made by the great sash windows behind the curtains, was herself in the dock. She was on trial, accused as the chief witness for Lisa being unfit to live with a child.

That was the QC's job, Mr Black said, to denigrate the character of the witnesses. Accused of being a lesbian, in itself an act of crime, and of corrupting the young Sophie, infuriated her.

No, Lisa could not, she would not talk to Dan. He shouted, and that made them laugh. How cruel they were – in truth, how frightened.

Under the old oak beams of its roof, the town hall clock said nine. A uniformed official, still half-asleep, opened the doors. The parquet floors echoed under their feet. Lisa had gone, Corinna made for the last seat in the row, waiting.

There was no talking, but the room was filling up with

people, friends of hers, friends of Lisa's, drifting in unbuttoning coats and peeling off gloves. Stevie and David sat by her, Stevie trying to fade out of the scene, strained and alert.

They smiled at Corinna, mouthing inaudibly. Margery was stuffing her gloves into her large pockets, her rosy cheeks puffed with hurrying, there was no sign of the wine and music and cake in the back room of her village store. Charles, bending towards her, was working on a new government committee, he whispered, on agriculture of all things – he was always standing for Labour in one constituency or another. Godfrey, her old colleague in the political office of the union journal, was still in touch with her old chief.

Lisa's friends sat separately, really because they wanted to whisper among themselves, too – there was the doubtful Ralph, subpoenaed by Dan and resenting it, homosexual and suddenly finding himself years later inexplicably falling in love, he said, with Lisa, and over-acting even here in the waiting room, to make sure no one would take him seriously. He was doing his best, it seemed to Corinna, to denigrate any testimony he might give.

Lisa's doctor, subpoenaed by Dan, like Ralph was furious at being called, and requested to be called as soon as possible as he had to get back to town. Lisa had told him she was in love with a male actor, a homosexual.

'Follow your heart,' he had said.

But she had also told him she had a lesbian friend. Obliged in all honour to defend Lisa he kept his eyes away from her now and studied the floor under his feet.

Corinna felt overwhelmed with emotion at their coming, all of them here to defend Lisa's character, and incidentally hers, either because they saw them both as something different from what they were, or because they felt superior to making such a judgement. She liked to think it was the latter.

Lisa alone saw the case inside the court, saw the witnesses come and go, and left them to tell each other outside what had been said – that Nell, Sophie's one-time nanny, had gripped the court in her forthright Scottish accent with her defence of Lisa. Godfrey had made the court laugh with his description of Corie as an attractive young woman who came to his house and he, a perfectly normal type, had tried it on because he liked her. Chuckling out of his massive black beard and with his beady spectacles, he made a most unlikely beau.

Later, she thought, *she must tell Lisa about that riot of an afternoon*. Godfrey, such a silly ass, unbuttoning his shirt, had been weak with laughter because he felt her awesome resistance.

When Ralph was called a note was passed from Mr Black to the magistrate, reporting that he had been heard boasting in the waiting room that he had been dancing with a young Indian the night before, the note destroyed his testimony on the spot.

He stood for one moment in the box with his hand at his breast, born actor that he was, his eyes closed in feigned indignation, then opened them to sweep his cloak round himself and stepped down.

She went into the box, she swept her eyes through the courtroom seeing nothing but faces white in pale daylight. The solicitor's clerk was holding up the Bible.

Words – her head full of unspeakable words. This is me I'm, not like you. I am of a different species. I reject your values and your judgement because you look at me with derision. What should I do? I am myself – should I be ashamed of being what your God made me?

'Take the Bible in your right hand,' the clerk said, 'and repeat after me.'

Yes – because she had to protect Lisa now, this was the

moment. She took the Bible in her hand.

'I swear to tell the truth, the whole truth and nothing but the truth – so help me God.'

She put the Bible down and waited for fate, determined as she was to tell what she had to as agreed with the solicitor by innuendoes, and with Stevie.

First, it was the child.

'The child, Sophie – tell the court how you feel about her.'

'I should take care of Sophie, with her mother.'

'And her education?'

Her solicitor, Mr Black, stood facing her.

'A Christian school?' he asked. 'Are we to understand you wish to bring her up as a Christian?'

Corinna looked at him intently.

'Yes – of course.'

That and where she slept, were the most important questions that could well be asked, he had warned her, introducing them himself.

How could she tell such lies. She stood astonished, thanking him with a glance for the talk with him a week before.

'Yes. I sleep on the divan in the drawing room.'

Sometimes I do.

'And Sophie? When she is at home?'

'Sophie has her own room in the front of the property.'

That at least was true.

Stevie may have been the greatest failure of her life but now she knew Stevie would fight for her like a tiger the second she entered the witness box for Lisa.

Stevie faced with Dan and the three learned lawyers in a battle of brains, emotions and sheer personality. Stevie enjoying it, shaking her dark hair loose away from her eyes and giving a subtle grin.

In the waiting room for much of the afternoon, Corinna

sat with Godfrey, taking turns to peep through the keyhole as the witnesses were disposed of.

'This is when you need your friends,' said Godfrey. 'I'd no idea it would be at such a level. That chap's a QC.'

Pretending all this behaviour was beneath him, David sat in a corner in the grip of a pained frown, Godfrey having defeated him on a legal point.

'I shall tell the truth,' David said. Fortunately, he was not called because any glimpse he might have had of the truth could be devastating.

She was waiting with Godfrey when the doors burst open and the reporters came flying out, voices calling.

'The wife to keep the child.'

She stood stunned into silence, trying to grasp what that meant and gripping someone's arm.

'The local press doesn't publish local domestic cases,' said Stevie.

Lisa came out, hot and tired, shining eyed and victorious, straight into her arms and all the hands came out to touch her. Surreptitiously, she kissed Lisa's ear.

Two of the best witnesses he had ever known, the QC told Mr Black. She and Stevie had won the case for Lisa.

'Good luck, and good acting, and sober lies,' she whispered to Lisa, holding her arm tight and leading her out into the fresh air.

'Certainly not the truth,' came Stevie's low mutter over her shoulder.

And yet, it seemed, nothing was very different. It depended on how one looked at life.

It was all back to The Lodge, to cheese rolls and mugs of beer, wine and coffee and fruitcake, prepared by the back room staff of relatives and friends not called to give evidence.

'The police got wind of that other business with Dan,' Stevie said, keeping well away from David. 'You needn't worry about losing Sophie now – that's something.'

Lisa was silent. She would never help to persecute Dan, whatever he did. Lisa had that sort of loyalty.

Dan had raced ahead of them and driven off in a frenzy. Later, he telephoned from London to say he was about – now – to shoot himself.

'Histrionics,' said Lisa. 'I'll get Harry to go round to see if he's all right. He'd miss himself in any case.'

Sophie home again with four weeks of the holidays to go, had an uncanny knack of talking about her father. What secrets were held in that pretty head?

'Do you think, Corie, that Daddy could come to live with us? Please would you let him, because I like it here. I don't like London. Please!'

'We'll think about it, Mummy and I.'

Without another word, Lisa knew.

'Ask Mrs Cartwright – she'll know if Dan's been prowling about.'

He had. The car had been seen, a Mercedes, in the lane with Sophie in the front seat with her father.

Lisa fretted through the night. Mr Black said nothing could be done to restrain Dan until Lisa had a court order, which put life back into turmoil.

'I shall kill him,' said Lisa, in tears. 'I'll never be free of him, Corie – never.'

Men have murdered for less, but it was ludicrous. Corinna laughed.

'You won't – I won't let you. He's her father. I'll talk to him. Or Mr Black'll do something.'

Two weeks after the court case, Lisa, unaided, coerced the police into escorting the car out of town for fear of Sophie's being kidnapped. Sophie was being taken to Amanda's out of Dan's way until he had quietened down.

Life had become exciting, almost theatrical, Corinna noticed, as life with Lisa was bound to be.

Chapter Twenty One

Corinna stood holding the letter, staring unseeing down the garden. It reminded her of letters Stevie had written to her before the court case – sad and painful. Across her vision came one clear memory, of Stevie long ago leaving her one day, waving goodbye, turning the motorcycle the wrong way round, making wild zigzags and she, Corinna, watching her, her own heart zigzagging with the bike, until it rose like a bird when Stevie took off. In her head came the words – the pity that lies in the heart of love.

And yet, she bore a vision of Lisa forever in her mind. A terrible pride she had that Lisa loved her, she was proud of her loveliness walking at her side, admired by masculine eyes and envied by pretty women for her loveliness.

She began to coax Lisa to break the silence with Stevie and ask Stevie and David to tea. Quite suddenly, Lisa did.

'Everyone's out upstairs,' Corinna said, tension spiralling in her. 'It's only a business meeting after all.'

'Business! I just don't trust her – never have and still don't!'

Lisa spat it out in her attempt to destroy the peace settlement before it began.

'Business means money – that's quite important to life.'

Corinna thrust her anger down, put her arms round Lisa and gently kissed her neck.

'Don't be so afraid. Stevie can't hurt you. I wouldn't let her. You don't have to be jealous – I swear.'

'I'm not jealous!'

Lisa snatched herself away.

'And they'll be here in one minute – Bill's sniffing round

the hall door. The bell!'

Stevie stood in the doorway of the great room, radiating satisfaction that it was all there as it had always been, in spite of Lisa. David turned his head away, vacantly staring into nothing, determined not to acquiesce.

Corinna closed the door behind her and walked after David to dive behind the table to sit facing the room, removing a pile of ledgers left scattered there after lunch to prepare the table for tea.

All this time, she mused, Stevie and David had stood about, getting out of her way and eventually sitting opposite her.

'Any new ideas,' she asked, eyes on Stevie.

There was a long moment of hesitation and David stood up as if to withdraw.

'Oh, please stay – let's all hear what you have to say.'

Her heart was banging with apprehension. All Stevie's hardness, that was what she wanted him to see, Stevie arguing on money. Personal relationships never come first with me, Stevie had always said.

David whispered to Stevie and pulled his chair back to the small wireless on top of the bookcase beside him.

'Just listen to the score,' he said, as if to show them all that what they did was of no significance to him. 'We went to a football match yesterday – Chelsea won.'

Corinna took this as a ruse to drag Stevie down to his own level.

'I've never known Stevie like any kind of sport, let alone football,' she said. 'Must've been boring for her.'

Daring she felt, and unafraid.

David half lifted himself out of his chair and shouted, 'Corie! If you don't mind!'

She shivered so much when he shouted that Lisa poured out a brandy and handed it to her to sip.

'It's only temper,' she muttered, taking it and fuming at

herself.

He was too pathetic for her to shout back, or even speak. Somehow she felt it wasn't altogether his fault he was so uncouth, he was showing off to Stevie.

'I finished with football when I was eighteen,' she said. 'I was sick to death of it at home.'

'Perhaps you should get immersed in it again,' said David icily. 'Stevie and I understand each other.'

'It's a funny thing, but that's how Stevie was with me, and she looked at me just as she's now looking at you.'

The smile vanished from David's face.

'I lived with Stevie for many years,' she said.

'I know,' he replied tersely.

Stevie ignored these preliminaries. She and David would like to raise money on their bungalow and on The Lodge, she said, or her half of it, to buy a Victorian house far bigger, but they could do that only if Corie would agree to an arrangement.

'I'm not interested in making money, Stevie, only in having enough to live on for Lisa and me, and Sophie, of course.'

The Victorian house could be bought on the deeds of The Lodge and the bungalow, the cost and profits could be shared between the two houses, with a stake for all of them, including Lisa and David. Stevie explained – no mortgage could be raised on it at that age.

'It can't fail,' said Stevie, tense with conviction, her eyes sharpened with ideas. David could see to all the legalities with Mr Black.

Corinna stood up to calm herself, saying, 'Let's get nearer to the fire. I'm sorry about that thumping upstairs – it's a new tenant having a party.'

'That's better,' said Stevie moving her own chair, sitting back and making great efforts to relax. 'I don't mind a gentle drumming in the background,' she said.

Now David's immaculate city suit could be seen, his legs crossed with his polished shoes pointing into the room. He looked like Pickwick – was it? – smiling benignly.

Refreshed, Stevie developed the details, that the total value of the whole would have to be put into the pool including the furniture of the flats, including those they lived in.

At this, Lisa sat bolt upright, her face red.

'I knew it! She wants to possess our home, all the furniture, *our* home.'

Lisa's face was pained with fear. She turned to Corie. 'You're going to let her do this! How can you? You're letting her interfere in our lives!'

Corinna sprang to her defence, but catching Stevie's eyes retreated.

'The Lodge is really Stevie's already,' she said, speaking quietly, trying to placate Lisa, who would not be placated.

'How can that be? We live here – there are laws—'

'It would be quite above board,' said Stevie. 'I have a rough draft here.'

Stevie walked across to Lisa holding out a sheet of paper, looking down at her with a grim smile.

'Don't get upset. Try to think it over – talk to Corie about it on your own. There's no hurry, except to decide on how to raise the money for the new property.'

'There's nothing to say! You've said it all in your letters!'

Lisa's voice rose to a new note, her eyes hard with hate. Corinna gripped the edge of her seat, the fury in Lisa turning on her.

'This is a trick and you can't see it! You sit there looking at her as if she's a god handing down the tablets – it's – it's ridiculous!'

A dark thin pole of manhood, David walked two steps to stand in front of Lisa.

'You must please be careful what you are saying to my

wife.'

No one answered him. Pompous beast. In sullen silence, Lisa stood looking at Corinna. Now she could see dark lines under Lisa's eyes as if she had not slept at all last night, and behind Lisa she could see Stevie's face wilting, wilting in pain under Lisa's attack.

'Did you really let her read my letters?' Stevie asked, her voice strained to breaking.

Corinna shook her head. She felt only half alive watching Lisa and Stevie, and confused because the idea was dangerously close to Stevie's idea that they should all live together, and she hadn't told Stevie how utterly impossible that would be. How Stevie could even think it meant she had never understood her nature. At least Lisa did that! And never would Stevie understand Lisa's indifference to money.

Stevie's face hardened. Obstinately, she pushed out her lower lip, her eyes as full of hate as Lisa's.

Lisa, apparently afraid of the gathering storm she had ignited, sat down silently, mechanically adjusting her wristwatch, moving to the window seat, shuddering under Stevie's gaze.

It was Stevie who broke the silence, sitting on her hands, the ethereal paleness of her features flushing with her apparent determination to keep cool, keep her eyes off Corie, and save the situation between her and David about the letters.

'I only came to talk business, that's all. Nothing to do with these personal matters, and Corie seems to have lost her tongue.'

'I know why you really came,' Lisa broke in. 'You know I understand about you and Corie, and you pretend to be innocent.'

'You seem to have read someone else's letters and failed to grasp what they said because you're so hysterical, carried away by your emotions.'

Stevie's voice trembled again, but she rallied visibly, determined to fight on. Stevie had none of the physical attraction that forgave Lisa all her transgressions, but Stevie twisted the heart.

'And you are trying to show me,' Lisa went on with surprising stubbornness, 'that this is your house, yours and Corie's, and nothing to do with me. You came here to make a quarrel.'

'Stupid child!'

Waving her hands violently, Stevie seethed with exasperation.

'If you twist everything I say, that makes all this impossible. I didn't come to talk about anything else but business, certainly not with David here.'

She put her hand on David's knee and patted it, pressing her hand on his.

'I don't believe you,' said Lisa haughtily. 'I shall not be careful about what I say – if I wish to shame you in my home, I will. I didn't freely invite you here!'

Stevie had returned to her proud self. She sat as if set in stone, words coming through tightly clenched teeth.

'It is you who are quarrelling, Lisa. I did think you'd have more sense than to do that when all I suggest is something to your advantage.'

The room hissed with malice. It was as if it were smouldering on a furnace. Lisa and Stevie were now deadly enemies where once they had been friends. Lisa raising the matter of the letters had broken forever any hope of a bridge with Stevie, obsessed as she was with them precisely because they would be like flaming torches in the air – and would end everything. Lisa's anger dominated the room, her voice choked with hatred.

'I asked Corie about you and her sexually,' she said boldly. 'She said long ago you ceased to have a truly close life together. She does love you – but it's a quite different kind of love – entirely.'

Stevie hesitated and turned pale, the effect Lisa must have desired. The word 'sexual' had shocked them all, but to Stevie it no doubt sounded like blasphemy.

'Yes, perhaps, but when I met Corie, we had a very close young love.'

Lisa's eyes lit up, pride in their depths, tossing her head with scorn at such childish nonsense.

'You must understand, Corie and I are happy together, as I have never been with anyone. You must understand what I want—'

'Tell me,' said Stevie quietly.

It was the way Stevie said 'Tell me' that caught the moment. Something had intruded. Stevie's voice had changed. She spoke softly, pleading almost, not speaking to Lisa in sarcasm, as she must have intended.

'Like a mother, not a lover,' Corinna said out loud in a spontaneous declaration.

The moment's silence hung in the air. Stevie stood looking up into Corinna's face with a wry smile, a new light in her eyes. The combat in those eyes had quietened down letting in the philosophical Stevie she held so dear.

'Yes.'

Silence.

'I understand. I see that's the truth of all this,' Stevie said.

'It's my way of loving. I loved Maurice and David and I love you, Corie. It's not a love that deprives anyone.'

'But the child has to be free, eventually,' Corinna said, hearing her voice shake, defying the gods.

Only then in the minute that followed did Corinna clearly see how she loved Lisa with adult love, as Lisa loved her, with the love of a lover. Lisa did not, could not, love her as Stevie did. She already had a child – Sophie.

'Tell me,' Stevie had said in the way of a mother wanting to know the truth.

But as she said the words, she turned not to Lisa but to Corinna, and now she began to answer herself.

'When we were young, we were comrades, in business we were clever and successful. But.'

Her voice changed.

'You have changed, grown up, perhaps.'

She stood still, thinking, a radiance surrounding her.

'Yes, you do still love me. All the things we have said to each other, all were true – as a child loves its mother. It's the sort of love that can't die. That is the only kind of love I know. It doesn't detract from others, but, in this moment now, I can see Lisa loves you as a lover. Yes. I understand.'

For a long moment of silence, Corinna kept her eyes on Stevie's fierce intelligent blue eyes boring back into herself, thinking.

'Yes,' Stevie went on. 'I do see it's something to do with me – the way I love. I love with my heart, not with my body or my head.'

Corinna stood back, sat in the nearest chair, sat in silence staring at Stevie, holding her breath to steady herself. Which was the truth? The letters, the stolen visits, the words said in the little bungalow by the river? Or Stevie now? This, she grasped, was the truth because David was there, his distant eyes miraculously bright and alert. Not the agony in Stevie's letters – the feeling of a storm of despair like a winter storm – because of her. Both could not be true – married to David and words of an angel – missing so much your Rupert Brooke face so dear. No – all that was fantasy. Stevie knew she could not hold fast. She gave to the one in front of her. She had to, she had such a need to be loved. Today, David was there – she, Corinna, was there. But David won. The secret love between herself and Stevie, the long letters of love, all that had to take second place.

Gripping the edge of her seat, Corinna sat as still as a statue, letting it all clear in her head. Remembering.

Remembering – how she had kissed her mother with passion, her face, her mouth, into her neck with deep long kisses. She had come to say goodnight, but these were the kisses of a lover. Her mother drew back.

'Stop that Corie! Come along, now. Bedtime.'

Ineffectually, the bent hand pushed at her. Ashamed she felt, as her mother must have been that her beloved little girl – in all her sixteen years – had not been affectionately inclined – and now this.

'Must be the northern blood, cool and loyal – like Granny's,' she would say.

It was the only way her mother could explain such things, the woman's journal she turned to for female education had not said anything to do with that. The push her mother had given her came back in the night, exaggerated beyond belief and woke her up in nightmares of torment. She couldn't breathe. She sweated and moaned. Jack in the Beanstalk rose out of the shadows, towering over her. She felt in herself, however, a new strong desire to drive her whole self through life. And so she had loved Stevie.

She had loved her mother almost too deeply, suffered with her the crippling increasing pain. She would wake in the night hot with anger against the doctors, the professors, all those in power who could not, for all their power and wealth, stop the pain, smooth out the bent and rigid fingers, the terrible weakness and swellings in the knees, the hunched up painful shoulders making sleep impossible, never mind lying flat. She had lived in a circle of pain.

Stevie stood in front of her. Corinna sat still, waking from her past – knowing afresh the love of her mother. She looked at Stevie's strong boyish little figure and breathed a gasp of relief. Stevie was her mother reincarnated, but in good health. Stevie, too, had tremendous strength of character, of intelligence, of moral fibre – her mother's eyes on her, her mother's eyes on Benjamin – weak and unable to play football, to run, or to swim. He pulled at her mother's heart. For that she had hated him, his going to a posh school, French, Latin. He had been her deadliest rival. And then came the war. She forgot him. Her mother died. She thought she would die then, but she had met Stevie, and her love for her mother flooded into Stevie, swept in by the excitement of war and Stevie's education and wit. She shut her eyes. Oh, my God, I'm seeing Stevie for the first time.

'That's right, isn't it, Stevie? The child must be free.'

Her eyes on Stevie, her mind in front of Stevie, she laid it all out explaining, knowing Stevie could read it all in her face. Nothing hidden.

'I understand,' said Stevie. 'You are no longer a child – you are awake to become a lover, to love Lisa. With us it was different.'

Bitter streaks were showing. Stevie shrugged, her eyes down.

'Well – you can't have – we can't have everything – no, not even I. Life has to be fought for everyday. If I taught you that, I've done well. I, too, have a life to live.'

What she would miss most about Stevie was the teacher in her – take exams – never wait and see – drive forward – read and read – the philosophy of Cowper Powys – *The Stricken Deer* – all of DHL – the four hundred classical novels of English literature – all.

'Don't forget, a little Latin everyday.'

Corinna kept her eyes on Stevie's face, now pale to the lips and trembling. Stevie's jealousy, unlike Lisa's, was silent and clenched. She was not able to conceal a bitter hurt at all that had been said, in spite of her apparent acceptance. Corinna swallowed the lump in her throat. The shock was over. Something had been torn apart. There could be no more trust between herself and Stevie because they now – because of the years – they now knew they saw things differently. Deep down, Corinna still felt the hollow where the pain had sickened and cured itself.

'Tea? Corie?'

Lisa had poured the tea. The cake had been cut, the knife, a wild-looking blade of steel, lay silent across the remains.

Grow up, Lisa said. Over and over. But now? Or had Corinna imagined it? Be the master of your fate – gentle Lisa who could never be the master of her own. She would take Lisa in her arms, free and demanding. That was what Lisa wanted.

After the remnants of drifting broken talk over the tea and the cake no more could be said. The fledging had been set free. Stevie managed a sarcastic laugh, talked in cut up syllables. She was letting go.

'Leave the mortgage and all that,' Stevie said. 'I'll think of something else David and I can do. On our own.'

It was over between them – their paths had broken apart. Her arm round Lisa, she watched Stevie take David by the hand and lead him out.

It was Stevie who first saw the fire. She stopped at the gate to glance back and saw the glow in a great cloud of smoke burst in the entrance, smashing the great doors open. A scream like a knife came through the roar and a thousand voices.

Corinna came through the smoke tugging old Bill by the collar, choking, trying to shout, to grab the phone as she passed. 'Lisa – where's Lisa!' pushing Bill into Lisa's outstretched hands.

'Cover your mouth,' Lisa shouted at her. 'For God's sake.'

A hand snatched the receiver away. 'Emergency – fire –

The Lodge.' It was David, control – control – control. He caught Stevie's arm and held the dog with the other hand, steering them out.

Lisa had turned, calling over her shoulder, 'Number eleven – the party's gone mad—' her voice flat and grim.

Old Smithie was running across the main landing, her face uplifted, defiant, holding a chair up in front of her, its legs out. Cushions came out of doors, books, everyone staggering about picking up possession as they ran. There was another scream – the girl from number eleven, smoke streaming from behind her, screaming hysterically, shaking the broken handrail, screaming herself silly, smothered in black, helpless with drugs, demanding help.

Corinna saw her fall, ran and caught her and held her. Someone had snatched the girl away, pushed the thin body down the stairs as if it were made of paper.

Another girl with hands outstretched stood under the arch. 'Lisa – what're you doing!'

'I'm not leaving you!' Lisa pulled her but it was impossible to breathe. 'I'm not letting you go,' she shouted.

The narrow staircase to the attic, the banister, cracked and fell apart,

'There's another girl up there.'

'Leave her! Corie!'

Corinna grabbed Lisa's arm, pulled her through the arch, hot wood trailing through her fingers, her throat blocked with smoke. Someone threw a cloth over the girl's head on the staircase and dragged her down as the staircase collapsed.

In the dust cloud a man's face rose, a fireman. 'About thirty people in that room,' he said, his mouth tight.

Corinna gasped at him in the smoke, 'Last week they had a party and left the carpet thick with pins.' But it all meant nothing. Not words or things or people. Faces came and went blackened, livid white. Voices stopped halfway and coughed. The broken banisters had fallen over the main landing.

'Corie!'

Corinna grabbed Lisa against her as the giant figure of the fireman came through the arch and in a flash lifted Lisa over the smoking timber in a long steady sweep, pushed her into Corinna's arms and was gone. The gap to the garden was clear.

The town, they already knew, in fact all the country towns as well as London, was a cell of drug traffickers. When the police came they found in the ashes of the roof poems written under the influence of heroin, and signs of LSD, which flung young people off the centre roof car park. All strewn in the ruins of the room.

Bewildered, the police seized the wrong suspects, left the instigators driving round the town bashing their horns, they stood in the smoking ruins with the fireman, shouting in tense voices conflicting orders at each other. They ground their feet in the burnt grass, glared up at the walls of the third floor rising like the skeleton of a broken ship after a storm at sea, unable to believe their ignorance of the invisible enemy destroying the old house she and Stevie had rebuilt. Destroying the young.

All through the night Corinna had sat against a fallen tree in the garden, leaning on Lisa's shoulder beside her, kissing her cheek, holding her tight, falling asleep and waking again, Bill at their feet.

The ambulances and fire engines had gone into the night. As had Stevie and David.

A damp soot lay on the grass, the air hung heavy with a bitter tang holding it still, rain clouds close overhead, creeping over, promising rain.

'We must have a plan,' she said. 'Set sail for France? Anything or I shall go mad. We could rebuild, a hostel, a headquarters for the Women's Movement?'

She stood up and a mass of birds rose from a field far below, rose and slowly swooped down to settle in the roof tops of the town. A wave of calm fell over her.

'We'll have money enough out of the insurance, it's all in order. That was a stroke of luck.'

Lisa was silently nodding, choked for speech. Corinna sat down again, her fingers rows of icicles dangling from her knees. Silence at last. She sat still but in her head was a ciné film of the disaster: fire engines, ambulances, tenants in tears.

'It's the roof, Lisa. It would mean the whole place being fireproofed, repaired. Cost a fortune.'

She could feel her feet heavy with exhaustion, heart still pounding at the closeness of death. She had reported the drugs – but no one would listen. There's no way to give the girl notice, said Mr Black, no court would listen to you. Mainly because she was a woman among greedy landlords – Mr Black wouldn't like to say that. It was part of the mission, the mission against despair at not being able to fit into the world – not man, not woman – not listened to. The struggle to be oneself, to rise above being an outcast.

'It's all in the fight to be free and equal, Lisa,' she said out loud. 'With no more than a stone in my shoe – as Stevie said, remember? And we just watch history rolling into one – men and women. It has to happen. All humanity equal and free.'

'Yes, I do understand,' Lisa said softly. She raised her voice, 'so long as I have a studio and time to spend in it.'

Corinna laughed. 'I promise, all the time you want. A new world for the world and a new beginning for us. It's as clear as the night sky last night, long fields of stars leading us.'

Lisa laughed at the poetry, standing up, brushing her skirt down, tossing back her hair. 'For now I'm starving – and I need a bath and a bed, please.'

Corinna kissed her forehead and clumsily hugged her.

'Time for breakfast, coming?' she whispered.

She looked up, calling out: 'Rain's coming! Look!' Clouds milky with rain opening over them.